"You could have been killed..."

Sydney's voice broke. "That was a bomb, wasn't it?"

"Shh, don't cry." Collin brushed the tears from her cheeks. "C'mon, help me up."

Sydney slid her hands under his waist, the heat from the blaze scalding her back. Relief filled her when Collin stood and leaned against her.

"This is because of me, isn't it? Because you're helping me ask about the murder." The realization horrified her. She traced his jaw with her finger. "I can't believe how close you came to being kill—"

He pulled her into the doorway, away from the neighbors' eyes, and captured her lips with his, cutting off her words, his mouth devouring hers as if he needed to feel her warmth as much as she needed to know he was alive.

The near brush with death, the flames hissing behind them, the memory of Collin hurtling through the air all culminated in a desperate need to hold him. She wanted all of him, wanted to feel his bare skin against hers....

But if Collin was in danger because of her, she would have to make him leave her....

Dear Reader,

I have been a mystery lover since I read the
Trixie Belden mysteries at age twelve, and a lover
of romance since I first picked up a Harlequin
novel. Discovering Harlequin Intrigue books
combined the best of both worlds. I'm excited to be
writing for this line.

One day, I saw a clip on TV about a man who'd
had a corneal transplant. The wheels of my
imagination started turning and I thought: What if
the man who donated his eyes had been murdered,
and what if the wife of the man who'd received his
eyes actually saw visions of the murder, and what
if the wife of the man who'd donated his eyes was
accused of the murder...?

Then I began to wonder if there was any possible
scientific way this could happen. My husband is
a veterinarian by profession and has worked with
pharmaceutical research for years. Advances in
medicine are mind-boggling, so with his ingenious
help I came up with the theory for *Her Eyewitness*.

I hope you fall in love with Collin Cash and are as
intrigued by this premise as I was.

Sincerely,

Rita Herron

RITA HERRON

Her eyewitness

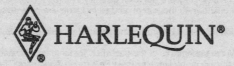

HARLEQUIN®

TORONTO • NEW YORK • LONDON
AMSTERDAM • PARIS • SYDNEY • HAMBURG
STOCKHOLM • ATHENS • TOKYO • MILAN • MADRID
PRAGUE • WARSAW • BUDAPEST • AUCKLAND

ISBN 0-373-47055-X

HER EYEWITNESS

Copyright © 1999 by Rita B. Herron

This edition published by arrangement with Harlequin Books S.A.

www.eHarlequin.com

Printed in U.S.A.

Special thanks to Debra Matteuci
and Natashya Wilson for their enthusiasm
over this premise. To my wonderful husband, Lee,
for his ingenious theory and for helping me
blend fact with fiction, and to my cousin and
childhood playmate, Sheila Samples, who has
undergone three corneal transplants and willingly
shared her experiences with me.

CAST OF CHARACTERS

Sydney Green—The prime suspect for her husband's murder, her life depended on uncovering secrets she didn't know he had.

Collin Cash—Regaining his eyesight made him an eyewitness to murder.

Doug Green—He was more trouble dead than alive.

Kelly Cook—Besides Collin, Sydney's friend and neighbor was the only person who seemed to believe in her.

Roxy DeLong—She'd expected to marry Doug before he chose Sydney.

Spade McKenzie—The mad scientist claimed Doug cheated him out of millions.

Darlene McKenzie—She wanted her husband to succeed—at what cost?

Marla Perkins—A friend of Doug's—how close had they really been?

Sergeant Raeburn—The policeman had no reason to look further than Sydney for the killer—and a good reason not to.

Steve Wallace—The CEO of Norvek Pharmaceuticals had suspected Doug might double-cross him.

Prologue

"Hurry up, Doctor," Collin Cash muttered impatiently, "remove these bandages. I'm ready to see again." The dark office seemed totally oppressive, filled with the scents of medicine and antiseptics. Smells that Collin had learned to hate over the past year. He was so nervous he could hear his own breathing rattle through the empty room. The past twelve months had been hell. First the shooting. Then the surgery. Then he'd awakened to a world of darkness. A world where he'd gone from being a fearless cop to a man full of fear.

He balled his hands into fists. A man who trusted no one, he'd been forced to accept help from strangers. To admit weakness, to admit he *needed* people.

The fear that he might always be dependent on others had been pure torture. Weeks of recovery and tests had dragged into months as he'd waited for the scar tissue to heal so he could have the corneal transplant. Then he'd finally gotten lucky.

Someone had died and donated their eyes.

A moment of sorrow and guilt attacked him. He shouldn't use the word *lucky*. He wouldn't be getting his sight back if someone hadn't given up their life.

Finally the door creaked open. Footsteps clicked on the

floor. He recognized the sound of Dr. Darber's hard-soled shoes.

"How are you doing, Mr. Cash? Feeling all right?" Darber asked with his faint Northern accent. "No headaches, dizziness, nausea?"

"I feel fine," Collin said. "A little anxious, maybe."

Darber chuckled. "Most of my patients feel that way." Collin heard the clink of metal as Darber worked. "Are you ready?"

Collin nodded, finally gaining the courage to voice his fear. "Will I be able to see right away?"

"Providing you haven't rejected the new corneas, yes," Darber said, clipping the bandages. "Although, at some point you may need glasses."

What if the transplant hadn't worked? Or what if he could see for a while, then his body rejected the corneas and he had to face blindness again? Could he handle the darkness forever?

"Remember what we discussed," Darber cautioned. "You could reject one or both of the corneas at any time. If you have headaches, blurred vision, double vision, any of the other symptoms I described earlier, call me right away."

Collin agreed, his breath tight in his chest as Darber unwound the bandages.

"Patients vary at how well they see immediately after the operation. First, you'll probably detect some light— shades of white and gray. Things will be blurry. Remember, the muscles in your eyes and the nerve cells going to your brain haven't worked in quite some time. They need retraining."

"One year, one month and eleven days." Collin exhaled loudly. The longest damn year of his life.

"It's important you take the drug I've prescribed. It's

still experimental, but it should lower your chances of rejection. And don't forget to use the eyedrops. Dark sunglasses will help in the sunlight, and you can wear the mesh patch I'll give you for a few days. You can see through it, but it'll protect your eyes while you heal."

"Fine, as long as I don't have to use that damned cane."

"Be patient. We have every reason to believe the corneas are a good match." Darber's cold fingers touched his forehead. "Remember, your eyes and the surrounding areas will look red, puffy and swollen. Your eyes will be bloodshot at first, but that should pass in a couple of weeks."

Collin didn't care about his appearance. He just wanted to see again.

"Okay, now open your eyes slowly."

Collin's breath whooshed out. He slowly lifted his lids. A sliver at a time. Fear knotted his stomach. What if…

Think positive. He was going to see again. The worst was over.

He opened his eyes a little more. A small white spot appeared, a thread of thin light. He blinked, squinting when the light's impact hurt his eyes. The light grew bigger.

"You're doing fine. Let it come back to you slowly."

The door squeaked open again. Darber's lab coat brushed his arm as he turned.

"I need to talk to you, Doctor."

In spite of the tension, Collin smiled at the woman's soft Southern drawl. It would be nice to *look* at a pretty woman again. He loved the South. He'd been born in Charleston, South Carolina. Would probably die there. *Had* almost died there this past year.

"I'm busy right now," Darber replied tersely. "Go wait in my office."

"Who was that?" Collin squinted, hoping he could see the woman. Her face registered in his vision, fuzzy and distorted, then faded into a blur as she shut the door.

"Just a nurse. Tell me what you see."

Collin blinked again, frowning when streaks of red replaced the dismal gray. Small bits of light. Patches of red. A blotch of dark crimson.

"Blood," he whispered.

"What?"

The shades faded. Shadows twisted and turned into an angry blur of red. A horrible image filled his vision.

Blood. Lots of blood. The halo of someone's silhouette shimmering in the darkness. Moonlight streaming in, casting the body in shadows. The silvery glint of a gun flickering off the bare wall. The weapon pointed at him. A hand closing around the pistol. The hand shaking. The fingers tightening around the trigger. The tremor of the hand. The gun fired.

He saw his fingers splayed across his body, blood seeping from the wound in his chest. An ugly bullet hole tattered his white shirt.

He tried to call for help, then saw himself falling, collapsing onto the hard, cold floor. More blood. Weak, in pain, he clutched his chest and moaned. His head lolled to the side. He struggled to see, to keep his eyes open, but all he could make out was the burning, fiery red of his own life flowing onto the rug. Then he closed his eyes and let himself drift into a world of nothingness.

He was going to die.

"MR. CASH, CAN YOU HEAR me? How do you feel?"

Slowly Collin awoke, his limbs languid. His eyelids ached, begging to be shaded from the glaring light.

"What happened? Where am I?"

"You passed out on me, Cash."

"What?" Collin tried to sit, but collapsed against the bed. Exhaustion pulled at his legs, his arms. Nevertheless he could make out a face.

Dr. Darber's face. White-haired Dr. Darber. He had leathery tanned skin. Wrinkles around his eyes. A prominent nose. My God, he could finally see again!

"I didn't know you wore glasses, Doc," he said in a husky whisper.

Darber laughed. "So, you *can* see. I was beginning to wonder..."

"It's a miracle." Collin looked for the nurse he'd heard earlier, but she wasn't in the room.

Darber frowned. "What happened? You started talking about blood and then passed out on me. I could barely find your pulse. Are you still dizzy?"

"A little bit." Collin struggled to remember the disturbing images. The gun, the vision of blood seeping from his body. "I was shot."

"Yes," Darber said with exaggerated patience. "Last year. The shooting caused your blindness."

"No, this time I was shot in the chest." Collin jammed a hand through his hair, confusion clouding his mind. At the same time, joy leaped inside him. He stared at the gray floor, stark white walls, down at his own hands, his legs, the chair—after staring into a black world for the past year, he suddenly had his eyesight back. His *life* back.

But what had he seen when he'd first opened his eyes? It had seemed so real. Like a murder—*his own murder.*

"Darber, how did the man who donated his eyes die?"

Darber folded his arms across his chest. "You know I'm not at liberty to discuss the donor."

"Just tell me how he died."

"He was shot, Mr. Cash." Darber regarded him through veiled eyes. "In the chest."

Collin forced air into his lungs. "He was murdered?"

A shudder coursed through Collin when Darber nodded in confirmation. The image tore through his mind again with vivid clarity.

No, it was impossible. Completely impossible.

Chapter One

"Sergeant Raeburn, I didn't kill my husband."

Sydney Green wiped at the perspiration dotting her forehead, wishing she could forget the image of Doug lying facedown in a pool of blood.

The detective's bold look of disbelief unnerved her. "And you have no idea who'd want him dead?"

"No." The wooden chair squeaked as she shifted her weight. Even two weeks later, the scent of death and the coppery taste of fear she'd experienced as she'd knelt beside Doug rushed back.

The paunchy, near-bald policeman paced, his heavy boots thudding against the wood floor. His incessant motion intensified the tension radiating through the small office. The stained, yellowed walls felt as if they were closing in on her.

Raeburn finally paused, planted one beefy arm on the scarred table and bent over so his face was only inches from hers. His breath smelled of cigarettes, his body of sweat. "You put on a good innocent act, Mrs. Green, but I'm not buying it."

The condemning look in his expression almost shattered her self-control.

"You said you came home around 11:00 p.m. and

found your husband immediately, but you didn't report it until almost an hour later. And no fingerprints other than yours and your husband's were found in your house.''

"Just what are you implying?'' Sydney asked bitterly, unable to believe anyone could think she was a killer. Raeburn had read her her rights the first time he'd questioned her, but she'd been in such a state of shock she hadn't realized the implications of answering his questions. Perhaps she should call a lawyer.

"I'm just trying to get to the truth.''

"I told you the truth.'' Her stomach clenched into a knot. "I came in and found Doug on the floor. He was pale, chalky-looking.'' She hesitated, twisting her hands in her lap. "I rushed to him and saw the blood. So much blood. He didn't respond to me. I jumped up to call for help...then someone knocked me over the head.'' She hesitated again, wondering if she could have done something different. Something that would have saved Doug. She tucked away the guilt, but not before she saw suspicion in the detective's feral eyes. "As soon as I regained consciousness, I called 911. You have to believe me! Why aren't you looking for the killer?''

Raeburn dug a toothpick out of his plaid-shirt pocket and stuck it in the corner of his mouth, chewing on it thoughtfully as he continued to stare at her. Sydney fought the urge to close her eyes. Every time she did, she saw the awful bloodstain that had soaked the carpet.

"What if I think I've got the killer right here?'' Raeburn asked in a deceptively calm voice as if he'd already tried and convicted her.

"Sergeant, I photograph babies and children for a living,'' she replied softly, swiping at her tears. "I believe in family and home and all that sappy stuff. I'm not a murderer. I had no reason to hurt Doug. I loved him.''

She stood, ready to leave. "And if you continue to harass me, I will call an attorney."

His eyes didn't soften. "So you're telling me you and your husband had a good marriage?"

Sydney prayed her voice didn't give her away. "Yes. Now I wish you'd leave me alone and let me grieve."

"Are you sure your marriage was stable? No problems? Arguments, money trouble?" The sardonic edge in his tone sent a chill slithering up her spine. "Everything okay in the bedroom, Mrs. Green?"

Sydney refused to let him coerce her into discussing the more intimate details of her marriage. Instead, she folded her arms across her chest and met his gaze, praying her voice sounded steady. "Not that our personal life is any of your business, but that was fine, too." She took a deep breath. "In fact, we were trying to have a baby."

For a fraction of a second, the steely glint in his eyes slipped. "Is that so?"

"Yes." Sydney looked away, picking at a piece of lint on her dress. "I wanted a baby more than anything in the world."

Raeburn leaned so close Sydney unconsciously retreated as far as possible against the table, ignoring the pain when the wood pressed into her hip. "Then why did your husband have a vasectomy?"

The breath whooshed from her lungs. *"What?"*

"You want me to believe you didn't know?"

Hurt, shock, then anger rippled through her. The tears she'd tried to keep at bay tracked down her face, unchecked, as she shook her head. "You're lying. That's not true. We were trying to have a baby. Doug wanted one as badly as I did. He said so."

"It is true, Mrs. Green," Raeburn said in a quiet voice. "I saw the autopsy report. He'd had a vasectomy."

Sydney pressed her fist against her mouth to hold back a sob as the detective's words sliced through her. Any hope she'd had that Doug had really loved her died immediately. She'd known her husband had secrets, had suspected an affair, maybe something illegal going on. But this...

Raeburn laid his hand beside the tape recorder and leaned forward. "You know what I think? I think you killed your husband, and you needed that extra time to get rid of the gun before you called 911." His voice lowered to a menacing pitch. "And I'll give you credit—you were good, even made a real lump on your head to throw suspicion off yourself. And now I know why."

A feeble protest died on her lips as she realized she'd fallen right into Raeburn's trap. The next time she spoke with him, she would definitely have a lawyer present. Because in her grief and her inability to hide her pain, she'd just confirmed she had a motive to kill her husband.

AS DUSK SETTLED around the small town of Beaufort, Collin removed his sunglasses, cataloging the details of the police station, trying to decide whether or not to get out of his Bronco, go in and ask questions. He'd come here to repay his debt to the man who'd given him back his sight.

After the bizarre vision, he'd hounded his friend and colleague, Sam, until he'd pulled some strings and found out the name of the donor. The short report Sam had faxed him about Doug Green said he'd been an entrepreneur, that he put together deals for start-up companies. He raised capital for them, then took them public.

Not only a smart man, but an honorable one—Green had donated a part of his body for someone else's benefit.

And Collin would never be able to thank him personally for it.

Green had been married to his wife, Sydney, for only a year. Collin shifted in his seat, unable to shake the feeling that had nagged him for the past few weeks and made him drive to Beaufort. Doug Green had been murdered. Why? Maybe there was something he could do to solve the crime, something that would make his nightmares disappear. Unofficially, of course.

The door to the station opened and a woman exited. *Sydney Green*. He recognized her from the snapshot in the newspaper article Sam had sent him. For a brief second she raised her head and seemed to stare right at him. Tears streaked her cheeks and his gut clenched at the sorrow in her heart-shaped face.

Her beauty and vulnerability struck a chord of longing in him he hadn't experienced in a long time. Slender, she wore a light blue sundress with spaghetti straps and flat sandals. Her sable hair fell in waves over her shoulders, and her eyes were as blue as the summer sky. He felt like an intruder, spying on her as she walked slowly toward a green Honda, her face pale, her shoulders hunched.

What had happened inside? Had the local police already solved the case?

If not, did they suspect Sydney Green?

The cop in him had dissected the case the minute he'd finished Sam's report. The prime suspect in a murder case was usually the spouse. Given the facts, this case looked classic—domestic passion gone awry. No break-and-enter. No struggle. Victim shot at close range with a .40 caliber gun. Amount of time elapsed before the wife reported the crime sufficient for her to hide evidence. Was Sydney Green a grieving widow in need of help or one hell of an actress?

Still unsure whether or not to tell her about the transplant or to go in undercover, he watched her pull away. He gripped the steering wheel, his mind cluttered with questions. Some small spark of awareness, an aching familiarity streaked through him, making him shift uncomfortably in his seat. She looked fragile, and he could imagine the kind of interrogation they'd put her through—the kind he would have put her through himself.

He started his Bronco and began to follow her at a safe distance. She wound through the streets of the quaint South Carolina town and crossed the bridge over the inlet, then eventually turned onto a graveled driveway that led to a small, white-clapboard church. He drove past the driveway, then parked at the side of the road and killed the engine. He watched her climb out of her car and pick her way across the weed-filled graveyard beside the church.

Faded plastic flowers filled chipped cemetery vases while other vases sat empty. His uneasiness grew. If he'd died, instead of being blinded, would anyone have brought flowers to his grave? He felt a momentary longing for someone to love and love him back, but he shrugged it off. Cops were loners. He'd always lived alone. He always would.

A light sprinkling of rain dotted his windshield. He pulled a pair of binoculars from his dash and rolled down his window. He watched her push the damp tresses of her hair away from her face, saw her tears mingle with the raindrops as she knelt at the tombstone. She was talking to the grave. A creepy feeling crawled up his spine, and an urge to go to her tightened his gut.

He climbed silently from his car, telling himself he would only go close enough to hear what she was saying.

Stuffing his hands in the pockets of his faded jeans, he walked toward her. Sobs racked her body now.

Emotions bombarded him. No one could stand by and witness such misery without feeling sympathetic.

"Doug, why did you lie to me?" he heard her whisper.

He hesitated at her comment, but unable to stop himself, he approached her slowly and laid a hand gently on her shoulder. She jerked and turned to stare at him, her reddened eyes wide with a mixture of fear, hurt, surprise.

"Who are you?" she choked out, quickly standing and putting some distance between them.

Collin released a strained breath, pausing when her gaze locked with his. He slowly peeled off his dark glasses, and something strange, surreal, passed between them, connecting them in a way he couldn't explain. It was almost as if she recognized him. Then wariness darkened her expression.

"I asked you who you are," she said in a shaky voice.

"My name is Collin Cash." He extended his hand and she simply stared at it, biting her lip. "I'm truly sorry for your loss," he said quietly. He'd frightened her. A twinge of guilt inched into his conscience.

She rejected his outstretched hand, so he dropped it and took a step back. She, too, retreated another step as if she was about to run, but a beige sedan pulled into the parking lot and an elderly couple climbed out, and she relaxed slightly.

Her skin glowed in the dimming light, looked smooth and silky soft. Raindrops clung to her eyelashes and hair. A tingle of awareness he didn't want to admit to raced through him. Even in grief, Sydney Green was a strikingly beautiful woman. Porcelain skin, hair like an ebony curtain, eyes a misty blue.

"I'm sorry about your husband's death."

Her eyes momentarily filled with renewed tears and he felt his gut clench. Should he tell her the truth?

"I gather you knew Doug," she said, her gaze raking over him in an uncomfortable way. A suspicious, cautious way, he realized, wondering about the direction of her thoughts.

"We had a mutual business acquaintance," he hedged.

"You weren't at the funeral?"

"No. I just arrived in town and wanted to pay my respects. I've been in the hospital…" He let his explanation fade into silence. "Is there anything I can do for you?"

Distrust flashed into her expression. "No thanks, I'm fine. I just need to be alone."

She didn't look fine. She looked vulnerable and sad, as if the *last* thing she needed was to be alone. He acknowledged her words with a slight nod. Maybe now wasn't the time to tell her the truth. It might come as too much of a shock. "I'm going to be staying at the Beaufort Bed-and-Breakfast. If there's any way I can help you, let me know."

Sydney retreated another step, hugging herself protectively. The elderly couple, having placed flowers on a nearby grave, walked past hand in hand.

"Look, I have to go now." She lowered her head and focused on the soaked leather of her sandals, then hurried away.

"I'll walk you to your car," he said, falling into step beside her.

"I'd rather you didn't." She cast him an anxious glance and he realized she really was afraid, so he slowed his steps. Was she always this fearful around men, or had her husband's murder spooked her?

If so, he could understand. And he felt even worse for

scaring her. A woman alone, at dusk, a deserted graveyard—the atmosphere gave *him* an uneasy feeling.

He purposefully kept his distance, the tense silence between them accentuated by the raindrops pelting the walkway and the soles of her shoes tapping on the concrete.
Just as she neared her car, an engine roared to life.
Strange, he thought. He stopped and scanned the area. The
elderly couple still stood by their car. He hadn't noticed
anyone else in the graveyard.

Near the street a utility van was exiting the driveway.
Suspicion snaked through him. But the truck made a legal
left turn and pulled onto the roadway, and he dismissed
the incident. It was probably a delivery truck or some kind
of work crew. Nothing to garner suspicion.

Then he glanced at Sydney and saw her stagger as she
unlocked her car door. He instinctively knew something
was wrong and hurried toward her. When he approached
the car, the glint of metal caught his eye.

And he knew it was a gun.

SYDNEY SPOTTED THE GUN lying in the passenger's seat
and froze in shock. The sounds and sights around her were
obliterated.

It was a small pistol, cold gray metal, and she instantly
remembered the gun used to shoot Doug had never been
found. Dear Lord, was this it?

Her legs felt rubbery and she clutched the car door for
support. The man who said his name was Collin Cash was
moving closer, and Sydney panicked. If he saw the
weapon, he might think she had something to do with
Doug's death and call the police.

She jumped inside, sliding her leather purse over the
pistol, then quickly glanced up to see if the man had no-

ticed. His gaze remained trained on something in front of him, his eyes unblinking, his complexion chalky.

She started the engine, put the car in gear and quickly sped out of the lot, checking her rearview window to see if the enigmatic stranger was following her. But he was still standing in the same spot with that blank expression on his face. She turned onto the road, breathing a sigh of relief when he disappeared from view. She didn't understand the eerie feeling, but something about him seemed odd—mysterious.

It was almost as if she'd see him before—as if she knew him.

THE IMAGE of the .40 automatic bore into Collin's mind. Sydney Green had a gun in her car, the same make that had killed her husband. The light around him faded and he blinked, feeling dizzy as he tried to focus. He shook his head to dislodge the shadows stealing his sight. What was wrong? Was he losing his vision again? Rejecting the corneas? The shadows melted into grays and he swallowed, glimpsing the silhouette of a person—in the feeble light.

A hand closed tightly around the revolver, aimed at his chest. "No," he whispered. "No, don't."

But it was too late. The gun fired, the jolt knocking the hand up. He clutched his chest and stared at the blood spreading across his white shirt. The shadow moved, aimed the weapon at him a second time, then fired.

This time the bullet penetrated his heart. His body bounced backward, and his legs jerked as he collapsed to the floor. Dark crimson gushed from his chest, soaking into the moss-green rug. Blood filled his nose and mouth and he gagged, his head lolling to the side. Darkness closed around him. He stretched out a hand for help, then saw shoes as the shadow stood in front of him. He watched, shocked, as the figure padded across the room to leave him. The door opened. A thin stream of light filtered in from the hallway.

He couldn't breathe. The darkness, the pain... His hand fell limp. His signet ring winked in the light. The door shut and he closed his eyes, helpless and alone.

Seconds later Collin shook himself as the images faded. His hands skimmed his body. His limbs were trembling, his pulse was racing, but he was alive. And he hadn't been shot. He was still standing in the cemetery parking lot. Had the sight of the gun in Sydney's car triggered the vision?

The gun. Sydney had rushed away, taking the weapon with her. Odd—.38s were most people's choice for protection, not .40s. And if she was the killer, why would she have the gun in her car? Surely she would have gotten rid of it. He had to find her. Had to know if it belonged to her, if it was the same .40 that had killed her husband.

He raced to his Bronco and climbed in. After starting the engine, he made a U-turn and accelerated quickly, fishtailing on the damp pavement. He floored the gas pedal and sped up the narrow road, his tires screeching as he passed a yellow Ford. His eyes stung when the driver flashed his headlights, and he blinked against the pain. Collin quickly turned on his own lights, vaguely aware dusk had settled into darkness. His eyesight was still foggy at times, and he knew he should return to the bed-and-breakfast. But seeing Sydney had changed everything.

He finally spotted Sydney's Honda up ahead. She was speeding, going way too fast as she approached the bottom of the hill before the bridge. Why didn't she slow down?

She swerved across the double yellow lines and an oncoming car blared its horn. Still speeding, she steered the car sharply sideways to dodge a stalled vehicle, almost rolling on two wheels. What was she doing? Trying to kill herself?

SYDNEY STOMPED on the brake and barely missed the truck parked in the middle of the road. Her car wouldn't stop! A low garbled sound tore from her throat. She was going to crash.

She gripped the steering wheel so hard her fingers ached, and then she downshifted, grateful for the sudden slowing of the car. Fear clogged her throat. She flew down the hill and spotted the bridge.

"Help me, God, please help me," she whispered, her heart pounding. The ocean loomed only a few hundred yards away. The car gained momentum, bouncing over the rough grooves of the road. Her body jerked against the constraints of her seat belt. She pumped the brakes, but the car accelerated as it raced down the hill. The inlet slid into view, the arches of the bridge, the water, it was so close...

She pumped the brakes again, but the car careened out of control. She swerved sideways, hoping to break the speed, but the car hit a pothole, then spun around. She screamed and braced herself. Metal crunched. The car screeched and skidded onto the opposite side of the road. Her shoulder and neck were wrenched painfully, and she inhaled the scent of burning rubber. Her head hit the window, and she tasted blood on her lip. Then she saw the metal rungs of the bridge, the roaring waves crashing against the shore. Water. Miles and miles of water, endless water...

A sob tore from low in her chest. And her last thought before she plunged into the ocean was that she would never have the family she wanted.

Because she would never survive.

Chapter Two

"Oh, my God!" Collin slammed on his brakes and screeched to a halt just as Sydney's car plunged into the water. He grabbed his car phone and punched 911.

His hands were shaking, his pulse racing as he waited for the call to go through. He had to hurry! He frantically unfastened his seat belt, dumped the contents of his pockets onto the seats and yanked open his car door, ready to run to Sydney as soon as the call connected. Finally an operator answered.

"This is an emergency! There's been a car accident."

"Can you give me the specifics, sir? The address?"

He swiped his hand over his forehead. Damn, no streetlights or signs anywhere.

"I don't know the street name," he said, near panic, "but a car crashed into the water on the north side of the bridge coming into Beaufort. Send an ambulance right away!" He threw down the phone and ran toward the ocean. What if Sydney was already dead?

Her car had nose-dived into the inlet and was slowly sinking. Kicking off his shoes, he plunged into the water, grateful he'd maintained an exercise program during his months of blindness. The car dipped beneath the crashing waves. He dove beneath the water, fighting the undercurrent, and swam as fast as he could, then nearly choked when he spotted the car with Sydney inside. A bloody gash marred her forehead, but she was alive!

And she was struggling to open the car door. Water poured into the sedan, the level dangerously close to her neck. Her eyes were stricken with fear, her dark hair swirling in a tangle around her face. Hoping his lungs could hold out, he tried to open the door from the outside, but the force of the water kept it from budging. Panic streaked through him. He saw the terror in her clenched jaw as she pushed at the door, then her chest heaved as if in defeat.

He banged on the window and motioned for her to try to roll it down. The moment she did, water would rush in over her head and he'd have only seconds to save her.

She nodded, her face pale as if the life was already draining from her. How much longer could she hold out?

Then she closed her eyes and leaned her head back, and he thought she was going to pass out. But she seemed to summon a second burst of courage, or maybe adrenaline, and jerked the window handle. He yanked on the door. Finally the window inched down. Her lungs obviously couldn't hold out any longer. She choked, coughing and swallowing water as she fought her way out.

He struggled, pulling her out the window, his lungs about to burst. Sydney's body went limp and floated toward him. He tucked his arm around her waist and swam upward, dragging her beside him. His chest ached, but he kicked and pushed against the water until they surfaced.

"Sydney, can you hear me?"

She sagged against him, her face ashen. It seemed like an eternity before he made it to the embankment, his body throbbing from the ordeal, his throat tight with fear. Finally his feet touched the pebbled ground and he dragged her onto the grass. Laying her down gently, he knelt and listened for a heartbeat.

Nothing.

He fought his panic and pressed his finger to her neck for a pulse. Still nothing.

"Damn it, Sydney, you're not going to die."

His own breathing was erratic and he took several deep breaths to calm himself, then tilted her head back and breathed into her mouth. The first time nothing happened. She merely lay there, the ghostly pallor of her skin making his stomach heave. "Come on, Sydney. Don't give up." He lowered his mouth again.

After several breaths, she coughed and choked. Her ragged breathing sounded wonderful to his ears. Then she began to spit out the murky water. He tilted her head to the side, brushing her hair away from her face. The scent of seawater and fish permeated the air, and he thought he might be sick himself. A siren wailed in the distance and blinding lights beamed across the bridge. *Thank God.*

"Don't worry, help is on the way." He stroked her face with his fingertips. Her cheeks felt cold and clammy, her skin so chalky it almost glowed white in the moonlight. She moaned and coughed again, and he wiped her cheeks with a soggy handkerchief, then pulled her into his arms, rocking her back and forth, trying to warm her. She tried to open her eyes, a hoarse whisper erupting from her lips.

"Shh, just rest," he whispered. "You're going to be all right." She closed her eyes, almost as if she trusted him, and succumbed to the fatigue. Then her slender hand curled in his lap and he gathered it to his chest, rubbing it in his own to warm her. She whimpered softly, and he blinked against the unwanted emotions churning through him.

The ambulance screeched to a stop and the paramedics

rushed out. They immediately took over. "I'm fine. Just take care of her," he ordered when one of the men wanted to examine him. He remembered the doctor's warnings about his recent eye surgery. The water could pose a problem, yet he hadn't given a thought to his own life when he'd dived in to rescue Sydney. He hadn't had a choice. Still, he'd call his physician when he returned to the bed-and-breakfast.

Another siren wailed, then everything happened in a blur. The police arrived and the paramedics placed Sydney on a stretcher. Collin moved close and took her hand. She gazed at him, her pupils still slightly dilated. He squeezed her hand. "They're going to take care of you now."

She nodded weakly. He grimaced at the blood matted in her hair and the dirt streaking her lovely cheeks. Her eyes drifted shut, and he struggled against the urge to stroke her face.

"Is she going to be okay?" he asked.

The paramedic nodded. "Yeah. We'll take her in for observation and tests. The doc might want to take some X rays."

Collin ran a hand through his own wet, tangled hair. He wanted to go with her, but he had no right. He didn't even know her.

"Take care of her. I'll question her later," the police officer said.

Collin felt oddly shaken when the ambulance drove away. A tall, heavyset cop sidled over to him, a small notebook in hand. "I'm Sergeant Raeburn. Your name?"

"Collin Cash."

"You got any ID?"

Collin reached into his pocket, then remembered he'd dumped its contents on the seat, so he walked over to his

Bronco. Suddenly exhausted, he sank onto the seat and handed the policeman his driver's license.

The man studied it, then him. "You're from Charleston? What're you doing out here, Mr. Cash?"

"Vacation," Collin replied, deciding this wasn't the time to spill his whole story. "I recently had surgery and need time to recuperate."

"You wanna tell me what happened here tonight?"

Collin described exactly what he'd seen, avoiding any details about his encounter with Sydney in the graveyard. "So you don't know Mrs. Green?"

Collin shook his head.

"Didn't see any other cars around, any reason she might have been driving so fast?"

"No. She swerved to avoid a stalled truck in the road, then veered toward the water as if her car was out of control." He thought back to the last few minutes before she'd crashed. At the graveyard she'd been upset, distraught, emotional, but still...

"I'll have the car towed in and checked."

Collin nodded.

"You staying in town?"

"Yeah. At the Beaufort Bed-and-Breakfast. I'm going there now to clean up."

Raeburn caught his elbow. "I might need to talk to you later."

"Sure." *In fact, I might need to talk to you, too—ask you what you've found out about Doug Green's murder.* But first he wanted to check on Sydney.

"It's a good thing you were behind her," Raeburn commented. "Must have been Mrs. Green's lucky day."

Collin stared at the sheriff, disturbed by his casual tone. "I'd hardly call having an accident and almost drowning lucky."

Raeburn shrugged. "I meant it was a lucky coincidence you came along."

Collin didn't like the man on sight. And he wasn't about to explain that it hadn't been a coincidence at all.

He needed to go back to the B-and-B. Instead, he climbed into his car and headed toward the hospital, telling himself he simply wanted to verify Sydney would be okay.

But deep down he had a terrible feeling he was lying to himself. He was a loner, a man who needed no one, a man who *wanted* no one to need him.

Which made him even more confused about the loss he'd felt when the doors of the ambulance had closed, taking Sydney from his sight.

SYDNEY TRIED TO OPEN her eyes, but fatigue clawed at her limbs and muscles. She snuggled beneath the blankets, vaguely aware she'd been thoroughly examined by doctors and nurses, dragged through X rays and bathed by a stranger. She was so tired she thought she might sleep for days.

But the memory of the accident and the scent of saltwater invaded her mind. The terror she'd felt when she lost control of the car. The water crashing around her, suffocating her, choking her. She jerked her eyes open, hating the fear bubbling inside.

"It's okay. You're safe now." A man's soft, husky voice startled her and she searched the shadows, finally discerning the tall figure as the stranger she'd seen in the graveyard. Collin Cash. Fear once again knotted her stomach. Just who was this man? And what was he doing here?

Then guilt attacked her. He'd saved her life. She should be grateful, not suspicious. Damn Doug for making her so distrustful.

"The doctor said you're going to be fine. A few cuts and bruises, a minor concussion and a little water in your lungs. You just need to rest."

Sydney nodded, feeling the pathetic sting of tears in her eyes. Furious with herself, she blinked to stem their flow, then flinched when Collin raised his hand and wiped the moisture away. His intense dark gray eyes studied her.

"Thank you for rescuing me," she said, her throat aching with every word.

Collin's frown deepened. "Shh. Don't talk."

She opened her mouth to speak again but coughed, and he shook his head. "I said don't talk. You need to rest." The look of concern disappeared. His expression grew blank. "The police are going to want to question you tomorrow about what happened with your car."

She tensed at the thought of Raeburn. Flashes of the horrible day bombarded her—being questioned about Doug's murder, learning about his betrayal, then the accident...

"I'll check on you later," Collin whispered. "Try to sleep now, Sydney."

She fisted her hands around the sheets as he closed the door. Collin knew Doug. Who was he and why had he come to Beaufort? On the heels of her suspicions, guilt warred with her distrust. He'd saved her life. He'd been her knight in shining armor.

No.

There were no knights in shining armor. Not in real life. In real life, men told lies. No matter what Collin Cash had done, she didn't want to talk to him, or anyone else. She wanted to sink into sleep. To forget about Doug's deception.

Because if Collin had known her husband, he couldn't be trusted, either.

COLLIN'S HEAD throbbed as he drove back to the inn, his vision blurring. Thankfully Sydney was all right.

You can reject the corneas at any time. Darber's words had haunted him, so he'd finally agreed to a checkup at the hospital before he left. He felt reasonably sure he hadn't damaged his eyes too badly tonight. Only time would tell.

His drenched clothes had dried. The stiff fabric chafed his skin and he smelled like fish. He needed a long, hot shower and a bourbon. Both would have to wait.

Because more than anything, he needed answers— needed to know what the hell was happening to him. The vision at the graveyard had completely unnerved him. Had he regained his eyesight only to lose his mind?

As soon as he reached the bed-and-breakfast, he phoned Dr. Darber. "Yes, I'm using the antirejection drops." He explained about his unplanned excursion in the ocean. The doctor listened quietly while he relayed the bizarre episode in the graveyard.

"I wasn't dreaming, Doctor." Collin's fingers tightened around the phone. "I tell you I was wide awake."

"Are you telling me you saw a ghost?" the doctor asked in a skeptical voice.

"No." Collin paced the length of the Victorian bedroom, his six-foot-two frame grossly out of place among the ornately carved furniture and lacy comforter. "I'm not sure what I saw. But I know it was real."

"But you *were* shot just over a year ago." Darber's tone sounded patronizing this time. "Perhaps you're confusing the incidents in your mind."

"I was shot in the head, not in the heart. And I was outdoors."

"Are you sure you didn't doze off and—"

"I was not asleep!" Collin raked a hand over his stubbled jaw in frustration. "That drug you gave me must be causing me to hallucinate."

Silence stretched taut across the line. Finally Darber said, "It's possible, but highly unlikely."

"Even though the drug is still experimental?"

The doctor sighed heartily. "Yes. I'm sure the anesthetic combined with the drug caused some of your strange dreams during and immediately following the surgery, but the effects should have subsided by now. That is, unless…"

"Unless what?"

"Unless you're drinking alcohol."

"For God's sake, I wasn't drinking," Collin snapped.

"You said yourself you were tired. You were in a graveyard. Maybe you…you know…"

"Let my imagination go wild?" Collin huffed in disgust. "I'm not imagining this, Doctor."

"Let me know if it happens again. And be sure to keep your follow-up appointment." He paused and Collin hoped he was thinking of some reasonable explanation for the strange visions. Instead, he hastily said goodbye.

Collin squeezed the handset as the line clicked into silence. Rubbing his temple, he shuffled into the bathroom, stripped off his filthy, damp clothing and turned on the shower. The hot water felt heavenly, but while he showered, he couldn't forget the image of Sydney plunging into the water. Or the fear that had gripped him when he'd thought she might die.

He staggered, feeling dizzy. Worried he might collapse, he turned off the water, toweled off, then stretched out on the bed completely naked, hoping the headache pounding at the base of his skull would dissipate with a few hours of sleep. And praying it didn't mean his body was rejecting the corneas.

Maybe the doctor was right. Maybe he'd imagined the whole episode earlier when he'd seen the gun. Stress, post-traumatic stress at seeing a weapon so similar to the one that had blinded him—something like that. Maybe he should consult a shrink.

Finally accepting the flimsy reasoning, he closed his eyes and drifted into an exhausted sleep. But instead of seeing murder in his dreams, he saw Sydney. Beautiful and sexy, with her long dark hair fanned out over white sheets. A dark green satin gown with spaghetti straps revealing full breasts and porcelain skin. He could almost feel her warm breath caress his neck as she leaned over to kiss him. She looked so sad, so incredibly sweet, so vulnerable. He wanted her...needed her...had to have her...

He moaned and awoke with a start, then blinked at the suffocating darkness of the room. For a moment the panic he'd felt during his blindness seized him. His breathing became erratic, his palms sweaty. He rolled sideways and turned on the lamp, exhaling sharply in relief when light spilled into the room and he realized he could still see. Thank God. He'd rather die than live in that dark world again. And he wouldn't allow himself to become dependent on anyone ever again.

He left the light on and closed his eyes, telling himself over and over he wouldn't get involved with Sydney Green. He'd *needed* people in the past year, needed them to teach him how to survive in a world of darkness, needed them to drive him places, to shop for him, to guide him on a simple walk around his neighborhood, to tell him whether his damn clothes matched or whether he'd worn a white sock with a brown one.

When he'd finally gotten his sight back, he'd wanted to call someone to share his good news. He'd thought about calling his old girlfriend, Debbie, but had instantly squelched the idea when he remembered her reaction to his blindness. He'd needed her to stand by him after the shooting, to love him in spite of his inability to see. But she hadn't. She'd found someone more virile, someone who didn't need a cane and a guide to find his way to the bathroom in a public restaurant.

Yes, he'd needed people. And he'd hated every minute of it. He absolutely would *never* let himself want or need anyone again. His partner had been suckered in by a beautiful woman and died because of it, in the very shooting that had taken his eyesight.

He gave his pillow a firm punch and put Sydney Green just as firmly out of his mind. He'd solve this murder case, then go back to Charleston.

He wouldn't get personally involved with Doug Green's wife. After all, she might be a murderer.

SYDNEY AWOKE the next morning, her throat raw, every limb in her body aching. The memory of the wreck, the nightmarish seconds before she'd passed out, returned in vivid detail. And along with them came images of Collin Cash saving her life, of his attempts to comfort her afterward.

Despite it all, she wasn't staying in the hospital a minute longer than necessary. If he came back, she would be gone.

A knock at the door startled her. She half expected, half feared the man would appear. Instead, her good friend and neighbor, Kelly Cook, rushed in, carrying a bouquet of flowers. "I couldn't wait to see you for myself." Kelly hugged her. "I was so worried when I heard about the accident."

"Thanks for the flowers." Sydney tried to sit up but

winced when her muscles protested. "Where's my god-child?"

"I left her with the nurse downstairs. You know how picky the nurses are about letting children in the rooms."

"I know, but I'd love to see her." Children in general cheered her up, and Kelly's baby, Megan, was a bright spot in any day. She loved the little girl like her own.

Kelly sat down in the chair beside the bed, her blond ponytail bobbing. "I can't tell you how I felt, Syd, when I first heard the news about your accident. I couldn't believe it. What happened?"

The sheets rustled as Sydney's fingers tightened around them. "I don't know. I lost control. The car sped up and I couldn't stop. It was awful."

Kelly's hazel eyes darkened in horror. "You mean your brakes failed?"

"I guess so. I kept pumping them but they wouldn't work." She shivered. "It all happened so fast."

Kelly patted her arm. "Thank heavens, it's over now, and you're okay. That's all that matters. The nurse said they're letting you go home today."

"Yes," Sydney said in a weak voice. "I can't wait to leave this place."

A man cleared his throat from the doorway.

Sydney groaned as Sergeant Raeburn lumbered in.

He scrutinized her from head to toe. "How're you feeling this morning, Mizz Green?"

"I've been better," Sydney said, guarding her expression.

"Sergeant, it was awful, wasn't it?" Kelly used her hands to punctuate her words. "Sydney's brakes wouldn't work." She turned to Sydney. "Didn't Doug keep the car serviced?"

"Usually. But he'd been traveling a lot before..." Sydney shrugged and bit her lip. "It might have been over-due. I'm not really very good at mechanical things."

Raeburn made a clicking sound with his cheek. "Is that right?"

"Yes. I don't know what went wrong." Sydney resisted the urge to squirm under his perusal. "The brakes have never failed before."

He jotted something in his notepad. "The wrecker service towed it in. We'll check it out."

Sydney suddenly remembered the gun on the seat of her car. Where had it come from? What if the police found it? What if they thought—

"I'll let you know what we find out." Raeburn repeated that irritating clicking sound as he strode from the room.

Sydney's mind raced with questions about the gun. Maybe they wouldn't find it. Maybe it had been washed out to sea.

Kelly smiled reassuringly. "I brought my car. As soon as the doctor releases you, I'll take you home."

"It's Saturday, Kel. I have a shoot this afternoon."

Kelly dismissed the idea with a wave. "I'm sure whoever it is wouldn't mind rescheduling."

"I know. But after all that's happened, I need to feel some sort of normalcy. I'll call Marla and see if she can come later today," she said. "Working might help me forget the accident."

"You've been through a lot lately, Syd." Kelly patted her arm sympathetically. "Promise me you'll rest first. And if you don't feel up to working, you'll cancel."

Sydney's emotions rose to her throat. "I promise. Hey, maybe you can bring Meg by and I'll take some photos of her, too. We haven't shot her portrait yet."

"Maybe," Kelly said in a noncommittal voice. "But I don't want you to overdo things."

"I won't. It'll be fun." Sydney squeezed Kelly's hand, grateful for her friendship. She'd felt so alone the past few months, even before Doug's death. Now, after learning about Doug's betrayal, knowing he hadn't wanted a child with her, she felt even more alone. Had Doug ever loved her at all?

COLLIN SLEPT FITFULLY through the night, finally rousing himself from his tortured dreams to find his headache had subsided. He shoved away the tangled covers, then realized in disgust that he'd slept the whole night through with the light on—like a damn baby.

Scrubbing his hand over his face, he ignored the pain in his sore muscles as he rose. He had too much to do to wallow in bed.

He showered and dressed in jeans and a denim shirt, determined not to think of Sydney Green as a woman, but as a lead—even a suspect.

Within a half hour, he'd connected his laptop to the police computer and run a complete background check on Doug Green. Doug was quite an entrepreneur. Jotting down a few notes, he decided to spend the rest of the day researching Green's business dealings, his investments, all the start-up companies he'd taken public. If his wife wasn't to blame for his demise, his business dealings might lend a clue. Money and greed were two of the most common motives for murder. And if Green was a self-employed entrepreneur, he obviously enjoyed the business of making big money. And big money often meant *big* trouble.

SYDNEY'S MIND SCREAMED with worry when she spotted the article about her accident on the front page of the newspaper. The report claimed the accident was under investigation. Once again, her husband's murder had been mentioned. Damn. Why couldn't that stupid detective find the real murderer so this nightmare could be over?

The article briefly mentioned the man who'd saved her life, but the reporter obviously had no details about him. She skimmed it further, her hands trembling as she finished and laid the paper on her desk. Thank God they hadn't named her as a suspect. And the article hadn't mentioned the gun.

Had the police found it? Were they planning to arrest her? But more importantly, where had the gun come from? And how had it gotten in her car?

Her nerves on edge, she showered and dressed in a pair of tan slacks and a black, short-sleeved sweater, hoping work would relieve the kinks in her sore muscles and take her mind off her problems. And off the enigmatic man who'd appeared at the graveyard, then later saved her life.

But she couldn't help but wonder how he knew Doug.

She walked to her studio and prepared the backdrops for toddler Beth Perkins's portrait, determined to forget him. She chose a high-key white background for one set of shots and a favorite backdrop featuring tall green grass with wildflowers for another set.

Four-year-old Beth bustled in with Marla, her mother. "Hey, Ms. Sydney." Beth twirled around, showing off her ruffled pink dress. A big white eyelet bow teetered in her waist-length brown hair.

"You look beautiful, Beth," Sydney said.

Beth gave her a hug, then pointed to Sydney's forehead. "What's that big purple spot?"

"It's a bruise," Sydney explained. "I had an accident last night, sweetie."

Beth's small face crumpled. "Did you get hurt bad?"

Sydney smiled and curved her arm around the little girl. "No, honey. I'm fine. It was really scary, though."

"Gracious, Sydney, I saw the paper! What happened?" Marla looked stunned.

Sydney explained, minimizing the details to avoid scaring Beth. "I'm fine, really. A little sore, that's all."

"I'm sorry," Marla said sympathetically. "Is there anything I can do to help?"

"Yes—let me photograph this little darling." She tickled Beth, grateful when the little girl's frightened expression disappeared and she collapsed into giggles.

"Thanks for fitting me in this afternoon," Marla said as Sydney adjusted the lighting. "I hate that you aren't feeling well, but I did want to have these ready in time for the family reunion in a couple of weeks."

"You know I love photographing Beth." Sydney changed the camera filter, then took several poses of the toddler against the white background. "Perfect," she said when Beth struck a silly pose. Then Beth flounced into a small rocking chair in front of the grassy backdrop and Sydney snapped some more shots.

"You did great today, sweetie," she said when they finished. "You're one of my favorite models."

Beth wrapped her arms around Sydney's legs and squeezed. "I wuv you, Ms. Sydney."

"I love you, too." Tears pricked at the backs of her eyes when Beth kissed her cheek.

A pang from her husband's betrayal hit like an icy dart. A vasectomy. He'd had one and never told her. She'd wanted kids so badly, and Doug had pretended to go along. All the times she'd talked about it, planned for the baby—he must have been laughing behind her back.

He'd never wanted a family with her. Never intended to have one. It had all been lies. And worse, he'd let her believe that her failure to conceive was her fault, that she'd been inadequate.

"How are you doing?" Beth's mother asked quietly. "I know your husband's death was hard on you."

"I'm okay." Sydney averted her gaze, avoiding the pitying expression on Marla's face. One she'd become very familiar with.

"Do the police know who killed him?"

Sydney shook her head, tensing. "Not yet."

"I do hope they find the person." Marla wiped at her own eyes. "Doug was such a handsome man. And brilliant, too, wasn't he?"

"I suppose so," Sydney said. At least brilliant enough to fool her.

Marla had an odd expression on her face. "We'll miss him at the club."

"The club?"

"Yes, you know, the Beaufort Health Club." Marla frowned again. "You did know he belonged?"

"Oh, right." Sydney feigned a smile. "With his traveling, I didn't realize he made it there very often."

Marla shrugged. "Well, even though he and Randy didn't hit it off, the rest of the staff liked Doug."

Sydney nodded, although she *hadn't* known Doug had belonged to the health club. And she didn't know anything about Doug having problems with Marla's husband, Randy. She was discovering a lot of things about her former husband she hadn't known.

Marla ushered Beth out the door. The memory of Doug's funeral surfaced, along with the memory of Marla's tearstained face. Just how well had Marla known Doug?

The telephone rang before she had time to contemplate the question. Kelly's friendly voice came over the line.

"Hey, Kel, where are you?"

"Meg's been fussy all morning," Kelly explained. "I think she must be cutting a tooth."

"Oh, poor baby." Sydney hated the thought of Meg in pain. "I hope she feels better. Do you have something to give her?"

"Yes, I've rubbed medicine on her gums. And now we're both going to take a nap," Kelly said with a laugh. "We definitely won't make it by for pictures today. Maybe we can get together tonight and order pizza."

"Sounds great," Sydney said, deciding she'd spend the afternoon in the darkroom catching up on some projects.

Kelly yawned and they said goodbye, then Sydney retreated to the darkroom, enthusiastic about developing the photos. Seeing the faces of smiling children immortalized on film always brightened her day. And she could certainly use some brightness.

A few hours later she hung the last of the shots up to dry and went out into her studio. She checked her appointment book, noting how few entries there'd been since Doug's death.

As she closed the shades on the floor-length windows, thoughts of her problems resurfaced, and an image of Collin Cash popped into her mind. When she'd first looked into his eyes, she'd felt drawn to him. Something eerie had passed between them, a sort of déjà vu.

Then he'd saved her life.

Still, she didn't trust him. Doug had been handsome, but he'd also been a liar. Her judgment about men was apparently off base, and she'd definitely seen trouble written in Collin Cash's sexy eyes. She glanced up in dismay as he sauntered through her studio door.

He leaned against the shadowed corner of the brick

wall, his masculinity filling the room. Broad shoulders, square chin, muscular thighs. That dark stubble of a beard.

He folded his arms and watched her. His dark hair gleamed in the sunlight, the long ends curling around his collar. And the faint lines around his bedroom eyes added to his mysterious, sexy persona.

She shouldn't be thinking that way, she realized, annoyed with herself. She was a recent widow, still mourning the loss of her husband. Her deceitful, dead husband. Who'd known this man.

Meaning she couldn't trust him, either.

The phone rang and she quickly answered it, relieved to have an excuse to delay talking to him. "Sydney's Custom Photography." She began to rifle through a stack of bills.

"Sydney, this is Steve Wallace at Norvek Pharmaceuticals." Steve's agitated baritone cut off her thoughts.

"Yes, hi, Steve. What can I do for you?"

"We've been working on securing that deal for the weight-loss product." A pause punctuated the tense silence. "But we have problems. We're missing part of Doug's paperwork, his material on the patent agreement."

"What?" She turned her back on Collin Cash and lowered her voice so he couldn't hear her conversation. "July was supposed to be the debut month."

"I know." Steve's voice crackled over the phone. Irritated, she pulled back slightly from the earpiece. "But after Doug's death, we postponed it. Now we're trying to get back on track, but we can't find the disk. The information on the hard drive isn't complete. Did Doug have any copies of his work at home?"

"I'm not sure," Sydney said, remembering the boxes she hadn't yet sorted through.

"Look, Sydney," Steve said, his voice edgy, "I'd like

to come by and look for it. How about in a couple of hours?''

She'd known Steve for months, and he'd questioned her before about Doug's personal things, each time sounding increasingly agitated. Could he have killed Doug and she'd come home before he'd had a chance to search for the files? ''Wait a minute,'' she said, stalling. ''I don't understand. Doug closed the deal months ago.''

''That's what he told us. But we don't have a copy of the licensing agreement. And I've heard that another health-care company has a similar product they're getting ready to unveil.''

''What? How can they?''

His voice faltered. ''I hate to slander a good man's name, but we wondered if Doug might have misrepresented us and sold the agreement to this other company.''

Sydney masked her shock by covering her mouth with her hand. ''You really think he'd sell out from under you?''

''I don't know,'' Steve said in a hard voice. ''But it's vital I find that document. So, I'll see you in a bit?''

''No. I'll look for it,'' Sydney said, uneasy about Steve poking through her possessions. ''And if I find any of Doug's files, I'll give you a call.''

''But Sydney—''

''Listen, Steve. I want this deal to go through as much as you do, so there's no reason I would hold back. I'll call you if I find something.''

Sydney hung up, baffled. Doug had worked on closing this deal for months. The weight-loss product tasted like soda and actually inhibited hunger. Filled with nutrients, it increased users' metabolisms, causing them to burn calories at a faster rate. Steve's financial board estimated it would earn millions from diet centers and health spas across the nation. Had Steve tried to cheat Doug out of his share?

Or had Doug tried to cheat his company?

Her husband's lies splintered though her mind. He'd betrayed her. Had he betrayed his company, as well?

Remembering her visitor, she turned to see him studying her intently, that probing, serious look in his sexy eyes. Another man she didn't want to deal with.

Yes, Collin Cash was *trouble*. Widowed or not, a woman would have to be dead not to notice his potent charm. While Sydney might be hurt, she might be confused, she might not ever want another man, she wasn't dead.

She had to find out what Collin Cash was doing here and how he'd known Doug. But she wouldn't get involved with the man. Because she wasn't a fool—or, at least, she wouldn't be fooled twice.

Chapter Three

Collin carefully gauged his reactions as Sydney hung up the phone. Despite her attempts to keep the call quiet, he'd been able to hear most of what she said. His theory about Doug's death being related to his work might be on target. At the library, he'd scanned numerous articles about Doug's business dealings. The man had acquired some pretty hefty accounts. The impending deal with Norvek Pharmaceuticals alone would pad his bank account into the millions.

But after making a quick call to Sam, he'd also learned Doug had a sizable life-insurance policy with Sydney as the benefactor. With the closing of this new deal, she stood to inherit a great deal of money. She definitely had a motive. And she'd found Green's body. It was a wonder Raeburn hadn't arrested her already. Probably waiting till he found the murder weapon.

When Sydney faced him, her expression immediately became guarded. Yes, she was definitely a suspect. What was she hiding?

"Hi." He made a production of admiring the display of photographs on the wall. "How are you feeling?"

"Fine," Sydney said.

"You have some great photographs here."

"Thanks." Sydney regarded him through veiled eyes—did she know who he was? "What are you doing here?"

He relaxed his stance, hoping to alleviate her anxiety. "I was passing by and saw your studio. Thought I'd drop in."

Sydney arched one dark eyebrow. "You were passing by?"

Collin sighed. "Okay, truthfully…I looked you up in the phone book. I had to see if you were okay."

"I'm fine," she repeated. She shuffled through some paperwork, jammed it into a leather briefcase and slung it over her shoulder, accentuating her point. She was ready to go home.

"Once again, thanks for saving my life." She rolled her shoulders as if her muscles ached. "But right now, unless you want a portrait, I need to go home and soak in a nice bubble bath."

"No, I don't want a portrait." Collin tried his best to maintain his calm, but the scent of jasmine invaded his senses, the sultry aroma pumping through his body. Sydney's gold hair clip dangled precariously to one side, causing strands of her unruly hair to sweep down against her cheek. The image of her lying in a bubble bath, her hair wet with his fingers combing through it—

"Look, Mr. Cash. I don't mean to be rude, but I recently lost my husband. I'm not up to dealing with anything right now. If you had business with Doug, you should take it up with his office. I can't help you."

He cleared his throat, her comment a definite reminder of his motive for being in Beaufort. "I understand, but I thought I might be able to help you in some way."

She simply stared at him. "How do you think you can help me?"

"I know what it's like to lose someone," he said softly. "I'm a good listener. We could go for coffee."

She chewed on her bottom lip. "I'd rather grieve in private."

"I'm not going to be in town long. Could we just talk about Doug?"

"I don't feel like it tonight, Mr. Cash."

His police instincts wouldn't let it go. For the first time since he'd been shot, he felt challenged and alive. That, on top of this unwanted physical attraction, made it impossible for him to get her out of his mind.

He wanted—no, he *needed* to learn more about her, to know if she was a murderer or if she herself was in danger. To learn if he really *was* witnessing Green's murder in his visions.

"Look, don't take it personally," Sydney finally said, flipping off a desk lamp. "I don't make it a habit to go out with strangers."

"Even ones who save your life?" It was a low blow and he knew it, but he was desperate.

Her hand tightened around the strap of her bag. "I already thanked you for that. Now I want to go home."

"You can tell me about the town," Collin urged. "It's my first visit here and I'd like to play tourist. How about breakfast tomorrow?"

Sydney headed to the door. "I have to work tomorrow afternoon."

"But you also have to eat. Come on, Sydney, it's only one meal. I know you and Doug were practically newlyweds. I'd like to hear about how you two met."

The dark circles beneath her eyes deepened in the light from the door as she turned to stare at him. Just when he thought he'd lost the battle, she replied, "And I'd like to hear exactly how you knew my husband, Mr. Cash."

Collin resisted the urge to wince. She might look fragile, but she was a tough lady. "Fair enough. We'll talk about it over breakfast tomorrow."

"Okay, but brunch, not breakfast."

"That sounds fine. Where can I pick you up?"

"Meet me at the Plantation Café. It's on Main Street."

"I thought you might need a ride. You haven't gotten your car back yet, have you?"

Sydney frowned and he silently chastised himself for reminding her of the accident. "No. But the café's within walking distance. And I've already contacted my insurance company and arranged for a rental."

"Okay. What time shall I meet you?"

"Eleven. They have a nice Sunday buffet."

"All right." Collin jammed his hands in the pockets of his jeans and nodded, pausing to admire a small eight-by-ten of a baby girl lying on a white rug, then another photo of a little boy riding a small tractor. The scene touched some deep emotion inside him, stirred a momentary longing for family, which he quickly dismissed. Sydney had captured the joy of youth in that one shot. Yet, as a cop, he'd seen the destruction of innocence so many times he'd become jaded. His own bout with blindness had hammered the realization into his head with undying clarity. "You do nice work, Sydney."

"Thanks." She relaxed for the first time since he'd met her, giving him a brief glimpse of how beautiful she was when unencumbered by grief. "It's easy with such cute subjects."

"You obviously like children."

"I freelance for magazines and newspapers, but I specialize in children and family portraits. I couldn't do my job if I didn't like kids."

Collin smiled again, an uncomfortable feeling eating at

him as he said goodbye, then walked outside and put on his sunglasses. Could this beautiful woman who captured the innocence of children in her pictures possibly be a murderer?

AFTER SHE LEFT the studio, Sydney walked to the rental place and picked up the small sedan she'd be driving until she heard more about the status of her Honda. Tension knotted her muscles. Had the police found the gun yet? Would they be at her door when she got home, ready to interrogate her further? Or worse, arrest her?

By the time she finally arrived home, she was jumpy and had a headache. With Doug's betrayal on her mind, she shuffled through a box filled with his belongings she'd found hidden in the back of their closet. After talking to Steve Wallace, she had to stop living in denial. As much as she'd wanted to believe Doug's murder had been a simple robbery attempt, deep down she'd always suspected another motive. Maybe something in this box would provide her with some answers.

She sorted through papers, a stack of bank-account statements, several notepads filled with information on start-up companies, a manila envelope containing disks. Wedged between package wrapping, she found a passport. Before their marriage had fallen apart, she and Doug had discussed taking a trip to Europe. Had he already obtained a visa? Had he planned to go without her?

She opened the passport and gasped at the picture. Instead of Doug's sandy brown hair and clean-shaven face, a mustache and thick red beard covered his face. But his eyes were undeniably the same dark shade of muddy brown. Her hands trembled. A driver's license fell from where it had been tucked inside the pages of the passport. The driver's license bore the same photograph. A wave of nausea crawled through her. Underneath both pictures Doug had used a different name—Doug Black.

Stunned, she searched further and discovered an airplane ticket with the same name. A one-way ticket to Brazil—dated the day Doug had died.

So Doug had planned to leave the country as Doug Black? And he'd intended to go alone? The questions and little incidents that had bothered her during the last few months of their marriage snowballed in her mind. And now the missing licensing agreement? What in the world had her late husband been involved in?

Her pulse racing, Sydney booted up the computer and popped in the first disk. Scanning the files, she discovered folders filled with financial statements. Doug had several Swiss bank accounts and an account in Brazil. Each held a sizable amount of money. He'd also opened an account in Charleston, which wouldn't have surprised her since he worked there and had commuted from Beaufort daily. But he had separate accounts in two different banks in Beaufort. Odd. "What were you up to, Doug?" she whispered, shocked at his duplicity.

After mulling over the possibilities, she inserted the second disk. Notes and files pertaining to his work composed the directory. She studied the data, but couldn't determine whether or not it was related to Norvek. Deciding she'd have to let Steve figure it out, she made a backup copy of the disk, then put the copy and the one containing the financial information back in the box.

With the first disk tucked in her purse and her nerves frazzled, she drove to Steve's office. Inside, she walked unsteadily into the elevator, her mind still reeling with shock. Did Steve Wallace have any knowledge of the fake passport and ID? And the plane ticket? Her earlier suspicions mounted. She had to be careful about how much she revealed to Steve. What if she said something to incriminate herself? And if Steve had killed Doug...

The elevator doors swished opened and people filed out. She sighed in relief, grateful to escape the claustrophobic space. Inhaling a calming breath, she adjusted the lapels of her linen jacket and squared her shoulders as she walked through the textured doors of the pharmaceutical company.

Peggy, Steve's secretary, greeted her. "The phone's been ringing off the hook today—the news about the delay has everyone in a state." As if to confirm her words, the telephone immediately trilled. Peggy placed the caller on hold and showed her into Steve's office.

"Come on in," Steve said. Expensive cherry furniture filled the office, which came complete with its own stocked wet bar and sitting area. Black leather sofas flanked an Italian-marble fireplace and two nude Oriental statues graced the mantel.

"Coffee, juice?" Steve offered.

"No, nothing," Sydney said, knowing anything she drank would upset her already tense stomach.

He poured himself a cup of coffee, then settled on the leather sofa, gesturing for Sydney to do likewise.

She did, forcing herself to relax. "I brought a file, but I'm not sure it's the most current one." She handed Steve the disk, then scooted to the edge of the leather seat. "Can you tell me something, Steve?"

"I don't know. Try me."

"Was Doug planning to go away on business before he died?"

Steve shook his head. "No. There was no need. Our marketing distributor and consultants handle the overseas work. Doug set up meetings in the States."

"I see."

"Tell me why you asked."

Why had Steve automatically assumed she meant Doug might be traveling overseas? He could just as easily have been traveling within the States. "I'm trying to figure out if what you said could be true," she replied. "You believe Doug sold the agreement out from under you?"

Steve's momentarily silence answered her question. "Maybe the file will tell us what we need to know."

A sick feeling ballooned in her stomach. "Who knew about the deal besides the people in the company?"

"Exactly my point." The lines of Steve's face grew taut around his eyes as he frowned. "I knew you were distraught over Doug's death, so I didn't come to you immediately, but we think Doug spread his idea to generate interest and auctioned it to the highest bidder."

Steve shrugged, his anger building. "Several companies would have loved to have laid their hands on that product."

Sydney picked at the hem of her jacket. "You really think Doug would cheat you?" He had several Swiss bank accounts, she reminded herself silently. What if it was true?

Steve's voice lost all its warmth. "Possibly. Millions of dollars were at stake. And Doug liked to make money."

The passport, the fake ID, the one-way ticket to South America—it all added up. Did Steve know about those? If she told him, would he use it against Doug? Even worse, could Steve be right? Could her former husband be guilty of such a thing? And could his business be the reason he was murdered?

"I haven't disclosed this to the public yet," Steve said. "At this point we don't have proof. Plus, the publicity might hurt us."

"So..."

Steve reached for her hand and covered it with his other hand. "If I were you, I wouldn't mention this to anyone. We've promised our patrons the greatest weight-loss product in the country and somehow we're going to deliver."

"And you're not going to involve the police?"

"Not at this point, although I have spoken with an attorney."

Sydney pulled her hand away and squeezed the sofa edge.

"I suggest you don't mention it, either," Steve added. "On the chance we're wrong, you don't want to destroy your husband's good name, do you?"

Sydney shook her head, her mind spinning. Part of what Steve said made perfect sense, yet she still felt confused. If they really thought Doug had cheated them, wouldn't they want the police to handle it?

But if Steve had killed Doug...

COLLIN WENT TO BED with one question on his mind—was Sydney an innocent woman or a murderer?

The next morning he awoke with the sheets tangled around his bare legs, his body rock hard, the image of Sydney naked beneath him still fresh in his memory. He'd dreamed about her again. Feeling frustrated and disoriented, he stumbled into the shower and turned on the cold water, letting the spray absorb the heat from his body. Why in the world was he dreaming about making love to a woman he barely knew?

Because for the past year, he'd been without a woman. After a year of celibacy, *any* man would react this way to an attractive woman like Sydney. But the dream had seemed so real, as if they had actually been together.

Like his visions.

He soaped his body and lathered his hair, then rinsed himself and stepped from the shower. Knotting a towel around his hips, he walked into the bedroom. The room had been decorated in period pieces—the Azalea room, the owners of the bed-and-breakfast called it. It was the kind of room a woman would love, the four-poster bed the perfect cocoon for making love, the sunken antique tub ideal for sharing a luxurious bubble bath and sipping champagne.

The anesthesia from his surgery must have affected his brain, he thought in disgust. He'd never in his entire thirty-five years taken a bubble bath. Or wanted to. But the image of Sydney's skin shimmering with moisture was enough to create a fantasy in any man's mind.

He fought off the images. He had to investigate her, use her to solve a crime. Prove he hadn't gone soft. That he could go back to his job. Instead of crawling into bed with her, he might have to arrest her and put her in jail.

He glanced at the clock and grimaced. Ten o'clock. He was definitely out of shape. At one time, he'd been able to go nonstop without sleep for days, but since the shooting, he'd had to learn to pace himself. Right now, he needed food and coffee. And to find out more about Green.

He walked to the Plantation Café, inhaling the salty air carried on the morning breeze. Decorated with a magnolia-leaf wallpaper and filled with white wicker furniture, the café oozed small-town charm. He felt as out of place as an elephant in a rose garden. But the magnificent view counteracted the feminine decor. The outdoor porch overlooked the marina. Ships sailed past, a shrimp boat chugged out to sea, a small cruise ship filled with tourists cast off from the marina—God, he'd missed seeing all those things.

He drank a pot of coffee and skimmed the *Beaufort Gazette,* grateful he could read the paper himself. Another small pleasure he used to take for granted. Local news featured a recent price rise for shrimp, a local arts-and-crafts show. He fished through the other stories until his gaze fell on an article about health care.

All the nutritionists and health clubs were clamoring over a weight-loss drink to be released in July by a company associated with Doug Green. However, the company, Norvek Pharmaceuticals, had delayed the introduction of the drink due to Green's death. He turned the page to finish the story and paused in surprise when he saw the photograph underlying the story. A picture of Sydney standing next to her husband.

He stared at Doug's picture, an uneasiness splintering through him. The fair-haired man had his arm draped casually around Sydney's shoulders. She looked radiant. Much different from the woeful woman he'd seen in the graveyard. And not suspicious and wary as she'd acted in her studio. He zeroed in on the signet ring on the man's right hand. Identical to the one he'd seen in his vision.

He fell back in his chair as reality knocked the air from his lungs. He really *had* been Green in his vision. For several minutes, he sat, stunned with disbelief, his mind unable to fathom the impossible. Beads of sweat gathered on his forehead, and his heart pounded in his ears. Dragging in a breath, he sipped some water to calm himself. He had to call Darber. And this time Darber had better listen and give him an explanation.

If it was true, if he really was *an eyewitness* to Doug's murder, he had to come forward.

He rubbed his temples with his thumbs, a headache threatening. Who the hell would believe him? He didn't know if he believed it himself. Besides, he hadn't actually seen the killer's face.

No, he needed a strategy. The last person anyone in the town would want to talk to was a cop, especially one babbling a crazy story like his. But if he told Sydney about the transplant, he could say he'd come to repay her husband for the gift of his renewed eyesight. She'd view him as a friend, and he'd glean more information from her. Of course, he'd have to ignore his attraction to her.

And if he discovered she was the killer? He'd just have to deal with that, too.

SYDNEY STARED at the man sitting at the table and almost bolted. But if she left, she'd never find out if he had something to do with Doug's murder. What if he knew Steve and the two of them had conspired to kill Doug? She'd found Doug's body. Maybe he thought she'd seen him the night of the murder.

Taking a deep breath, she forced her feet to move toward him. "Thanks for ordering the coffee," she said, slipping into the seat across from him.

Collin snapped the paper closed, her soft Southern drawl jolting him from his disturbing thoughts. "I didn't think you were going to show."

Sydney's stomach fluttered as he took in her appearance. Her sleeveless white shell top, navy wraparound skirt and sandals were meant for comfort, but he was looking at her bare legs with an appreciation that surprised her, a male appreciation that made her blood flow hot. She fanned her face, grateful for the ocean breeze. "I almost backed out."

"I'm glad you came. We have a lot to talk about."

She thumbed her silverware, then spread her napkin in her lap.

"I don't mean to make you nervous," Collin said.

Sydney shrugged, running her fingers through her hair. "The last few weeks have been difficult—"

"Since your husband died."

"Yes." Sydney twisted her hands in her lap, thankful that the waiter interrupted and told them about the buffet. She took her time filling her plate with the spicy food, omelets, breads and shrimp grits. Why, she didn't know. Her stomach was so twisted in knots, she didn't think she could eat a bite.

Collin devoured the heaping portions on his plate while Sydney picked at hers, raking the items around on the china. When the tension became unbearable, she sipped her orange juice and spoke up. "You're not from around here, are you?"

A shadow darkened part of his face, but she thought a smile twitched at the corner of his mouth. "Charleston. Not really that far."

"Tell me how you knew Doug. Did you do business together?"

"In a way. I'm interested in his research."

"Are you an investor?"

"Possibly."

He was lying. Sydney didn't know why he was lying, but she could tell by the way he avoided eye contact that he wasn't telling her everything. Plus, he kept winding his pasta noodles around his spoon, only pretending interest in his food.

"Doug and I never actually met, but I'm familiar with some of his companies." Collin paused, regarding her thoughtfully. "You said you had to work this afternoon. Do you always schedule Sunday appointments?"

"No. There's a local arts-and-craft fair today. The paper's featuring a special section on the kids' activities during the festival, so I'm taking photos.''

"You and Doug didn't have children of your own?''

Surprised at his question, the pain of Doug's betrayal blindsided her. "We wanted a family, but it didn't work out that way.''

"Not everyone's meant for marriage and family, Sydney.''

The compassion in his voice startled her. "I take it you're speaking for yourself.''

He made a noncommittal sound, his gray eyes gazing past her at the sidewalk where a young mother pushed a baby stroller.

Then the moment was lost and Collin deftly changed the subject. "So, how did you meet Doug?''

Sydney studied his handsome features, wondering if he could possibly be as deceitful as Doug. "It was a fluke meeting. I was at the beach, barefoot, walking along taking photographs. I glanced up and saw this man watching me.'' The memory flashed into her mind with bittersweetness. "I sat down on one of the jetties and he joined me. We started talking and...'' Sydney shrugged as a blush heated her neck.

"Love at first sight, huh?''

Sydney laughed softly. "Not exactly. I thought he seemed arrogant and too sure of himself.'' *And now I know why. I should have listened to my first instincts.*

"But Doug was persistent?''

"Yes. He could be charming, kept telling me I was—'' Sydney broke off suddenly, embarrassed at the silly memory. Especially in light of what she knew about Doug now. Every word had probably been a lie.

"You *are* beautiful,'' Collin said quietly.

He brushed his knuckle over the top of her hand and Sydney shifted, a sliver of awareness riveting through her.

"Dessert? More coffee?" the waiter offered.

Sydney withdrew her hand and patted her mouth with the linen napkin, declining. Collin accepted more coffee, and she made small talk about the town, suggested a few places he should visit, hoping he would shed some light on the reason he wanted to see her.

"Sydney?"

"Yes?"

"Thanks for coming." He covered her hand with his and an exhilarating warmth curled low in her belly. His bedroom eyes seemed to be searching her out, waiting for a reaction. If she hadn't sensed he had an ulterior motive for questioning her, she might be drawn into their bottomless depths, might be tempted to wipe that tiny bit of Hollandaise sauce from his lower lip. And she might be tempted to follow up on the passionate promises in his voice.

But he wasn't being honest with her. She didn't know why or what his real purpose was, but he had secrets. And she would never again get involved with someone who would deceive her. She was still dealing with the lies Doug had dished out. Suddenly the need to find out Collin's real purpose in Beaufort faded in comparison to the compelling need to escape from Collin. He was dangerous. If Steve was a killer, this man might be, too.

"I hope you enjoy your vacation," Sydney said, abruptly rising to her feet.

"I'd like to see you again while I'm here, Sydney," Collin said in a low voice.

His husky murmur beat a path over her frayed nerve endings. Maybe he didn't have anything to do with Doug. Maybe he simply wanted a relationship, friendship...sex.

"I don't think so, Mr. Cash. Besides the fact that I'm not ready for any personal involvement right now, you've asked me dozens of questions about myself and my husband, yet you've failed to tell me anything about yourself or how you knew Doug. In fact, you seem to avoid the subject, as if you're hiding something."

Collin's face tensed, his eyes smoldering with emotions she couldn't name. Anger, hurt, confusion?

"Goodbye, Mr. Cash." She gave him a curt nod, wanting to escape to her house where she could be alone. Alone with her secrets. And far away from the attractive, unsettling Collin Cash.

But Collin surprised her by grabbing her hand. In a quiet but compelling tone he urged her to stay. "I'm sorry, Sydney. You're right. But if you sit down, I'll tell you how I knew Doug. I swear."

The timbre of his voice drew her in, made her wonder at the tormented expression twisting his strong, chiseled face, and she couldn't refuse him.

"Please, I know this is hard for you, and I know you were the one who found Doug's body." He hesitated, his voice troubled. Then she noticed the newspaper lying on the table and realized he'd probably been reading about the murder. "Tell me what happened that night, Sydney." His hand trembled as he thrust it through his hair.

She sank back into the chair. "Not until you level with me." Sydney narrowed her eyes. "Why did you come here? And what were you doing at the graveyard?"

Collin drummed his fingers on the table, the sound of a ship's horn echoing in the distance. "I came to pay my respects. And I am sorry about your husband's death. That's the truth."

"I don't understand."

Sorrow registered on his face. "I don't know how to

tell you this, except just to come out and say it. It may come as a shock...."

"What?" Sydney's breath hissed out as the tension became unbearable.

"You were aware your husband was an organ donor?"

His change of conversation threw her. "An organ donor?"

"Yes, you know, on the back of his license, he checked the organ donor spot."

"Uh, I...I didn't know."

Collin's hands clenched and unclenched on the table in front of her. "You must have signed release papers at the hospital."

"I don't remember." Sydney gestured with her hands. "I was in shock...the police, the doctors, everyone was talking at once."

Collin caught her hand and stilled it. "Anyway, I told you that I recently had surgery and I came here to recover."

Sydney wanted to scream. Why was he stalling? "Yes. But what does that have to do with Doug?"

"I had an accident last year and lost my eyesight. I underwent surgery, months of recovery while the scar tissue healed. Meanwhile, I'd been put on a transplant list."

"I still don't understand—"

"Bear with me, Sydney." Collin angled his chair back, sunlight flickering off his bronze skin. "Three weeks ago I received a phone call. A man had died, and he'd donated both corneas. I had the transplant immediately."

Three weeks? Her throat went dry.

"I wanted to know the name of the donor, but the hospitals and doctors won't release their names. They try to protect the families."

Sydney nodded mutely, her stomach churning.

His voice grew deeper, barely controlled. "I'd been through hell the last year. Thought I might never see again. I couldn't work, couldn't..." He let the words trail off, then started again. "Anyway, when I had the transplant, it was a second chance at life. A miracle."

"Why are you telling me this?" Sydney asked in a shaky voice.

He met her confused gaze, his tone low and strained. "Because I did find out the name of the donor, Sydney. It was Doug. Three weeks ago I received his eyes."

Chapter Four

"What?"

Collin braced himself for Sydney's reaction. He wasn't surprised when the color drained from her face. "I know it's a shock, but I received your husband's corneas." He paused, giving his words time to register, then continued in a quiet voice. "I'm sorry to spring this on you, but being able to see again is a miracle to me and I wanted to thank you."

Sydney's hand trembled as she reached for a glass of water. His eyes were riveted to the plain gold band around her third finger, a definite sign she still loved her husband.

Her throat muscles worked as she tried to digest his news. Then her gaze swung up to his and locked. She stared into his eyes and he saw her searching...for what? Her husband?

His chest tightened with anxiety as the silence between them grew taut. An uneasy feeling seeped through him, a thread of recognition and familiarity, as if he knew her, as if he'd been close to her once but they had drifted apart.

"I can't believe it," she whispered, bringing her hand up to her mouth, her eyes wide. Then she tilted her head sideways and crinkled her forehead as she studied him, and his uneasiness escalated. "I...it's true, isn't it?"

He nodded, his heart pounding as he searched her face for acceptance, for rejection, then for other feelings he didn't want to put a label on.

"I thought there was some…something familiar about you," she said in a husky whisper.

He exhaled a shaky breath, finding it odd she'd chosen the very word he'd used to describe his feelings toward her.

"But your eyes, they aren't the same color as his."

"No. In a transplant, you only receive the clear cornea, not the iris, so the color of your eyes doesn't change."

Her hand tightened around her glass. "Doug's eyes. It's strange, I can't believe it…." Her words trailed off and she stared at him again as if she wanted to say more but couldn't force the words out.

The intensity of her look cut him to the core. His palms grew sweaty. His pulse raced. What was she thinking? How did she feel?

"I didn't come to Beaufort to upset you," Collin said quietly. "But I needed to know about your husband." He paused and saw her bite her lower lip. "I feel as if I owe him something, Sydney. And when I heard the man, my donor, had a widow, I thought maybe there was something I could do for you. Some way I could help, you know, with money or something."

"You don't owe me anything." She twined her hands in her lap, absentmindedly pushing her wedding band in circles around her finger. "And I don't want your money."

Once again the silence grew thick between them. Collin watched her wrestle with her emotions. He reached over the table and covered her hand with his, hoping to comfort her. Instead, the warmth of her skin beneath his palm sent a spark of desire through his body. A desire he had no right to feel, and certainly couldn't act upon.

"Yes, I do owe you," he said, making a concerted effort to focus on the fact that she was a recent widow. He'd seen her sorrow at the graveyard. "You can't know what it was like to suddenly be blinded, to have to give up everything, my job, my independence, and adjust to a world of darkness." He shrugged, smiling when she started to shake her head. "I never thought about the donor before the operation—I was only hoping to have the surgery. Then when I had the surgery...well, knowing I had a part of someone else really shook me up." His voice grew husky and he hesitated, realizing he'd told her more about the feelings he'd had over the past months than he'd told anyone.

Her gaze swung back to his again and he saw the compassion and understanding he'd hoped for. She was a remarkable woman, all strength and soft vulnerability at the same time. Her eyes glittered with unshed tears and her rosy lips parted in a sigh.

He cleared his throat and continued, "It's a weird feeling, knowing I can see now because a man died. It makes me feel guilty."

"I don't know what to say." She relaxed her fingers beneath his. "Except, I'm glad you have your eyesight back. It must have really been an ordeal."

"It was. And thank you for listening," he said, glancing at their hands, fascinated at how her fingers seemed to fit into his. "But I am sorry that getting my sight back was at someone else's expense. Mainly yours and your husband's."

Sydney grew quiet as she curled her hands into fists. Collin's hand tightened over hers. He wanted to gain her trust. He wanted to believe she was innocent.

An image suddenly flitted through his mind, and his throat closed, the words dying on his lips as Sydney's face appeared in his mind. Like a choppy out-of-focus video, bits and pieces of a meeting between Sydney and Doug scattered through his vision, obliterating the world around him.

Sydney arguing with him…heated words…his mocking laughter…tears streaming down Sydney's face….

Collin's gut clenched at the disturbing image. He pressed one of his knuckles to his temple, massaging his head, trying to bring himself back to reality. Somewhere in his subconscious, he knew Sydney was talking to him, calling his name. But then another image drifted into his mind.

Sydney standing in the dim glow of candlelight, a slither of silk floating over her soft, feminine curves as she smiled seductively, calling his name…calling him to bed….

He released her hand, his fingers suddenly cold and stiff.

Sydney's startled voice jolted him back to reality. "Collin, are you all right?"

He scrubbed his face with his hands, then took a sip of water and swallowed, willing the images away. His vision retreated into darkness, then blurred for several seconds, shades of black and gray reminding him of the fear he'd lived with during his blindness. He blinked again and finally Sydney's face and the restaurant slid back into focus, fuzzy at first, then slowly details sharpened—Sydney's incredible blue eyes intense with fear, her sable hair falling like a waterfall around her shoulders.

"Collin? What's wrong? Are you ill?"

He was surprised to see the look of concern on her

delicate features. "Uh, nothing," he said. "I had a...sort of a blackout."

"Are you all right?"

"Yes, I'm fine now," he said to reassure himself, as well as her. "I just have these spells occasionally."

"The operation—was it totally successful? Is your vision okay now?"

Collin gave a slight nod. "So far. Although there's still a chance of rejection, and occasionally I have blurred vision, but it's improving daily." The concern on her face deepened. "My vision is really clear, considering that three weeks ago, I couldn't see anything."

"That's good." Sydney wrapped her arms around her middle. "I hope you'll be all right now." She stood up as if to say goodbye. "And please don't feel you owe me anything. Actually I'm glad you told me. It's nice to know that at least something good came of Doug's tragic death."

A lump formed in his throat at her sincerity, and he wondered again how deep her feelings ran for her deceased husband. He struggled for words to keep her near, not certain why it was so important, but knowing he had an urge to reach out and hold her hand again.

But she'd had a shock. First her husband's death, then the accident, now his news. She needed time, he told himself. He mustn't push her.

"I need to go now." Sydney glanced nervously at the door. "I have some work to do this afternoon. I hope you enjoy the rest of your stay, Collin."

She was dismissing him. Too many conflicting emotions raged between them. Whatever reasons she had for running, he felt bereft at the thought of her leaving. He couldn't let her go. "That's right, you're photographing the festival this afternoon."

She checked her watch. "Yes, the activities should be starting soon."

"It sounds nice. Mind if I tag along?"

She hesitated and took a step back. "I guess that would be okay. But I really have to work, Collin. I promised the editor photos for the morning paper tomorrow. And I have a photography booth set up. A friend of mine is running it. I may need to relieve her for a while."

"No problem." He picked up the check. "Just let me pay the bill and we'll go."

She twisted her purse strap in her hands, biting on her lip again. She was nervous about being with him. Was it because she felt this strange chemistry between them, too? Or was she hiding something?

"THIS AFTERNOON is going to be a scorcher," Sydney said as they strolled down the sidewalk toward Bay Street. She slung her camera bag over her shoulder, grateful she'd dressed in a cool outfit. The sun was already blistering. No rain today. Only the beating rays of the summer sunshine and a gentle breeze off the water to stir the humidity.

The man beside her wasn't helping matters, either.

Her nerves felt like frayed rope. Thank God he didn't work with Steve. But a part of Doug lived in Collin. How was she supposed to feel about that? Goose bumps skated up her arms in spite of the heat. Making small talk after Collin's bombshell seemed somehow ridiculous—and eerie. It was as if Doug had come back to stalk her from the grave, to haunt her. As if he was mocking her as he watched her learn about his betrayal.

They passed two elderly women from church. She waved, not surprised when they appeared startled that she'd caught them staring. She'd heard whispers and seen the odd glances people gave her. Some people felt sorry for her, others had morbid curiosity about the details of the murder—and others gossiped that she'd killed Doug.

"The townsfolk really get into this festival, don't they?" Collin gestured toward the variety of booths set up along the town square.

"This festival is held during our peak vacation season." She paused, smiling at two children eating cotton candy who stood enthralled by a clown tying balloons into animal forms. Wanting to capture the children candidly, she quietly raised her camera and snapped a few shots.

Balloons and banners decorated the storefronts, and tents had been set up along the waterfront near the open park where a giant jungle gym provided entertainment for a rollicking group of kids. Adults and more kids roamed through the arts-and-crafts displays, some browsing, others buying decorative items for their homes or works from their favorite artists. She snapped pictures of everything, chatting with several families as she passed. Music wafted from a stage where local acts were scheduled for the day. Vendors sold everything from snow cones to funnel cakes to seafood plates. A country line-dance instructor called steps over a microphone, and people joined in the dance as the lively music picked up.

Collin seemed to be enjoying himself. But he kept watching her with those arresting dark gray eyes. Doug's eyes had been a dull brown—emotionless, she now realized. But Collin's were intense, searching, full of secrets and…passion. Sexy. Bedroom eyes. It was as if he could see inside her head, as if he knew things about her she hadn't told him.

A heavyset woman in a red-and-white-checked apron called to them from a small refreshment stand. "How're you doing, Ms. Sydney?"

"Fine, Lucinda. How about you?" Sydney snapped a shot of the woman serving two children.

"Great. If I can just keep myself from eating the merchandise." She patted her round hips and laughed.

Sydney grinned, grateful the woman didn't offer a comment about Doug. Then Collin stepped up beside her and Sydney introduced them, wondering if being escorted by him would feed the gossip vine.

Lucinda smiled in greeting. "What would you like this afternoon?"

Collin's arm brushed against Sydney's as she studied the selection. Sydney wiped a drop of perspiration from her brow, the afternoon heat becoming more unbearable with his nearness.

"The butter pecan for the lady and mint chocolate chip for me," Collin said automatically.

Sydney's camera bag clambered down her arm as she dropped her hands in surprise. "How did you know what I wanted? How could you possibly know I—"

"You always order butter pecan?"

Sydney nodded slowly, his husky voice sliding over her skin like a lover's caress. Intimate, knowing. *Too* knowing.

She jerked her camera up and stepped back.

"I...don't know. A lucky guess, I suppose." He shaded his eyes with his hands, squinting at her. Then, as if he couldn't bear the light, he slipped on a pair of aviator sunglasses, and she could no longer see his eyes.

Doug's eyes.

No, the fact that he'd guessed her favorite kind of ice cream couldn't be related to the transplant. The idea was preposterous.

But as he accepted the treats, tension tightened his jaw. A breeze caught the short strands of his dark hair, tumbling a lock over his forehead. His features radiated masculinity that reminded her of Harry Connick, Jr., a face she'd like to photograph. A dangerous thought—sex appeal oozed from Collin just as it did from her favorite musician. And it had been a long time since she'd felt sexually alive.

But he had Doug's eyes—it was eerie.

On the heels of awareness rode guilt. She had no right to be thinking how attractive this man was when she'd recently buried her husband. *But the marriage ended long before he died,* a voice whispered. First they'd fought over Doug's traveling so much, then she'd found hotel receipts and phone numbers in his pocket that had made her suspect he was having an affair. Several times she'd phoned his office to find he wasn't where he'd said he would be.

"I'm impressed with the number of artists here," Collin said, interrupting her thoughts.

"They come from all over," Sydney said quietly.

He followed her down the steps and Sydney licked her ice cream, pointing out landmarks. "The bed-and-breakfast where you're staying is one of the oldest houses in town," Sydney said, trying to distract herself from watching Collin's mouth as he licked at his own cone. "Although it's only four bedrooms, it's one of the most popular because of its mom and pop appeal."

People milled along the sidewalk, couples hand in hand, women and men pushing strollers and carrying little ones on their shoulders. Sydney photographed a group of women working on a quilt, then moved on to a pottery-and-leather-goods exhibit. Finally they reached Sydney's booth, where Kelly was working. Megan slept in her stroller under a tall oak tree.

Sydney stopped to brush her fingers over Megan's chubby cheek, then introduced Collin to Kelly.

A slight frown marred Kelly's face as she greeted Collin. "You sold a couple of prints, Syd."

Collin wandered to Sydney's right, studying some of her photographs while she and Kelly talked business.

"I like your sea-animal shots," Collin said, his voice filled with surprise. "Those sea turtles are so vivid I can almost touch them."

A blush warmed Sydney's cheeks, adding fire to the already sweltering heat. "I like to dabble in nature photos and marine wildlife."

Collin took his time scrutinizing the prints, commenting on the shadows, angles and lighting of each shot. He was a complex man adding to a complex situation. But his admiration for her work pleased her.

"I bet Doug liked your work," he said.

Sydney shifted uncomfortably. "He admired it in the beginning, but he was so busy last year he wasn't around a lot." He'd even wanted her to quit, to devote more time to being an executive's wife, something she'd been unable to fathom. Then they'd talked about having a baby, and their marriage had improved for a while. He'd obviously been placating her with false promises.

"This sunset is fantastic."

"I took it by the marina," Sydney said, her pride swelling. "The oranges and reds were great that night, but that streak of purple intrigued me." It was also the same night she'd realized her rocky marriage to Doug was over. He'd come home smelling like cheap perfume and admitted he'd been with another woman, had said it was just one time, but she'd suspected there were others, would always be others.

"I'd like to buy it." Collin removed it from the display.

Sydney stiffened, aware Kelly was watching their interaction. Megan started to fuss and Kelly picked her up, propping her on her hip.

"I told you earlier you don't owe me anything," Sydney said, remembering his comment about repaying his debt.

Collin's smile faded. "I'm not buying it because I owe you. I'm buying it because I like it. It'll be perfect above the mantel in my apartment."

Sydney folded her arms across her chest. "Really, Collin, I don't want you to feel like you have to—"

"You don't understand, Sydney." His voice dropped to a whisper. "All those months I was blind, I missed seeing things like this." He motioned toward the wall of photographs, then toward the ocean behind them. "I used to try and remember places I'd been, what the ocean looked like, the mountains, but it wasn't the same." He pulled off his sunglasses and gazed into her eyes. "Now, I appreciate them more. I know how much I missed." His voice cracked slightly. "I know it sounds corny, but can you understand that?"

Sydney's heart melted. His mouth curved into a lopsided, almost embarrassed smile. Warmth radiated through her body at his words, teasing her senses, making her forget she was a recent widow. He'd described her feelings about the pictures she took, the reason she'd gotten into photography years ago—she wanted to capture the beauty of the world around her forever. Only, lately life hadn't been so beautiful.

The thought jerked her back to the moment and she noticed Kelly watching her, frowning. Other people joined them at the booth and Sydney dragged her gaze away from Collin. He did the same, although she sensed he was as reluctant as she to break the spell.

Kelly wrapped the picture and promised to hold it for him to pick up later.

"You want me to man the booth for a while?" Sydney asked, noticing several potential customers.

"No, Jean's coming to get Megan in a few minutes," Kelly explained. "She's baby-sitting this afternoon."

Sydney cooed and brushed Megan's baby-soft curls away from her forehead. "Hey, sweetie, how's my little angel?" Megan made a gurgling sound and curled her chubby hand against Sydney's chest. The scent of baby powder wafted from her, and Sydney felt a painful tug on her heartstrings for the child she'd never had. And for the dream of a family that had died with her unhappy marriage.

Suddenly she felt someone watching her. She glanced up to see Sergeant Raeburn glaring at her across the crowd.

COLLIN DIDN'T UNDERSTAND what was happening to him. Every time he met another local, strange feelings bombarded him. Nothing concrete, no real images, just a slight rattle of his nerve endings hinting that something peculiar was happening to his body. And with the town. Sydney's face paled in the bright sunlight, and he turned to see what had upset her.

Raeburn. Watching the two of them like a hawk about to swoop.

He'd probably discovered Collin was a cop by now. What else did he know?

Collin raised his hand and waved. Raeburn tipped his hat, then sauntered off. Sydney clamped down on her lip with her teeth and cuddled Megan. He instinctively reached out to touch the little girl's chubby, soft cheek.

"Hey, there, pudding."

Sydney's eyes widened.

"What is it, Sydney?"

The breath seemed to catch in her throat. "That's exactly what Doug used to call her."

He froze, his heart skipping a beat, and racked his brain to remember where he'd heard the silly nickname before. He couldn't recall ever hearing it.

A little girl of about four ran up, an elderly man in tow. "Take my picture, Ms. Sydney," the child said, her big brown eyes mesmerizing.

Sydney laughed and photographed the little girl while the elderly man stood by. Then she carefully eased Megan back into her stroller and kissed her cheek. The oddest sensation struck Collin at the gesture. Strange, since he'd never paid much attention to kids before, had never had the desire for a family of his own, but for just a minute... He blocked the ridiculous thought. Must be all this small-town stuff.

A tall, attractive blond woman approached. On her blouse she wore an unusual sea-horse pin with an emerald eye that glittered in the sunlight.

"I'm taking Beth to ride the ponies now," the elderly man, apparently the little girl's grandfather, said to the woman. Beth grabbed his hand again and quickly dragged him away.

The woman gave Sydney a questioning look as Sydney introduced her to Collin as Marla.

"Where's your hubby?" Sydney asked.

Marla's smile faded. "I didn't want to mention it at the studio, with you just out of the hospital. He and I separated last week." She traced a circle on the ground with the toe of her shoe. "He went to Atlanta on business. We're going to talk when he gets back."

"Oh, I'm sorry." Sympathy softened Sydney's face. "I hope you guys can work things out."

Marla shrugged. "Me, too. Beth will be devastated if her dad moves out permanently." Looking as if she regretted saying so much, Marla added an apology and hastily left.

"A good friend?" Collin asked.

"An acquaintance," Sydney answered. "I take Beth's portraits a couple of times a year. Why?"

Collin shook his head. "I don't know. Were you and Doug good friends of theirs?"

"Not really," Sydney said hesitantly. "Marla and Randy belong to the club where Doug worked out. We didn't socialize, though."

Collin rolled his shoulders, wondering about the uneasiness he'd sensed with Marla. The town certainly appeared friendly, but looks could be deceiving. "Do you have any idea which one of these people might have killed your husband?"

Sydney's startled eyes touched a chord of guilt inside him, reminding him of a time in his life when he'd been less skeptical of others, more trusting. A time before he was a cop, witnessing the dregs of society. Sydney had that innocence about her, but her husband's murder had obviously tainted it.

Still, he could have kicked himself for being so blunt, especially when Sydney's blue eyes turned wary, their earlier ease disintegrating.

"I'm sorry. I didn't mean to upset you."

Sydney gestured toward the crowd, her voice quivering as she said, "These people are my friends. I trust them."

He reached out to comfort her, but she backed away. "I apologize for being so tactless. I just wondered if Doug had any enemies."

"I don't know," Sydney said cautiously. "Why are you asking so many questions?"

Collin winced, realizing he'd overstepped. "I'm sorry, I didn't mean to pry." He shrugged. "I guess it has me rattled to know that the man who gave me back my eyesight didn't die by accident."

Shadows played across her face as she retreated further. He silently told himself to move slowly. To give her space and himself time to think like a cop, not like someone personally involved.

But he *was* personally involved, he admitted to himself. Ever since his operation.

Two middle-aged men approached Sydney. The taller one wore khakis and a polo shirt and held out his hand in greeting. They offered condolences about Doug, then asked about Norvek Pharmaceuticals and when the company would release the new weight-loss product.

"I don't know, John. I'm sure Steve Wallace will have an announcement soon." She tucked a strand of hair behind her ear, the sun highlighting the curve of her chin.

"Keep us posted," both men said.

Sydney introduced them, and Collin committed their names to memory. John Armstrong and Bill Daniels. A couple of Doug's acquaintances to check out. Collin's eyesight blurred slightly. As he shook John's hand, he experienced a quick vision. *The man arguing with him...accusing him of falsifying FDA information.*

When he managed to shake off the image, Collin was sweating, his mouth dry. The men retreated toward a health-care booth at the far end of the street. He hadn't noticed it earlier, but a tent had been set up for free blood-pressure checkups, and a barrage of health-care companies congregated there to answer questions and give other types of free screenings.

"I'm going to take photographs of the entertainment,"
Sydney said. "Why don't you check out some of the other
booths?"

He wished he could control the images bombarding
him. And he wished Sydney would stop looking at him
as if he were a ghost.

"I'll see you later?" he asked.

She shrugged, then hurried off, obviously wanting to
get away from him. He'd definitely spooked her with his
questions and probing looks. While Sydney took photographs, he wandered around the booths, picking up snippets of information and gossip about the town, carefully
keeping one eye on Sydney.

"Poor girl," he heard an older woman whisper to her
blue-haired friend. "You knew her husband was running
around on her, didn't you?"

"I thought as much," the second woman said, her
bracelets jangling as she talked with her hands. "They
say the wife's always the last to know."

The gossip stirred new questions in Collin's head. Just
what kind of a man and husband had Doug Green been?
Did Sydney know he'd been unfaithful?

"I think he had more than one slip on the side." The
first woman tittered.

"I heard they were headed for a divorce. She'd already
filed the papers. Didn't surprise me a bit."

Sydney had filed divorce papers? The news hit him like
a truck. Did Raeburn know this? Was that why he didn't
seem to be looking past Sydney for the killer?

"I always told my girl not to trust a pretty-boy face.
And that Doug Green had one if I ever saw one."

"Lying eyes," the blue-haired woman added. "The
windows of a person's soul. And that man's soul had the
devil in it."

Collin pressed his fingers to his temple as the realization sank in. They were talking about Doug Green's eyes. The eyes that now belonged to him.

SYDNEY TOOK SEVERAL more snapshots, feeling Collin's dark gaze burning into her back as she wove through the crowd. He'd planted a seed of doubt in her mind about her friends, and she didn't like it at all.

Thank God she'd escaped without bumping into Raeburn. He'd been too occupied with the police safety booth to hassle her.

Glancing over her shoulder, she sighed in relief to see Collin had finally gone on without her. She needed to put some space between them. She headed down the street, anxious to retreat to her home for some privacy.

But when she finally reached her walkway, an eerie premonition crawled through her, raising the hair on the nape of her neck. The door to her garage was open. And her front door stood slightly ajar. What was going on? Could someone be inside? Beaufort had always been such a safe town.

Until Doug's murder.

Her heart thudded to a stop as she peered inside the open doorway. Her house had been broken into. She could see into the den. The room had been ransacked. Magazines, books, her couch cushions, all her belongings lay in disarray.

Then she staggered backward in horror as a tall, wiry man appeared in the doorway and pointed a gun in her face.

Chapter Five

"Who...who are you?" Sydney stammered.

The thin hand holding the gun trembled. "Come in, Mrs. Green. I've been waitin' on you."

The strong scent of his musky cologne and cigarette smoke filled the air. Sydney wanted to gag. "What do you want?" She fisted ner hand around her keys and tried to remember the self-defense class she'd taken. If she stomped his foot first, then stabbed him in the eyes with her keys—

"I said come in, damn it." The man's growl and wild-eyed expression made her rethink her plan. If the gun went off, she'd be dead. He jerked her arm, yanking her through the front door. Her legs wobbled as she stared into his beady green eyes. Was this Doug's murderer? Had he returned to kill her?

Determined not to let him succeed without a fight, she struggled against his grasp, stumbling backward. Suddenly Collin Cash materialized behind her and caught her. He reached for the gun, but the stranger pointed the weapon at Sydney's temple. Collin froze, then raised his hands in surrender. Sydney's heart pounded, but Collin's presence sent a wave of relief rushing through her.

"What's going on?" Collin's steely voice startled the

man, who waved the gun back and forth between the two of them.

"Who the hell are you?"

Collin eased up beside Sydney, then placed himself in front of her. "I'm a friend of Sydney's. Just stay calm, mister, and put down the gun."

"Be quiet!"

Sydney tried to mollify him, "If you want jewelry or money—"

"Shut up!" he yelled in a high-pitched voice, shuffling from one worn leather loafer to the other. "I don't want your damn jewelry. I want what's rightfully *mine*."

Sydney shuddered. "What are you talking about?"

"The formula for the weight-loss drink." He pushed a copy of the newspaper article in front of her. He looked like a mad scientist, Sydney thought, irrational and out of control. "It's mine. I demand you give me credit for it."

"I don't understand, Mr...."

"McKenzie." He flattened his palm over his chest, punctuating his words as he pulled a formal-looking document from his pocket. "I'm Spade McKenzie, Mrs. Green. I'm sure your husband told you about me."

"No, he didn't," Sydney said, striving for calm. "And even if the formula is yours, my husband secured the licensing agreement for it."

The man's eyebrows drew together in a scowl, his right eye twitching nervously. "Your husband *stole* it from me at the university. He must have copied it from my files. Imagine my surprise when I opened the paper and read he'd sold it." His eyes flashed with rage. "Now I want you to talk to the company, tell them it's mine and make sure I'm paid the money due me."

Collin held up a warning hand. "Settle down, man, and put away the gun."

Fear ballooned in Sydney's chest, then settled into a dull ache. Was McKenzie telling the truth? Had Doug stolen it? Or had this crazy man seen the article and decided to take the credit and money for Doug's accomplishments?

"Listen, Mr. McKenzie, you need to talk to the president of the company," Sydney suggested in a shaky voice. "I didn't have anything to do with the deal."

"Now put down the gun before you hurt someone," Collin coaxed in a quiet but threatening tone.

"Don't tell me what to do!"

Sydney clutched Collin's elbow at the panicked look on McKenzie's face. Collin squeezed her hand, but sent McKenzie a scathing look.

McKenzie's hand was trembling so badly now she was afraid the gun would discharge. "I tried talking to the people at Norvex, but they wouldn't even see me."

"Why don't you get a lawyer?" Collin suggested.

"That'll cost me a fortune." McKenzie wiped his forehead with the back of his hand. "Just read this document. I got the patent six months ago."

"But Doug's been working on this deal for over a year," Sydney argued.

"If you look at this paper, you'll see I talked with Triset Pharmaceuticals about the product, not your husband," McKenzie explained. "I worked so hard on that formula, took so damn much time to get it right."

Sydney's hand shook as she accepted the paper. If McKenzie was telling the truth, Doug hadn't been the man she'd thought he was. But then, she already knew that. He had an alias. What else would she discover about him?

"I don't see how I can help you," Sydney said, fighting tears. "I didn't work with Doug or the company, Mr. McKenzie."

He gestured toward her computer. He'd already turned it on and had been snooping through her file manager. "You know where your husband's files are stored. Show me and I'll prove he copied it from me."

"Mr. McKenzie—" Sydney hesitated, forcing a calm into her voice she didn't feel "—that computer is mine. I store my bookkeeping for my photography business in it. Doug kept his computer and files at his office."

Collin laid a gentle hand over hers and Sydney took a deep breath. Collin's entire persona radiated danger and anger, but she felt nothing but tenderness in his touch. And protectiveness, a sensation that both puzzled her and left her feeling vulnerable in a whole different way.

McKenzie's fingers tightened around the automatic, his complexion turning ruddy with anger. "I want my name on that formula. I deserve to have it."

"Then get a lawyer," Collin suggested again, his voice deadly this time. "Mrs. Green can't help you."

McKenzie stalked toward Collin, his mouth twisting nastily. Collin gently pushed Sydney behind him, then pounced on McKenzie. One minute McKenzie's hand was holding the weapon, the next Collin landed a punch to his arm and stomach that sent the gun flying to the floor. Sydney jumped back, clutching the side of a chair. McKenzie doubled over and dropped to the carpet, groaning.

Collin retrieved the gun, reached for the phone with one hand and kept his booted foot pressed against McKenzie's neck. "I'm sure the police will be interested in hearing how you barged in and threatened Mrs. Green."

McKenzie whimpered and gaped at Sydney and Collin with hate-filled eyes. "It's not my fault. It's that cheatin' husband of yours."

Sydney pressed a shaky fist to her mouth as Collin dialed the police. Then they waited for them to arrive.

"You know, McKenzie, the cops may decide you had the perfect motive to kill Sydney's husband." Collin gestured at the ransacked room. "And now you returned, searching for Green's files to destroy them and cover your tracks. Then you intended to kill his wife, too."

Spade McKenzie's face turned even paler. His big eyes bulged with fear. "I didn't kill him," he said in a shrill voice. "I didn't."

Collin clenched his jaw. "Tell it to the police."

"And I...I wasn't going to kill her," McKenzie protested. "I only wanted my money...and the credit for my work."

Sydney wrapped her arms around herself at the man's pathetic whine. A siren wailed in the distance and she experienced a sense of déjà vu; memories of the horrible night Doug had died flooded her mind. Her chest ached and her throat felt raw, but she slowly rocked herself, trying to maintain control. A hand gently massaged her shoulder and she sank onto the sofa, her knees buckling.

"Are you all right?" Collin's low, intimate voice ignited a subtle warmth that replaced the chill in her body.

Sydney nodded, her throat too dry to speak. The police pounded on the door and yelled for her to open it. Collin shook his head at her, silently telling her to stay still and allow him to handle things. Emotionally drained, she relented, already dreading another encounter with the police. McKenzie started to stand, but Collin pointed the gun at him more aggressively, and McKenzie slumped back onto the floor. Then Collin let Raeburn and a uniformed woman officer in.

"So, what's going on here, Mizz Green?" the sergeant asked, maneuvering his bulk toward her.

Sydney tensed as he surveyed the room. "This man broke into my house. He pulled a gun on me."

Raeburn's questioning gaze traveled from McKenzie to Collin. "You're the one who dragged Mizz Green from the wreck, aren't you?"

"Yeah."

Raeburn's bushy eyebrows shot up. "I thought you two didn't know each other."

Sydney realized the implication. Apparently so did Collin. "I'm vacationing here," Collin explained. "I ran into Sydney at the festival, then walked over here afterward. When I arrived, this man was waving a gun in her face."

Raeburn and the other officer listened while Sydney repeated McKenzie's threats.

"I have my rights," McKenzie whined. "And her husband cheated me. I only want what's mine."

"Can it!" the woman officer snapped.

"Cuff him," Raeburn ordered. "We'll take him in and book him."

Sydney breathed a sigh of relief. She'd feared Raeburn wouldn't believe her.

The accompanying officer handcuffed McKenzie and helped him to stand. He struggled with the cuffs, a feral gleam in his eyes, but the woman jerked his arm and shoved him toward the door.

"This isn't over yet!" McKenzie yelled.

"Get him outta here," Raeburn said coldly.

Sydney recoiled at McKenzie's crude reply.

Raeburn turned to Sydney. "Care to shed any light on McKenzie's accusations, Mizz Green?"

Once again Sydney felt the implications underlying his statement, and anger churned through her. He thought she was holding back; he'd made his opinion clear the last time he'd questioned her. "I don't know anything about

Doug's business deals. He didn't share his files or details about his ventures with me," she said. "And I've never heard of that man before tonight."

Raeburn stuffed a piece of gum in his mouth. "I see. Seems you're always winding up in trouble and don't know why, don't it, Mizz Green?"

Sydney clasped her hands in her lap, the day's events taking a toll. He made her sound like an idiot. "I told you everything I know, Sergeant. I was photographing the festival today and when I returned, my place had been ransacked. That man was waiting inside my house with a gun."

"The lady answered your question," Collin cut in. "Now why don't you do your job and find out about that lunatic who barged in here and threatened her."

Raeburn's fat cheeks reddened with anger. Collin sent him a steely look. Once again Sydney wondered just who Collin Cash was. He certainly wasn't afraid of fighting a crazy, dangerous man like McKenzie or standing up to a cop like Raeburn.

"I'll be in touch." Raeburn pointed a beefy finger at Sydney. "And don't leave town, Mizz Green. I'll need to talk to you again once I've interrogated McKenzie." He tipped his head, indicating the things strewn on the floor. "Oh, and make a list of anything you find missing. We'll need it for the report."

Sydney nodded curtly. Raeburn turned to leave, but Collin stopped him at the door. "Did you learn anything else about Mrs. Green's car when you hauled it in?"

Sydney's fingers dug into the edge of the sofa cushion as she waited for Raeburn's reply. Surely if he'd found the weapon, he would already have arrested her. The sergeant was obviously looking for some way to pin everything on her, and the gun was probably the only thing he needed to lock her up.

"As a matter of fact, we did," Raeburn said in a gravelly voice. He shot a punitive gaze her way.

"And?"

Raeburn popped his gum between his teeth. "It looks like the brake lines on the car were cut."

The air in Sydney's lungs collected in a hot pool and gushed out. "What?"

"So somebody intentionally tried to hurt her," Collin supplied.

Raeburn lifted his massive shoulders in a slight shrug. "Don't know for sure, but we're checking it out."

"I certainly hope you are checking it out. Because if it was intentional, then today makes the second time someone's tried to harm Sydney."

Sydney dropped her head forward and closed her eyes as Collin walked Raeburn outside. A shudder passed through her. Raeburn still believed she'd killed Doug. And that madman, McKenzie, might have killed her if Collin hadn't shown up.

Why was all this happening? Even if Doug had been in trouble, why would someone want to harm her?

COLLIN TOOK A DEEP BREATH, bracing himself as Raeburn knotted a fist around his shirt. "I did some checking on you, Mr. Cash." Raeburn's voice turned hard. "Why didn't you tell me you were a cop?"

Collin picked Raeburn's hands off his shirt. Apparently the sergeant wasn't as incompetent as he'd thought. "I see you've done your homework."

"Damn right. Now be straight with me, Cash."

Collin conceded with a slight grunt, "Because I didn't come here on business." Not officially, anyway, he thought. "I came here on vacation. I told you the truth about having surgery."

Raeburn made a hissing sound of disbelief. "And you just happened to wind up in the middle of a murder investigation?"

Collin nodded, but Raeburn's expression reeked of anger. "I don't believe you, Cash. Now tell me the real reason you're here, 'cause you're out of your jurisdiction."

"If you checked up on me, then you know I've been on disability leave for over a year," Collin said. "I was shot last spring and haven't worked since."

Raeburn's stance widened. "I'm not buying this vacation crap, Cash. It's too coincidental." He snapped his gum. "And I'm warning you, this is my town. Stay out of my way. If you botch this investigation, I'll throw you in the tank myself."

"I'm not going to botch anything." Collin squared his shoulders. "Tell me why you're not searching harder for Green's killer."

"Maybe I think I already know who it is."

"Maybe you're wrong. Why don't you look somewhere beyond the obvious?"

Raeburn gave him a nasty smile. "You mean beyond Mrs. Green?"

"Yeah. Surely you've investigated Doug Green's past. His business dealings. The guy made a bundle of money on his deals—plenty of motive for murder."

"Yeah, and guess who gets it all now he's dead?"

Raeburn's question silenced him. He knew there was more. He just hadn't figured it out yet. "What about protecting Sydney?" Collin asked. "You don't believe she cut her own brake lines, do you?"

A muscle ticked in Raeburn's jaw. "We're taking

McKenzie in. And other than that, I don't owe you any explanation. This matter is police business."

Collin had hit a brick wall. "How about having a car patrol the neighborhood tonight? I'm sure that would make Sydney feel better."

Raeburn mumbled an agreement, then jacked up his pants and sauntered away. Collin gritted his teeth. He wouldn't botch the case—he was determined to find Doug Green's killer.

Even if he had to butt heads with Raeburn. And even if the murderer turned out to be Sydney.

SYDNEY BARELY GLANCED UP when Collin knelt beside her. "Are you okay, Sydney?"

He laid his hand at the back of her neck, and Sydney swallowed, refusing to look up. Pain rolled through her in waves. Too many unanswered questions tumbled through her head.

Doug had obviously played her for a fool. And now Wallace and McKenzie both suggested he'd cheated them. She'd been so caught up in wanting a family that she'd seen only the things she wanted to see. Besides the horror of his murder, one nasty, dark secret after another about her husband kept popping up. What would be next?

Collin gently brushed aside her hair, then massaged the tense muscles at the base of her neck. "It's okay, you're safe now."

Sydney trembled, fighting the overwhelming sense of fear invading her. She also had to fight her attraction to this man. It would be too easy to lean on him, to accept his comfort—the way she had Doug's.

"Come on, Sydney, take a deep breath," Collin murmured. He kneaded her shoulder muscles and stroked her neck again, and Sydney shuddered, a low sob escaping her. Collin rubbed his hands up and down her arms, the rich cadence of his voice soothing and warm.

"I'm sorry," Sydney said, hating the way her body quivered.

"He scared you. Hell, he scared me, too," Collin said with a self-deprecating laugh. "It's a normal reaction, Sydney." He paused, their breathing the only sound in the room. "And it's also normal to release the fear once the danger's over."

Sydney knotted her hands around a small cushion. She had to tell him to leave, had to tell him she could take care of herself. But like a traitor, her mouth ignored her.

"Shh, it's okay." Collin pried her hands from the cushion, coaxing her with gentle murmurings. At first she resisted, but he crooned soft, comforting words and she felt herself relenting, giving in to the emotional pull of his husky voice.

His strong arms tightened around her and she sagged against him, the past two months' worth of anger and hurt welling up inside her. Tears spilled from her eyes, and her shoulders shook with unreleased sobs. She clutched his shirt and buried herself against him, drawing in his masculine scent and taking solace in the heat from his body, in the rapid rhythm of his heart beating beneath her cheek.

He stroked her hair and back, held her securely against the hard wall of his chest, and whispered soft words of understanding that soothed her nerves like kisses she might plant on a child. Finally, after what seemed like hours, the torrent of emotions ebbed and the rush of tears subsided. Embarrassed at her outburst, she huddled against him, not knowing what to say.

"I hope that SOB rots in jail," Collin muttered. "He had no right to barge in here and scare you half to death."

The harsh edge to his voice was so at odds with the tender way he held her that tears pooled in her eyes again. But she pressed her fist to her mouth and took several deep breaths to keep them at bay. Collin held her closer, his warm breath fanning her cheek.

"I wish you'd talk to me," Collin whispered. "Tell me about Doug's business dealings. Maybe I can help you."

Sydney shook her head, relaxing slightly when he threaded his fingers through her hair and lifted the strands away from her face. She barely even knew this man, yet she felt closer to him than she had to her own husband.

During the past few months of their marriage, her feelings for Doug had waned. When they'd first met, she'd been ready to settle down and have a family. Doug had said he wanted the same things. He'd been so charming.

But shortly into the marriage, Doug's vows had become nothing but empty words. Being old fashioned and believing in commitment, she'd tried to make things work, had hoped things would get better. But they hadn't.

"Sydney, I really do want to help," Collin repeated softly. He trailed his fingers down her arm and Sydney shivered again, this time a slow arousal building in her. Collin's strong, virile body was pressed against hers so tightly she could feel his chest rising and falling with every breath. She could smell his masculine scent. She could almost taste the understanding and yearning in his voice. She wanted to succumb to the long-dormant desire awakening inside her, stroke his jaw, then bury herself even more deeply in his warm embrace.

But she had too many problems to deal with now. She barely knew Collin. She couldn't bare her soul to a stranger. Mentally scolding herself, she eased out of his arms and wiped her face with her palms. Then she looked up into Collin's eyes and saw a tenderness she'd never expected. On the heels of understanding, something like desire flickered in the gray depths. His eyes simmered with heat, with longing. His eyes—Doug's eyes.

The thought jerked her back to reality with a soul-deep pain. He wanted her to talk to him, but how could she tell him she thought her husband, the man who'd given him back his eyesight, might be guilty of the things McKenzie had said? And that he'd deceived her, maybe cheated on her, had an alias and had bought a one-way ticket to Brazil the day he died?

She could no more do that than she could reveal the humiliating sting of finding out he'd had a vasectomy and acted as if she was a failure because she couldn't bear a child. She had to tell Collin to go back to his home, to his own life and leave her alone. Because every time she looked at him, she saw her husband in his eyes.

COLLIN KNEW the second he lost her. One moment Sydney was cradled against him, warm and trusting, accepting his comfort, and his mind was going berserk trying to refrain from kissing her fears away. The next she pulled away, looking wary and confused and leaving his body with an aching emptiness he didn't quite understand. He balled his hands into fists against his thighs to keep from dragging her back into his arms.

When he'd seen McKenzie holding a gun on her, he'd almost gone ballistic. Thank God, his police training had kicked in and he'd used his head. If he hadn't they might both have been killed.

He had a second chance at life now, and he didn't want to blow it. He didn't want to blow things with Sydney, either. So he sat patiently, trying to give her time to feel in control again. He understood how vulnerable it felt to be a victim. God, the whole past year of his life he'd felt victimized.

There was something else wrong, though, something she wasn't telling him about Doug. Something that had hurt her so badly she didn't want to talk about it. She was trying to distance herself, trying to decide whether she should trust him. She must have been desperately in love with Doug to want to protect the man this way.

"You should go," Sydney said in a low voice, standing and putting even more distance between them.

He cleared his throat, biding time while he studied her pale face. "I don't want to leave," he said. "Not until I know you're all right."

"I'm fine." Her chin lifted a notch as if to prove it.

But she didn't fool him. "I'd still like you to tell me about Doug's business dealings," Collin said. "I might be able to help you."

"How? Are you in the research business?"

Her question threw him and he realized he was wading into water he wasn't yet ready to swim in. "No, I haven't worked in a while—I'm on disability. But I could ask around, find out some information about McKenzie."

He looked at her and could still feel the warm impression where she'd cuddled next to him. Now his body felt suddenly cold.

"I'll let the police handle it. I'm really tired right now. I think I'll go to bed early and get some sleep."

He straightened the pillows on her sofa and righted the coffee table, remembering Raeburn's news about her brake lines having been cut. The thought of her being in danger sent a surge of panic through him. "I can stay if you want," he offered quietly.

Her startled gaze shot to his.

"I mean I could bunk on your couch or something…you know, so you'll sleep better."

She bit her bottom lip and he knew without a doubt she was shaken. But she was going to refuse his offer. He'd delivered quite a shock to her himself earlier when he'd told her about the transplant.

"I don't think that's such a good idea, Mr. Cash. But thanks for saving me…again."

"Call me Collin. Please." He smiled, hoping to alleviate her anxieties about him. She was standing so close he could smell the jasmine scent of her cologne. Like an aphrodisiac, it bled through his senses and sent desire rocketing through him. She stared at him, all sweetness and courage wrapped in one small, dark-haired bundle, and he reached out and tucked a strand of her sable hair behind her ear.

He gestured toward the items on the floor. "Let me at least stay until you have a shower. I can tackle this mess and help you clean up."

Sydney's troubled gaze swept the floor. "Thanks…that would be nice. I'll go through things later and see if anything's missing."

He wished there was something else he could do. Short of telling her more lies.

Sydney disappeared into her bedroom and he pushed his feelings aside. He quickly put the room back in order, his body tightening with desire as he heard the shower kick on. Unwanted lusty thoughts crawled through his head—Sydney naked, her slender body glistening with moisture, rivulets of water streaming down her long legs.

You can't do this, Cash. You can't let her get to you. She's a suspect in a murder case.

By the time he'd gotten his libido under control, Sydney emerged wearing a terry robe that covered her from head to toe. Unfortunately, knowing she might be naked underneath fueled his hunger again.

"Thanks for cleaning up. And for staying." She tightened the sash around her waist and walked him to the door.

He couldn't help himself. He reached out a hand and rubbed a strand of her wet hair between his thumb and forefinger. "Are you sure you don't want me to stay, Sydney? I won't bother you—I'll take the sofa." He paused, then added, "Scout's honor."

Her shoulders relaxed slightly. "I'm sure. Besides, you don't look like a Boy Scout, Collin."

He fought a smile. "You can lock your bedroom door if you're afraid I'll ravage you."

The corners of her mouth tilted upward and the magnitude of her smile struck a nerve in him that hadn't been touched in ages. She had a rare kind of beauty that made his heart clench, made him want to wipe all the fear from her eyes and see her smile forever.

For a second she faltered, glancing back at her bedroom as if she might be tempted. Her lush lips parted slightly and her eyes darkened with a longing that he felt burn through him like fire on ice, melting away the loneliness he'd felt for the past year, igniting desires in him like a match to dry kindling.

Then her smile disappeared into shadows of fear. "They have McKenzie in custody now," she said, breaking the spell. "I'll be fine."

Collin felt the loss of her trust like a hole being bored into him. Still, he wanted to protect her. "I asked Raeburn to have a car patrol your neighborhood tonight. He agreed."

"Thanks. That makes me feel better."

He nodded, then went out the front door and let her close it behind him.

He stood outside her cottage-style house and surveyed the neighbors' yards, the streets, the woods beyond, searching to see if anyone lurked behind the bushes waiting to hurt her. McKenzie might be in jail, but if he hadn't cut the brake lines of her car, someone else had. And Collin intended to find out who.

Because if he hadn't rescued her, she would already be dead. And though he barely knew the woman, the thought of losing her scared the hell out of him.

Chapter Six

Dear God, what was happening? Sydney leaned against the door, fighting the urge to open it and run after Collin. She was so very tempted to ask him to stay, to be with her all night, to help her forget her painful marriage.

But getting involved with him, the man who'd received her husband's eyes? She'd have to be crazy to do such a thing.

She secured the dead bolt, stumbled away from the door and stared at the remaining mess in her living room. Collin had righted the bulk of it, but magazines and papers still littered the floor. The idea that someone had violated her privacy fueled her temper. She gathered the books and magazines into a stack, then quickly collected the papers on her desk. She would go through everything later. Right now she couldn't think rationally enough to remember what had been on her desk, anyway.

Finally she checked all the locks on her doors and windows, then made some tea and retreated to her bedroom. The day's events rifled through her consciousness, scraping her already fraught nerves like shards of glass ripping through silk. Collin Cash's announcement about his transplant had made her come unglued; then she'd looked into his eyes and seen the soul of a kind man through the eyes of a deceiver.

And her brakes had been tampered with. But why?

Numbness settled in and she welcomed it, focusing on the new, soothing colors of her walls. Thank heavens she'd had Kelly help her redo the room after Doug's death. The brass bed Doug had insisted on had become a symbol of the baby she wanted but couldn't have, and later of the man who had once wanted her, but who rarely slept there. She'd wondered if he'd found another woman, had broached the subject a couple of times, but his anger had frightened her. He'd accused her of being paranoid. Now he was gone.

The telephone jangled and she jumped, chastising herself for her overreaction, then picked it up on the second ring.

"Hey, Sydney, it's Kelly." Sydney heard Megan fussing in the background and wished she could hold her, feel her chubby cheek against her own.

"Syd, are you there?"

"Oh, yeah, sorry."

"What's going on over there?" Kelly sounded petrified. "I saw a police car at your place earlier. Did they find Doug's killer?"

"No," Sydney said. "I wish they had."

"That sergeant wasn't bothering you again, was he?"

"Not exactly. In fact, this time I had to call him."

"What happened?"

Sydney tugged at the collar of her robe, not anxious to relive the evening. "I had a surprise visitor when I got home from the festival." She slumped into the armchair and wound the phone cord around her fingers while she told the story about her intruder.

"Oh, my God, he held a gun on you? Was it the same

kind that killed Doug? Do you think this man was the murderer?''

"I don't know." Sydney kicked off her slippers. "Maybe Raeburn will find out. Anyway, he's in custody now, so everything's fine. But if Collin hadn't come by, I'm not sure what would have happened." Her earlier tremors threatened to return with the memories, but Sydney willed them away. Still, she peeked out the window to make sure no one was lurking in the yard, then closed the curtains.

"Do you want me to come over and stay with you?"

"That's really nice, Kel, but I'll be fine. Besides, Meg will sleep better in her crib."

"Then you can come over here," Kelly offered. "I'm worried about you."

"Thanks, but I'm already settling in and Sergeant Raeburn's having a police car patrol the neighborhood. I think I'll go on to bed."

Kelly relented. "Okay, but promise me you'll call if you need anything."

Sydney laughed softly. "I'll put the phone right by the bed. Now kiss Meg for me. I'll see you guys tomorrow."

"All right, good night, then."

Sydney heard Kelly croon to Megan before she hung up, and she pictured Kelly rocking the baby to sleep. Another surge of longing swelled inside her. At last, more exhausted than weepy, she shrugged off her robe, pulled on a nightshirt and climbed into bed, tugging the covers up to her chin. But she stared at the ceiling for a long time, unable to shake the feeling of danger surrounding her.

Just before she finally drifted into sleep, she remembered the way Collin had held her in his arms, and she ached for his strength to get her through the night.

COLLIN SAT IN HIS CAR for the better part of an hour with his eyes on Sydney's house, guarding it like a watchdog. Adrenaline pumped through his veins, the way it always had when a case heated up back home.

A slight headache was starting to beat at the base of his skull and his eyes burned, two warning signs the doctor had cautioned him about. He needed sleep. But he refused to leave until the patrol car showed up.

He silently retraced the details of the visions he'd had. The person who'd shot Doug was either a small man or a woman. Which meant if the person who'd shot Doug and tampered with Sydney's car wasn't McKenzie, Sydney was still in danger.

By the time the patrol car Raeburn had promised drove up, his vision had started to blur drastically, so he was glad to call it a night. But as he drove back to the B-and-B, he wished like hell he was with Sydney. He couldn't stop thinking about holding her and wiping the sadness off her face with pleasures that would keep them both awake long into the night.

Back in his room, Collin punched in the number for his friend in the Charleston police force.

"Hey, buddy, what's up?" Sam asked, sounding groggy with sleep. "And why the hell are you calling me so late? You been partying or something?"

"Or something," Collin said with a grin. He knew his friends had worried about how he'd handled the inactivity during his blindness.

"Sounds great, man. Using those new eyes to check out the babes?"

"Yeah, right." Collin chuckled. "Listen, Sam, I've got a favor to ask."

"Sure. Anything for you, man."

"I need you to check out somebody. Off the record."

Sam hesitated. "What's going on, Collin? I thought you were on vacation."

"I am, but I may have stumbled onto something. Anyway, there's this woman—"

"Say no more. You want me to make sure she doesn't have a husband who'll hunt you down?"

"Not exactly." Collin leaned his head back and closed his eyes, his chest tight. "You know the information you gave me after I left the hospital?"

"About the donor?"

"Yeah. Well, I came to Beaufort—"

"Jeez, man, you didn't!" Sam tacked on an expletive and Collin held the phone away from his ear, wincing as Sam vented.

"I had to, Sam."

"What do you think you're doing, Cash? That information was supposed to be private. I went out on a limb to find out the donor's name for you."

"I know that—"

"I thought you were going to send a thank-you or donate some money to the man's favorite charity—"

"Just shut up and listen, would you?"

Sam exhaled audibly.

Collin let the silence stretch between them until Sam said, "Okay, go on."

"Good. I came to Beaufort planning to offer the man's widow some money or see if I could help her out, but things are complicated."

"Uh-oh. What does she want?"

"She doesn't want anything," Collin said, irritated. "But she does need my help."

"How's that?"

"They haven't made an arrest in her husband's murder."

"And you're working on the case," Sam muttered.

"Look, Sam, the man's wife was the one who found her husband. Now she's in danger."

"Is she a suspect?"

Collin hesitated.

"I can't believe it, Cash. You've got a thing for his wife! You know better than to get personally involved in a case," Sam bellowed. "Remember what happened with you and Tim."

"How could I forget?" Collin sighed. His partner had been killed and he'd been blinded. "But I can't help it this time. I am involved, Sam. The man gave me back my eyesight." He paused as the silence stretched between them again. "But it's not what you think," he explained. "The woman's still grieving for her husband. There's nothing going on between us."

"Yet," Sam added, sounding annoyed.

Collin undid the buttons of his shirt and tossed it to the floor, knowing he didn't believe it, either.

"Will you find out anything you can on Doug Green?"

"Sure. You want me to check out the wife, too?"

Collin hesitated, shucking his shoes and socks. "Not yet. But run a check on a man named Spade McKenzie. He's a food scientist or something like that, worked with the University of South Carolina. And dig up anything you can find on a company called Norvek Pharmaceuticals and another company, Triset Pharmaceuticals."

"Sounds like some vacation." Sam whistled between his teeth. "She must really be good-looking. Be careful, man."

Collin gave Sam his phone number. It was more than Sydney's drop-dead body and beautiful face that drew him to her. He couldn't explain it, but when he'd seen Mc-

Kenzie threaten her, he'd known he'd do anything to save her from harm, even if it meant jeopardizing his own life.

SYDNEY ROLLED OVER in restless slumber, nightmares of Doug's lifeless body invading her peace. Death surrounded her, its dark, cold shape engulfing her in its nothingness. The pungent odor of blood seeped into her nostrils. She clutched at the sheets of her bed, twisting them into a frenzied knot at her sides, then shrieked when the peal of the telephone startled her awake.

Jackknifing up, she needed several seconds to realize she'd been having a nightmare. For the moment she was safe. Still, shadows hung in the room. A tiny sliver of moonlight sliced a jagged line through the curtain. She squinted at the clock—3:00 a.m. Who would be calling her now?

Her hand trembled as she reached for the receiver. It was Kelly, it had to be. Meg had probably awakened, and she might be sick. Sydney said hello and was greeted by silence, then a gush of heavy breathing. "Don't go poking your nose into Doug's affairs."

Sydney lost the breath she'd been holding. "What? Who is this?"

"Let Doug rest in peace," the muffled voice murmured again, more sinister now. "Leave it alone, Sydney."

"Who is this?" Sydney shouted. The heavy breathing reverberated over the line again and her pulse rate climbed off the charts. "Tell me who this is. What do you know about Doug?"

"Enough. You and your friend better not stir things up," the caller threatened with an oily laugh. "Or you'll end up just like your husband."

Sydney gasped, her fingers tightening around the receiver, the blood roaring in her ears. Then the phone clicked into silence. The ticking of the clock on the bedside table seemed to intensify. What if the person were waiting outside?

Panicking, she dialed the police and reported the call.

"It was probably a prank," the female officer said. "If you'll feel better, contact the phone company tomorrow for caller ID."

"Will you please at least record my complaint?"

"Yes, ma'am, we always keep a record. You can call back tomorrow if you want to talk to a detective."

Sydney agreed, then sighed in defeat and hung up. The walls felt as if they were closing in around her. Shadows danced in every corner. The distant sounds from the street seemed magnified.

She took several deep breaths, trying to calm herself. She wished she'd asked Collin to stay. He would keep her safe. He would hold her through the night.

The horror of the past few weeks rippled through her in waves. She lay back down, pulled up the covers and stared at the curtain fluttering in the breeze of the fan. She was safe, she reminded herself. A police car was patrolling the neighborhood.

But what if the person came for her? What if he snuck past the police car? And what if the caller had been Doug's murderer just waiting until she was alone?

COLLIN SWALLOWED the painkillers the doctor had prescribed, used his antirejection drops and leaned against the bathroom sink, his head throbbing. He was glad he'd made the phone call to Sam, but the extra few minutes had added to the tension building behind his eyes. He was starting to feel dizzy and nauseated. He pressed a cool cloth to his forehead and closed his eyes, fighting to stand as the room spun around him, praying his body wasn't rejecting one or both of the corneas.

The antirejection drops… Some small nugget of information nagged at his brain, and he squinted at the label on the bottle. *Triset.* The name of the pharmaceutical company on the paper that madman McKenzie had been waving around.

Staggering toward the bed, Collin collapsed on it, kicking back the comforter with his feet. If Doug Green had been associated with Triset, it made sense he'd become a donor. But had the guy really stolen the licensing agreement from McKenzie? If so, what kind of man did that make Green?

Collin groaned and massaged his temple, the pain slightly dulling as he forced himself to relax. Tomorrow he'd call Sam and find out what he'd uncovered. But how would he feel if Green had been less than aboveboard? Probably one reason the doctors didn't reveal the donor's identity.

He ticked off the doctor's orders on his fingers. The ocean water could have been damaging. And he shouldn't have carried Sydney—he wasn't supposed to lift anything over twenty pounds for six weeks. But damn it, he hadn't had a choice. Surely that one time wasn't enough to cause serious damage.

A dull, relentless ache settled behind his left eye and he groaned, willing himself not to give in to the pain, forcing himself to relax. He would go to sleep. Then he'd wake up and the headache would be gone. Sydney would be fine tonight, McKenzie was in jail, the police would do their job. Troubled, disoriented thoughts drifted in and out of his subconscious as the pain medication took effect. The shooting, the surgery, the first few moments when he'd awakened and realized he couldn't see, might never see again.

He groaned and rolled to his side, but it made the nausea worse, so he returned to his back. The memories shuffled in and out, the darkness haunting him, the fear... being confined to his apartment for days at a time, the therapists and counselors teaching him basic coping skills, the long days of emptiness, of feeling isolated and useless...

He couldn't lose these eyes, not again, not now. He had to find out who murdered Doug Green, who was trying to hurt Sydney....

Finally the pain medication dulled his senses and he drifted into a troubled sleep, floating somewhere between consciousness and semiconsciousness. A few minutes of peaceful bliss, of nothingness...

Then he was choking, the darkness suffocating him. He tried to open his eyes, but the room blurred and his eyes stung. It was hot, burning up, so hot he shoved at the covers. The musty smell of smoke filled his lungs. Sweat drenched his hair, his feet were melting...

He struggled to see through the darkness, but couldn't. Dear God, he was blind again! The room disappeared into black, gray patches that clogged the air in front of him. Then a flash of bright light caught his eye.

No, he wasn't blind. A thick haze of smoke circled above him. Heat scorched his body. Orange flames swirled from the floor and licked the walls, shooting toward the ceiling.

He jerked upright, realizing in horror he wasn't dreaming. A raging fire had engulfed the room. And the flames were spiraling all around him.

Chapter Seven

Collin's lungs ached as they filled with smoke. Panic trapped him momentarily as death called his name. But he fought the fear, his mind spinning for an escape. Three of the four walls blazed around him. The fire gained momentum as it lapped up the antique furnishings and trailed a path around the edges of the upholstered chair and sofa. He had to hurry. The flimsy white curtains caught fire next. Wood crackled and popped. He coughed violently.

Think, man, think. Get down low.

He yanked the pillowcase from the bed, tied it around his face to cover his mouth, wrapped the comforter around him, then rolled from the bed. His heart pounded as he searched for the best escape.

The smoke was so thick he couldn't see a foot in front of him. Fire hissed, then engulfed the pine armoire. Next, the door erupted into flames. He backed away toward the window. Fire raged all around him, spitting out heat, singeing his hair and body. He had to get out.

He coughed again, the smoke and fumes almost overpowering him as he crawled toward the window. Once he broke the window, the oxygen would feed the fire like gasoline. He would have to go right through it.

Jerking the comforter around his head, he stood and

ran. Heat clawed at his body. Then he dove through the glass window. The pane shattered, sending shards of glass spraying outward. He yelled out for help as the scorching flames licked his body and he rolled onto the grass.

THE HEAT WAS OPPRESSIVE.

Sydney sat up in bed, soaked in sweat. She stared at the clock as early-morning sunshine peeked through her window. Perspiration trickled down the sides of her face, and she wiped it away with the edge of her sheet. Had her air-conditioning stopped working?

No. She'd turned it off so she could listen for an intruder after that terrible phone call.

Unable to stand the tension any longer, she picked up the phone and dialed the bed-and-breakfast inn. She wanted to talk to Collin. She didn't know exactly why; she just needed to hear his voice. But the phone gave an odd signal, then the operator broke in and said the line was out of order. Strange.

Feeling even more anxious, she climbed out of bed. She had to see Collin. Her nerves were stretched to the limit, and even though Collin frightened her, he also made her feel more secure. Something she didn't understand, but something she desperately needed right now.

She dragged on a pair of denim shorts and a T-shirt, pulled on her tennis shoes and grabbed her house key, then hurried out the door. A knot of tension wormed into her stomach when she noticed the deserted streets. What if someone wanted to hurt her? What if someone was out here waiting?

I am not going to be frightened all the time. McKenzie was in jail. There weren't any bogeymen waiting, no ghosts hiding behind the azaleas. Besides, there were a few neighbors out, walking and jogging. She slid into her rental car and locked the door.

Feeling more relaxed as she drove, she even managed to wave as she passed Mrs. Bailey's. The sweet old lady brought freshly clipped roses to anyone in town who was ill. Real small-town hospitality. Beaufort was the perfect place to raise a family. At least, Sydney had thought so before Doug had been murdered in their bedroom.

A siren wailed in the distance, followed by another, and she frowned, searching the streets for an accident. A fire engine honked its horn and she spotted a thick haze of smoke billowing above the buildings in the heart of town. The fire engine careened down a side street at full speed and an ambulance whizzed by on its tail, tires screeching. Suddenly nervous, she drove faster.

The stream of smoke rose, and her gaze fastened on its source. Bay Street. Her mind raced with possibilities, her pulse jumping in her throat. The florist shop, the bakery, the small grocery, the bed-and-breakfast.

Where Collin was staying.

The threatening phone call played over and over in her head and took on new significance. Only, why would someone want to hurt Collin? To get to *her?* But how would someone connect the two of them?

It seemed an eternity before she crossed the town square. She drew in a deep breath, afraid to round the corner, knowing in her gut the source of the burning inferno. Orange and yellow flames lit the sky, thick smoke hurling like a funnel cloud above the city. As she parked, pandemonium surrounded her. Sirens screeched. People shouted. A scream that made her blood run cold pierced the air.

Panic grasped her in a choke hold. She covered her

mouth with her hand, fighting the stench of the smoke. *God, don't let anyone be trapped inside,* she prayed.

Collin? Where was he? Mr. and Mrs. Davenport, had they escaped? Clenching her hands into fists, she searched the crowd of people in the street. She thought she heard someone mention arson, then she spotted the Davenports.

They stood huddled in blankets, staring wide-eyed and shocked at the ball of fire destroying their home. But they were alive.

Sydney watched as firefighters dragged hoses and sprayed water onto the leaping flames. Others shouted into the house, yelling to see if anyone was trapped inside. Paramedics stood ready. A rescue worker carried a small child from the back of the burning building. A young woman with dark hair raced toward the girl, arms outstretched, sobbing. Sydney's breath caught, then she heaved a sigh of relief when the tiny girl raised her head and hugged her mother. Her throat thick with emotions, Sydney hurried forward, twisting her hands anxiously. Where was Collin?

The roof suddenly collapsed with a thunderous crash. Mrs. Davenport broke into sobs and sagged into her husband's arms. Firemen shouted orders, trying to contain the blaze, and the roar of fire and crackling wood escalated to an almost deafening pitch. Sydney's heart stilled when the paramedics emerged from the back of the inn carrying a stretcher.

"We need oxygen!" a paramedic shouted.

"Clear the way!" a fireman yelled.

Sydney raced toward the ambulance, oblivious to the heat radiating from the blaze, her eyes riveted to the dark-haired man on the stretcher. Fear clutched at her chest when she recognized him. Collin.

COLLIN STRUGGLED to breathe in the air from the oxygen mask. The paramedic ordered him to lie still, then shouted something about smoke inhalation. A roar of noise and confusion surrounded him, reminding him of his brush with death. But he was alive, and at the moment that was all that mattered.

He saw a flash of orange and red, and he shuddered, remembering the burning inferno he'd awakened to. He squinted through the smoke-filled air and focused on a woman staring at him. No mask, no hat. Porcelain skin, sable hair, rosy lips. Blue eyes filled with terror.

"Collin, it's me, Sydney." He felt his hand being lifted and realized she'd picked it up and was nestling it between her own. "Are you all right?"

He tried to speak, but his throat was so dry he couldn't force out any words, and the effort only made him cough.

"We'll take him to the hospital for observation," the paramedic told Sydney. She nodded. Collin wanted to touch her, to let her know he was okay. But exhaustion pulled at his limbs, and he had to struggle to even keep his eyes open.

"It's okay, sir, we're taking you to the county hospital," the rescue worker said, patting his arm.

Collin's eyelids closed. He was being lifted and carried somewhere. He forced his eyes open and saw Sydney walking beside him, felt himself being jostled, then lost sight of her again.

Where had she gone? He strained to find her, listened for her voice, thought he heard her whisper, "I'm sorry." Then a feather-light kiss brushed his forehead.

Her face filled his vision again and he tried to smile. Her lips were pinched, her face troubled and anxious-looking. *Don't worry,* he tried to say, but the words got lost in his raw throat and the oxygen mask, and he wasn't sure she saw his efforts. Then he lost her again as the paramedics hoisted him into the back of an ambulance.

SYDNEY'S STOMACH clenched as the ambulance drove away, carrying Collin to the hospital. Thank God he was alive. And from what the paramedic had told her, everyone else was safe, too.

Why should she care so much about Collin Cash? she wondered, startled to find moisture in her eyes. She'd wanted to go to the hospital with him; she'd even kissed his forehead, but the driver had asked if she was family and she'd had to say no. She had no connection to the man, other than the fact he had her husband's eyes. And she didn't feel like sharing that bit of information just yet.

Then again, he had saved her life—not once, but twice. How could she not care a little bit about him? At least enough to not want him to die.

Furious with herself for being so emotional, she brushed away the tears, then glanced up to see Sergeant Raeburn studying her. He was standing beside his police car, one arm draped over the door, his radio in his beefy hand as if he was waiting for something to come over the air. Their gazes caught and he nodded, the kind of curt nod a Southern man gave when he wanted a woman to know he'd seen her, the kind of unfriendly nod that tortured her nerves and made her suspicious about his thoughts. Surely he didn't think she had something to do with the fire.

One of the firemen approached him, and Raeburn angled his face away from her. Knowing there was nothing else she could do and unable to push Collin from her mind, she turned and hurried to her car, automatically driving toward the hospital.

An uneasy feeling mushroomed in her stomach. Another incident had destroyed the peace of her small town. And if last night's phone call hadn't been a prank, if the fire had been arson, if someone had wanted to hurt Collin because of her...

Minutes later she rushed from her car into the emergency room. "Please, can you tell me if Mr. Cash is okay?"

An elderly woman smiled sympathetically. "Honey, they're examining him. Are you his wife?"

"No, a friend. But I have to know if he's all right."

The woman patted her hand. "I'll check on him, dear. You sit down and try to relax."

The clock on the yellowed wall ticked by at a snail's pace. Sydney paced the room, twisting her hands together. The smell of antiseptic and alcohol permeated the air, making her feel nauseated. If he hadn't been hurt seriously, wouldn't they tell her? What if he'd been burned? What if the smoke had damaged his eyes? What if he'd gone blind again? That would be awful for him.

Soft-soled shoes padded into the room and the nurse gestured for her to follow. "He's being put in the intensive care unit for a while. But he's stable."

"Can I see him?"

"We're not supposed to let anyone but family go in there."

"I don't know if he has any family," Sydney explained. "I'm the only person he knows here in Beaufort."

The nurse studied her for a long minute, her hazel eyes sparkling with understanding. "Okay, dear, but just for five minutes. The gentleman needs his rest."

Sydney swiped at a tear she didn't know had surfaced, then followed the nurse down a long corridor toward the ICU. When she reached the unit, she thanked the woman and slipped into the room, swallowing her nerves as she stared at the tubes and oxygen attached to Collin.

Except for the slight rise and fall of his chest, he didn't move. His skin was pale, strands of his hair singed, tousled in disarray against the stark white pillowcase. His bare arm lay on top of the sheet, a hospital gown covering his chest. His face and arms had been cleaned, but his skin was covered in bruises, scratches and small red patches where he'd been burned.

He could have died, she thought in horror. She slowly, tentatively reached out and took his hand in hers. She rubbed her fingers over his knuckles, stroking the soft dark hairs on the top of his hand. "I'm sorry, Collin. I'm so sorry."

His eyes flickered open briefly and his gaze locked with hers. She couldn't read his emotions. Then she felt him squeeze her fingers and realized he was trying to reassure her. Fatigue lines fanned beside his eyes, and he coughed, letting the oxygen mask feed him air. Her chest ached with emotions she didn't understand, and she leaned over and brushed a kiss on his forehead again. The nurse motioned it was time for her to leave. She slowly brought his hand to her mouth and kissed his fingers, wondering what she would have done if he had died.

"Oh, my God, did you hear about the fire?" Kelly met Sydney on the sidewalk in front of her house, almost hysterical.

"It was awful." Sydney climbed the steps to Kelly's front porch and reached for Megan, her heart warming when the baby batted her chubby hand against her cheek. "The whole place burned to the ground, Kel. I've never seen anything like it."

"You mean you were there?"

"Yeah, I woke up early and couldn't sleep, so I went for a drive, then saw the smoke." Megan curled her tiny fingers around Sydney's, and Sydney kissed Megan's soft curls, her heart gripped with emotion.

"I heard about it on the radio," Kelly said, cradling a cup of coffee in her hands. "I couldn't believe it."

"I feel so sorry for the Davenports." Sydney settled into the porch rocker with the baby. "They lost everything."

Kelly sank onto the porch step in front of her and blew into her coffee. "That's terrible. Was anyone hurt, Syd? The radio didn't give a lot of details."

Sydney patted Megan's back, smiling when Megan cooed and kicked her legs up and down. "The Davenports made it out okay. And there was another family staying there. They had a little girl."

Kelly gasped. "Was she okay?"

Sydney tucked Megan's feet into the blanket, gently rocking her back and forth. "The firemen saved her. But the mother was a mess. She was crying and hugging her daughter." Tears gathered again. "It was awful."

Kelly wiped her own eyes and put her coffee down, then held out her arms for Meg. "I know what you mean. I couldn't stand it if anything ever happened to Megan." A fierce frown touched her face. Then the frown disappeared and Kelly stroked the baby's soft cap of curls. "I'd do anything for Meg, Sydney. One day when you have a little one of your own, you'll understand."

"I'm sure I will," Sydney said gently. Single motherhood had been hard on Kelly. She never talked about Megan's father, but Sydney knew he'd hurt her terribly. And she knew how much Kelly loved Megan. "Megan's lucky to have a mom like you, Kel."

Kelly cradled Megan and Sydney thought she saw fresh

tears in Kelly's eyes, but Kelly blinked them away. "So no one else was in the B-and-B?"

Sydney folded her arms across her middle, feeling empty without Megan in her arms. "Collin had a room there, too."

"The man from Charleston?"

"Yes. The paramedics took him to the hospital. He's in the ICU for observation, but they said he'd be all right."

Kelly frowned. "Poor guy. What a rotten vacation."

"Yeah, it wouldn't surprise me if he went back to Charleston now."

"I wouldn't blame him, either," Kelly added sympathetically.

Sydney shrugged, wondering why the idea of Collin leaving bothered her so much. He was just a man. Another man who might break her heart if she got involved with him. And he had Doug's eyes.

Exhausted, she closed her eyes and leaned her head against the rocker, fear pressing her chest as the image of his pale, bruised face floated through her mind. It shouldn't have hurt so much to see him like that.

Maybe she was already too involved.

"YOU WERE LUCKY," the doctor told Collin the next morning as he checked his eyes. "You suffered smoke inhalation, but your eyes look good, and you didn't sustain any serious burns."

Collin gripped the hospital sheets, relieved but tired of all the prodding from the well-meaning nurses and doctors. Tired of hospitals in general. He'd had his fill the past year, and today wasn't helping matters.

"Was anyone else hurt in the fire?" he asked, his voice hoarse.

Dr. Cramer shook his head. "Nope, thank the Lord for that. Although I thought we might have to treat Mrs. Davenport for shock."

Collin grimaced. "It was pretty bad all right." He sat up, ignoring the elderly man's raised brows. "I'm okay, Doc. I'd really like to leave the hospital."

"I'm not sure you're in any condition to drive," Dr. Cramer said.

"I'll drive him."

Sydney appeared in the doorway, looking worried and incredibly beautiful in a white cotton blouse and bright floral skirt. Just the medicine he needed.

Cramer stared first at Collin, then at Sydney. "You two can discuss it while I finish up this paperwork. You'll need more antirejection drops before you leave. And I'll send in a specialist to look at your eyes." He indicated Collin's chart and left the room.

"Are you really up to leaving?" Sydney asked, cautiously moving into the room.

"I don't like hospitals," Collin said. He tried to sit up, but the sheet fell away from his shoulders and he realized he was wearing only boxers. Too exhausted to care, he laid his head back, hating his weakness.

Sydney twisted her hands in front of her. "You look better. Are you sure you're all right?"

Something softened inside him at her quivering voice. Without thinking, he reached out, motioning for her to move closer. "I'm okay. See." He patted his bare chest, aware her eyes were riveted to the dark hair tapering down the middle and veeing into his shorts. "No real burns," he said, his own voice low. "Some scrapes. Hair's a little singed, but I got out in time."

Sydney paused beside his bed. "I couldn't believe it

when I saw you on that stretcher. And the fire, it was… terrible.''

"Shh, don't think about it." Collin covered her hand with his. "It's over and everyone's safe. That's all that matters."

Sydney's lower lip trembled. "And your eyes?"

"They seem fine." A smile twitched at his mouth. She was actually worried about him. "I told the doctor about the transplant and he examined me. We'll see what the specialist has to say."

She sighed softly and his gut clenched. He vaguely remembered her being in the ICU when they'd brought him in. Or had he imagined it?

"Some vacation you're having. I guess you'll be leaving Beaufort?"

Collin wrestled with telling her the truth. She looked so lost and vulnerable, so utterly sexy with all the worry in her eyes. She couldn't possibly be a killer. "I don't know what I'll do."

"I'd like to know your plans, too, Mr. Cash."

Collin's head snapped up at the harsh sound of Raeburn's voice. Sydney curled her arms around her middle in a protective gesture. "I'm not sure," Collin replied slowly.

Raeburn lumbered in, his thumbs tucked in his belt loops, his uniform reeking of smoke. "The doc release you?"

"He's going to. He said for me to rest. I inhaled a little smoke and my throat's raw, but other than that, I'm fine."

Raeburn angled his head, his penetrating gaze traveling back and forth between Collin and Sydney. "Seems the two of you are always close by when there's trouble around here."

Collin's jaw tightened. "What's that supposed to mean, Sergeant?"

Raeburn's shirt stretched across his girth as he folded his beefy arms. "Means, it has me wondering…"

"Wondering what?" Collin asked, fighting a cough.

"About the connection between the two of you."

"What?" Sydney asked in a choked voice. "There is no connection."

"I told you I'd never met Sydney until I came to town. Do you really think Sydney tried to drown herself in the ocean by cutting her own brake lines and that I set the Beaufort Bed-and-Breakfast on fire, then barely crawled out alive?"

Raeburn's dark eyes glinted with anger. "I don't know what to think. All I know is this town used to be nice and safe." His mouth worked, chewing on a wad of gum. "Then Green was murdered and all sorts of things are going on. And I don't like it."

"Then do your job and find out who's causing all this trouble," Collin snapped. He broke into a coughing fit, then took several deep breaths, striving to control his temper. "How did the fire start?"

"As a matter of fact, that's why I'm here." Accusations hardened Raeburn's gaze.

Sydney dug her fingernails into the flesh of her arms. "It was an accident, wasn't it?"

"It don't look like it was, Mizz Green." Raeburn leaned his bulk against the doorjamb, ankles crossed casually. "It looks like someone set the place on fire."

"What?" Sydney stumbled backward. Collin wanted to reach out and help her sit down, but Raeburn would misconstrue the gesture. Besides, the damn IV kept him from moving.

"Looks like arson," Raeburn continued in his gruff voice. "In fact, someone used chemicals to start the fire." He angled his head toward Sydney. "The sort of chemicals used to develop pictures."

Chapter Eight

Sydney stared at the sergeant in shock, her earlier fears escalating.

"How can you be certain the fire was started with photo-developing chemicals?" Collin asked in a tone Sydney knew wasn't as casual as he'd made it sound.

"Fire marshal found a rag soaked in acetone and a charred can of developer." Raeburn's fat jowls worked his gum into his cheek. "He's running tests to make sure. Said he may be able to narrow it down to the name brand."

Tension tightened Sydney's throat muscles. "I don't understand. Why would someone want to burn down the Davenports' bed-and-breakfast?"

"You got me on that one." Raeburn shrugged. "But then, there's a lot of things been going on lately I haven't figured out yet. Strange thing is, the fire was started in the wing where you were staying, Mr. Cash."

Raeburn's gaze cut to Collin, then back to Sydney, razor sharp and probing. "Any theories, you two?"

The air whooshed from Sydney's lungs. Then it *was* conceivable that whoever had set the fire wanted to hurt Collin.

Collin frowned. "You're the investigator—you tell us."

Raeburn smirked. "Think about it, Cash. You come here on vacation. Then you hook up with Mizz Green, a suspect in a murder case, and you almost die. Doesn't that strike a funny chord with you?"

Collin shrugged.

"Think about it," Raeburn said as he turned and strode out the door, leaving the pungent smell of smoke and suspicion hanging in the air.

Sydney forced herself to remain calm, fighting panic at Raeburn's implications.

"Do you still want to give me a ride?" he asked.

Sydney jerked her head up, surprised he wasn't accusing her after what Raeburn had implied. Her gaze met his and locked for a brief moment. A tingle of awareness and some other emotion she couldn't name warmed her insides. He didn't think she'd started the fire.

"You still want to ride with me?"

"Sure, but I need a favor first." His husky voice soothed her nerves and caressed her with a tenderness that obliterated the horrors of the morning.

"A favor?"

He gestured at his boxers. "I need some clothes. Everything I brought was destroyed in the fire."

Her gaze riveted to the wide planes of his bare chest, to the soft, dark hair curling on his forearms. A faint scar ran in a thin line across his flat belly, and another small round one graced his right side near his collarbone. Otherwise, his body was perfect. But the thought of the fire immediately sobered her, and she dragged her gaze away, embarrassed when she noticed he'd caught her staring. "Sure. I...I still have some things of Doug's you could borrow."

"I'll return them when I buy some more clothes," he said a little tightly.

She nodded, wondering how she would handle seeing him in Doug's clothes. "Okay. I'll be back with them shortly."

His eyes darkened with something that at any other time or place, she might have construed as male interest, even desire. But given the hospital, the fire, Raeburn's implications…she must be misreading him.

Dismissing the idea from her head, she walked slowly from the room, wondering where she would drive Collin once she returned. After all, he couldn't go back to the inn. And with her attraction to him, it would be dangerous for him to stay at her place.

COLLIN STUDIED Sydney's slender figure as she disappeared from the room, anxious about her leaving. Knowing the fire at the inn had been set deliberately made him nervous, but he couldn't believe that Sydney had anything to do with it. He'd seen the fear in her face when she'd arrived. He'd felt it when she'd stood beside his bed.

The realization that she cared for him did crazy things to his insides. Heat suffused his body. In spite of his injuries, he'd had a hard time not pulling her down and kissing her. Then Raeburn had shown up. Damn. What the hell was going on here?

The fire hadn't been set to hurt Sydney. So how could it be related to the person who'd cut her brakes? The photo-developing chemicals were definitely used to frame Sydney. Who wanted to see her in jail?

Raeburn obviously suspected Sydney, but why? Other than the insurance policy, did Raeburn know something about Sydney and Doug's relationship that he, Collin, hadn't discovered? *Had* Green had an affair, a mistress, that would give Sydney another motive?

The memory of his partner's death surfaced quickly. What if he was making a mistake in trusting Sydney?

What if she found out that you're a cop, that you lied to her, that you came here hoping to solve Doug's murder? What if you're getting too close to her and she's scared you'll discover the truth?

A knock at the door broke into his disturbing reverie. A young doctor wearing small, wire-rim glasses walked in, a clipboard wedged beneath his arm.

The doctor introduced himself as Franks, a specialist from an eye clinic in Atlanta, and mentioned that he'd spoken with Darber, Collin's doctor. "I'd say you were a lucky man." He pushed his glasses up on his nose.

Collin grimaced. "Believe me, I know."

The doctor did a brief exam then removed the IV. "Are you having trouble with your vision? Headaches? Any of the symptoms your doctor warned you about after your surgery?"

Collin told him about the headache the night before. "But my head's better today."

"Any other problems?"

"Dr. Franks, have you had much experience with transplant patients?"

"As a matter of fact I studied with a European physician. He was involved in experimental eye procedures in France."

Impressed, Collin decided to tell him about the visions.

"You believe you're actually seeing something that happened before?" Franks asked when Collin finished.

"I know it sounds nutty," Collin said. "But I see Green being shot, and it's as if it's happening to me. I've also met people in the town and remembered talking to them…as Green."

Franks stroked his chin with his forefinger. "You know, Dr. Barringer encountered a couple of similar incidents in his research."

"What? You mean you believe me?"

Franks laughed. "We haven't yet discovered all the ramifications of transplant surgery, Mr. Cash. And Barringer has been researching the effects for several years."

Collin nodded. "So, it *could* be possible—I mean, medically?"

"Let me explain the theory we developed." Franks folded his arms over the clipboard. "People have neurotransmitters present in the anterior chamber of the eye. When the cornea is harvested for transplant, some of the neurotransmitters are transferred to the corneal-transplant recipient."

"So I received some of Green's neurotransmitters as a bonus?"

Franks grinned. "I guess you could put it like that. Anyway, if Green lived for a while after he was shot, it's possible that when his corneas were removed, some of the neurotransmitters that hold memory were also transferred."

"Unbelievable." Collin collapsed against the back of the hospital bed. "So I'm not hallucinating?"

Franks shook his head. "The antirejection drug you're taking is supposed to increase vascularization and decrease rejection, but it causes the neurotransmitters to be absorbed. These neurotransmitters, the ones you received from the donor, convey the memory of the trauma to your brain."

He was actually witnessing Doug Green's murder. It took him a moment to absorb the news.

"Are you all right?" the doctor asked.

Collin ran a hand over his jaw. "Yeah, but it's wild, isn't it? I not only received the man's eyes, but part of his memory."

Is that why I'm so drawn to Sydney?

"It's modern science." Franks tapped his pen on the clipboard. "But it's really nothing compared to all the genetic research being done. Soon we'll be cloning people."

"Will these visions fade with time?"

Franks shrugged. "Maybe. Mr. Cash, you should contact Darber so he can document the effects of the experimental drugs."

A soft knock interrupted them, and they looked up to see Sydney standing in the shadow of the door, holding a plastic bag. No doubt her deceased husband's clothes, Collin thought, which she'd brought for him to wear home. The doctor excused himself, then smiled at her in passing. Uncertainty pulled at her face as she walked farther into the room.

He had some of Doug Green's memory. Did it include feelings for Green's wife? Could that be the reason he was so attracted to her?

The muscles in his forearms hardened as he reached for the bag of clothes. A wave of apprehension gnawed at him. It seemed he was becoming more and more entrenched in Doug Green's life. And he wasn't sure he liked it.

SYDNEY HESITATED beside Collin's bed, her palms sweaty. She gave him the bag. Did he feel as awkward as she did about him wearing her husband's clothes?

She wondered if she'd made a mistake in coming. But how could she not? She felt drawn to Collin, connected to him by some power she didn't understand, but couldn't resist.

"I appreciate your doing this," Collin said quietly, his gray eyes settling on her face warily.

Their fingers brushed slightly, his mere touch awakening feelings she thought had died long ago. All the way from her house to the hospital, the memory of the fire had consumed her, the image of his body being carried from the burning inferno shaking her to the core.

His mouth quirked in a half smile, and she stifled the thoughts as he dug inside the bag, dragging out a pair of shoes, brand-new socks, faded jeans and a chambray shirt.

"I only brought one outfit," Sydney said. "I don't know your size, but I figured these would do until you could go shopping."

Collin unfolded the shirt. "Doug never wore that," she said. "He told me he didn't like the color."

Collin's gaze locked with hers and she felt as if he'd read her mind—she hadn't been able to bring one of Doug's worn shirts. Too many bad memories, too much heartache. Thank goodness, she'd found this new shirt in the closet, still in the package. She'd bought it for Doug's birthday. He'd said he was going to be working. When she'd gone by the office to surprise him, his secretary had informed her he hadn't been in all day.

"Thanks, Sydney. I'll change and then we can go."

When he started to stand, Sydney realized he still wore only his boxers. A blush crept onto her cheeks.

"Oh, sorry. I'll wait outside."

"It's okay."

But Sydney spun around and strode toward the door. Seeing Collin bare-chested and watching him dress seemed too…intimate.

Every time she looked into Collin's eyes, she saw part

of Doug. But he was nothing like Doug. His jaw was stronger, his wavy hair much darker, his body more muscular. Doug had been easy on the eyes, but Collin was a man who would turn any woman's head. A man who made her pulse clamor and her mind forget that she was a widow.

She closed the door and leaned against the wall, her heart beating frantically. She'd trusted Doug. She'd promised herself to him in marriage. But he'd painted her a fool. She couldn't afford to care about another man. Not now. Not ever.

COLLIN QUICKLY DRESSED, wondering if it had been painful for Sydney to sort through her husband's clothes and have another man wear them. The grief in her eyes was so overwhelming that guilt plagued him for the desire he felt for her.

He had to get a grip, solve the murder case and get back to Charleston, away from the woman's alluring body and arresting eyes. He didn't need anyone, didn't want to become involved with any woman, much less a troubled widow who quite possibly saw him as some sort of re-incarnation of her dead husband.

Raeburn's news about the fire worried him. He needed to talk to Sam, find out if he had any new information. He coughed again, then tucked the stiff shirt into the jeans, noting they were too short and the shoes too tight.

Stuffing his hands in the denim pockets, he started to leave the room, but he found a small paper in the pocket. Hmm, a motel receipt. The date, a month before Green had died.

The hotel, Red Baron Inn, popped into his head, and his eyesight blurred, replaced by a quick flash of a door opening. He reached for the wall to steady himself, trying not to fight the vision——*He was walking into a hotel room, a woman wearing a shimmering red dress sashaying in front of him.* Collin strained to prolong the image, to clarify the woman's face, then the room dimmed into darkness. *The red dress slipped off her shoulder. He saw his hand touching the delicate column of the woman's neck, pushing back the long red strands of her hair....*

Sydney's voice brought him back to reality, and he realized with sickening clarity that the woman Doug had been with had not been his wife.

"Are you ready to go?" Sydney's slender face slid into focus. "Collin, are you all right?" She moved quickly, appearing at his side.

"Yeah, let's go," he said, his voice sharper than he'd intended.

She paused, her slender fingers tightening around the doorknob. "Are you sure you're okay? I can call the doctor again. Or maybe you should stay here and rest."

He hesitated, wondering if he should speak to Dr. Franks, then mumbled he was fine and hurried out the door. If the vision he'd just seen had been true, then Doug Green had definitely cheated on his loving, trusting wife. If he discovered the other woman had something to do with Doug's death, he didn't want to have to be the one to tell Sydney.

And if he told Raeburn, he'd have to admit Sydney had a motive besides money for killing her husband. He might as well slap the handcuffs on her himself. Raeburn would take her in in a skinny minute.

"IF YOU WANT, we'll go back to my house and you can phone around to find another place to stay," Sydney suggested as they drove from the hospital. "That is, unless you're going back to Charleston."

Collin stared out the window at the passing scenery, watching the relentless June sunshine beat against the tall, dry grasses, thinking about the man who'd donated his eyes. Should he go home and leave the murder in the hands of the local police? He'd always thought a person who'd donate their organs for another human was honorable, selfless. But the more he learned, the more he *saw* of Doug Green, the more he disliked the man. Maybe he didn't owe Green anything, after all.

It was obvious from the depth of Sydney's grief at the graveyard that she'd loved him deeply. If he kept digging, what else would he find out about the man? Something else that would hurt Sydney?

"Collin, did you hear me? I said I'll take you back to my house so you can phone around for another place to stay or make arrangements to go home."

Sydney's fingertips pressed into his arm. He jerked sideways. "I'm sorry. I guess I'm just tired." He rubbed his neck wearily. His hair smelled, his skin, everything about him reeked of the fire. Even the shower he'd taken at the hospital hadn't been able to completely erase the odor. "I appreciate the offer, but first, could you take me by the B-and-B? I want to see if anything was left from the fire and get my car."

"Sure. Then are you leaving?"

Sydney's troubled glance pulled at him. He couldn't leave, not until he discovered the truth. "No, I'm staying."

"I can't imagine how awful it was to have been trapped in that fire." She shivered and he had the urge to reach out and massage her neck, to release the tension in her shoulders.

"It was pretty scary," he admitted.

She bit her bottom lip. "I couldn't believe it when I

saw the flames. I just knew…'' Her words trailed off and he remembered the moment on the stretcher, right before they'd hoisted him onto the ambulance, when he'd thought someone had kissed his temple. Then in the ICU…

"How did you know the place was on fire?"

"I couldn't sleep that morning," she said in a low voice, her fingers tightening around the steering wheel. "So I went for a drive, then I noticed the smoke. It was billowing everywhere. I drove toward it and saw the flames. I had to know if anyone was hurt."

He studied her worried frown. There was something she wasn't telling him, but what?

She didn't speak again until they'd turned down the street that led to the inn. "When I saw the paramedics carrying you, I wasn't sure you'd made it out alive."

A tender spot opened inside him at the concern lacing her voice. The charred ruins of the beautiful antebellum house came into view. Collin was stunned at the sight of ashes and debris littering the once perfectly manicured lawn. The flowers and azaleas had been trampled by the firemen. Nothing had been saved.

"My God," Sydney said in a strangled whisper as she cut the engine. "I can't believe everyone survived."

Yeah, Collin thought grimly, shuddering at the extent of the damage. A couple of policemen and a man Collin suspected was a fire marshal walked the property, obviously scouting for more evidence. Yellow police tape encircled the lot. "Can you think of any reason someone would want to burn down the inn?"

Sydney shook her head. "The Davenports are nice people. I'm sure they're devastated over losing the house. It's been in their family for years. They recently spent a lot of money refurbishing some of the original moldings and other historical aspects.'' She rolled her shoulders as if relieving tension. ''I can't think of any reason someone would do this. It doesn't make sense at all.''

Possibly to get money from the insurance claim, Collin speculated. The Davenports could have overextended their credit and found themselves drowning in debt, then decided to torch the place and collect the insurance.

But that answer didn't satisfy him. Too many coincidences.

He climbed from the car, the scent of smoke and ashes permeating the air.

''If you want to come to my house and use the phone, the offer still stands.''

''I plan to,'' Collin said. ''I'm going to talk to the cops for a minute, then get my car and follow you over.''

She agreed and he approached the nearest investigator, his gaze scanning the broken and charred remains of furniture, the metal appliances that had melted to the ground. ''You can't go in there.'' The man held up a hand to keep him from entering the taped-off area.

''I know,'' Collin said, frustrated because he wanted to check out the damage himself. ''Have you found anything yet?''

The officer paused, a small piece of metal in his hand. ''We're taking samples. It'll be a few days before all the test results are back.''

It was fruitless to continue until the guys had done a thorough sweep of the ruins. He crossed to Sydney and told her he was going to stop at a store and pick up some toiletries and extra clothes and meet her at her house. He also had to call Sam and tell him about the fire. Not that it was related to Green's death, but too many weird things had been going on in Beaufort not to search for a connection.

When he arrived at Sydney's later and she ushered him in the door, the house seemed eerily dark, the only light coming from the den. Sydney turned to him in the foyer, her blue eyes raging with emotions, like liquid pools of water. "I'm glad you're okay," she whispered. She lowered her head, kneading her hands. "Collin, I have to tell you something. Someone called in the middle of the night, before the fire. I don't know if it has anything to do with the fire...."

Fear inched its way inside him. "Who was it?"

"I don't know. Only that it was a man, I think." She began to toy with the gold band on her ring finger. "His voice was muffled, as if he was holding something over the receiver."

Collin gripped her arms just below the shoulders. "Did he threaten you?"

Her big blue eyes lifted to his. "They said that my friend and I should leave Doug's murder alone. Not to stir up things or I'd..."

Her voice broke and Collin stroked her arms soothingly, willing her to continue. "Or what, Sydney?"

"That I'd end up like Doug."

She trembled and Collin's resistance snapped. He pulled her into the safety of his arms. "It's okay, honey. No one's going to hurt you. I promise." He nuzzled the silky softness of her hair. She smelled like jasmine, sweet and delicious. And so precious. Like she belonged in his arms and always would.

"I stayed awake, wondering who called, wondering why he'd do this," Sydney said in a choked voice. "Then I called you and the phone was dead, so I drove over to see you and saw the fire. And you...you were lying on that stretcher so still, and I wondered if it was my fault...but why would someone hurt you to get at me?"

Collin closed his eyes, hugging her to him, the tremor in her voice knotting his stomach. She was upset because he'd almost died.

"I don't know, Sydney. There's probably no connection." God, she'd been through so much lately. "Shh, it's all right. I'm fine. No one was harmed." He brushed a strand of silky hair from her forehead. "It's not your fault."

A shudder rippled through her and he stroked the long indentation of her spine, running his hands over her shoulder blades and down the curve of her waist, rocking her back and forth, until he felt the trembling in her body cease. Then awareness warmed his fingers, and his senses sizzled with the imprint of the feminine curves pressed so intimately against him. His body instinctively hardened with need. She sighed, snuggling into his warmth as if she needed a safe haven from the dangers of the outside world. And for a moment, he forgot that he wasn't her savior, that he was a man who couldn't let himself get involved.

Driven by the heat pulsing through his veins, he became lost in her small hands stroking his back, in the rise and fall of her chest, in the trusting way she curled into him. Then she looped her arms gently around his waist, settling them on his hips, and her breath whispered hotly against his neck, igniting the fiery passion in his body.

Her need mingled with his, silent, beckoning, calling his name through the dim recesses of his mind, begging him to take her. Forgetting all the reasons he shouldn't kiss her, he lowered his head, knowing it was all wrong, but knowing that if he didn't taste her at least once, he would die.

Chapter Nine

Sydney melted into Collin's embrace, shocked at her eager response to the touch of his lips. Her need for comfort quickly built into a need for him, and when his hand cupped her chin, she parted her lips and met his kiss. His lips brushed her mouth like velvet, then his mouth hardened, slanting and seeking hers hungrily. Desire swirled in the pit of her stomach. She burrowed into the coccoon of his arms, drowning in the sensations flooding through her as his hands drew her closer. His mouth covered hers greedily, his body hard and straining toward her. Heat, desire, excitement all tingled along her nerve endings. She inhaled the heady scent of his body and dug her fingers into his back, whimpering as his lips left hers to nibble at her earlobe.

Aroused from his tender touches, she arched forward, savoring the low moan that escaped his lips. His fingers slid down her waist, seducing her as they tugged the hem of her skirt up, then feathered over her bare thighs. She sank her hands into his hair, clutching his arms for another kiss as passion rocked through her.

His tongue traced her mouth, seeking entrance and she parted her lips again, inviting him inside, her head spinning as his hunger touched her soul. His kiss became more frantic, hard and demanding, and her heart raced. He tangled his hands through the long tresses of her hair and then his lips traced a path down her neck. Involuntary tremors of arousal shook her, shattering the shell she'd built around herself since Doug's death. She ached for more. It had been so long since she'd been touched, held, since she'd felt truly desired. But the thought of her former husband and the painful memories of their marriage sobered her, bringing back reality and, with it, guilt and remorse. And fear.

"Incredible," Collin mumbled against her neck. "I've wanted you since I first saw you." The sound of his husky voice and the raw evidence of his arousal pressing into her belly sent liquid heat through her body. But she pulled back, bracing her hands on his shoulders, fighting the emotions churning through her. She couldn't do this, couldn't get involved with another man, especially with the murder of her husband unresolved.

Collin seemed to sense her withdrawal immediately. His hands loosened, slid to her waist to gently hold her. He lowered his head to hers, his eyes filled with confusion. His shaky breath brushed her cheek, still tempting.

But even as she told herself it was all wrong, that it was better she'd stopped, she drank in his masculine scent and craved more. In his arms she felt protected, cherished as she'd never before felt. But what if it was just sex—or all a lie, as it had been with Doug?

"I'm sorry, Sydney," he said in a hoarse whisper. "I don't know what to say."

"It's not your fault," Sydney said, her own voice strained. "I shouldn't have." She pushed the tangled strands of hair from her cheeks and turned away from him. "I...I'll bring you the phone."

"Sydney." He caught her by the arm, his intent clear.

He wasn't going to let her run away. They stood silently for several seconds, the tension between them almost palpable. Sydney closed her eyes, once again fighting her desire as his breath bathed her cheek. What must he think of her? She'd just buried a husband, and now she'd melted in his arms.

"That kiss was inevitable," he finally said, hunger still simmering in his voice.

She opened her eyes and her gaze searched his. The longing in his expression touched the hollow, lonely places in her heart, places that yearned for tender words and fiery passion, places that craved the kind of heat only a man could build and extinguish. He could fill that emptiness if she would only let him. But she couldn't.

"You must know I'm attracted to you," he said quietly, surprising her with his honesty. "But I know it's too soon for me to push you. And I know you loved Doug."

His comment brought another surge of guilt. She stared at his long, strong fingers where they circled her wrist, wishing things were different. Wishing she'd met him at a different time in her life.

"I know it's better if nothing happens between us," he said, his voice gruff. "But we might as well admit we have this chemistry between us. It's volatile, Sydney, it's…hot, and I'm not sure I can control it."

Startled at his choice of words, she wet her lips with her tongue.

His eyes smoldered as they followed the movement. "We do have to control it, don't we?" he asked, with a slow smile, as if he hoped she'd say no.

She nodded slowly, her only concession to his admission. Then, in spite of her discomfort, a smile tilted at the corner her mouth. "You're right—we're connected," she said. "But only because of Doug."

He released her arm, his expression suddenly grim. "I don't intend to push you into anything, Sydney." He raked a hand through his hair. "This situation between us, me and you and...Doug—it's weird, I realize that." His voice grew rough. "But the police don't seem sympathetic to your cause and somebody tried to hurt you. Besides, you were threatened. I told you I felt like I owed you, and I'm going to stay and make sure you're safe."

She opened her mouth to protest but he pressed a finger to her lips, silencing her. Her throat closed with emotions.

"Now, I'd better make a few phone calls or you're going to be stuck with me all night."

COLLIN SAT DOWN on shaky legs and ran a hand through his hair, struggling to control his libido as he ticked off the calls he needed to make while Sydney fixed him a sandwich. Get new ID, credit cards...banish Sydney from his mind. Impossible.

It had been a long time since he'd been with a woman—way before his accident—but no one had ever affected him the way Sydney had. Just the thought of her delicate skin beneath his fingertips turned his body hard, and the way she'd come apart in his arms—jeez, he'd never experienced anything like it.

Damn Doug Green. The man had been unfaithful to her. Green hadn't deserved her, and Collin wasn't going to feel guilty for wanting her himself. But he supposed he should be grateful for Sydney's caution. Hell, if it had been up to him, he wouldn't have stopped until he'd had her naked and writhing beneath him on the floor. But they had enough lies and secrets between them. Making love to her would complicate an already impossible situation.

She still had no idea he was a cop, and he still didn't know if she'd been involved in Doug's murder. He didn't think she had, but...other cases—the last one he'd worked on—flashed through his mind. His partner, Tim, had fallen for a woman he was supposed to be protecting. Collin had warned him not to trust her, but he'd stuck by Tim when he'd gone to a deserted alley to meet an informant.

The informant was supposed to testify to the woman's innocence and turn over the name of a major weapons dealer. Only, his partner had been set up. The woman's boyfriend and fourteen-year-old brother had shown up and killed him. And Collin had awakened in the alley, blinded by a shot from the brother's gun.

The sound of dishes rattling in the kitchen jerked Collin back from his thoughts, and he picked up the phone, anxious to talk to Sam. He dialed the precinct, then connected to Sam, his gaze scanning the room as he waited for Sam to answer. A cozy armchair in a green-and-white-striped fabric faced the fireplace, and a pine sofa table sat behind the leather sofa. There weren't any pictures of Sydney's former husband, not even a photograph of their wedding. Odd, with Sydney being a photographer, he'd expect her to have a roomful.

"What's up, man?" Sam asked.

"It's been a hell of a day," Collin said, then filled him in on the fire.

Sam cursed. "You okay?"

"Yeah." Collin rubbed his neck. "No one was hurt."

"You must have nine lives," Sam said. "First the shooting, now a fire. Either that or you're jinxed, Cash. Do they know what started the fire?"

"The police sergeant said it was arson. Found a rag soaked with acetone and a can of photo-developing chemicals."

"Any suspects?"

Collin considered Sydney but shook his head. "Not yet, but I'll keep you posted." He paused, almost dreading to ask the inevitable. "So, what did you learn about Doug Green?"

Sam gave a long-suffering sigh. "You sure you want to know? It's not a pretty picture."

Collin leaned against the back of the sofa, crossed his ankles on the coffee table and closed his eyes, exhausted. "Yeah, spill it."

"This guy Green was an interesting character. Had a few aliases."

"He had a record?" Collin's eyes popped open and he checked the door for Sydney.

"Yeah, some white-collar stuff. A couple cases of fraud, insider stock trading, income-tax evasion. He didn't serve any time, though, probably bought his way out."

"I see."

"Aliases were Doug White, Doug Sanders, Doug Waters, and the latest that shows up is Doug Black."

Collin whistled between his teeth. Did Raeburn know all this, or had he not felt the need to look past Sydney? "Busy guy."

"I'll say. He worked with more than fifteen start-up companies, took three public and made a bundle off stock options. But get this—a couple of years ago he was accused of falsifying FDA records."

"To speed up the process for the offering?"

"Exactly."

"Anything on McKenzie and the pharmaceutical companies?"

"The companies are legit. McKenzie's supposedly some eccentric genius scientist. Triset markets a wide variety of drugs to hospitals internationally. Norvek works with health-related products, but Green's the fascinating one.''

"Yeah?''

"Seems the guy had been married before, too. Lady named Gina Waters, lives here in Charleston. She has a kid—don't know if it's Green's or not.''

Collin grabbed a pad and pen from the sofa table, wondering if Sydney knew about the ex. "Give me the address, Sam.'' Collin wrote it down, along with Doug's aliases.

"A couple of girlfriends were arrested with him,'' Sam continued. "Sounds like a real ladies' man. But one of the ladies must have been pissed off, 'cause she sicced the IRS on him for tax evasion.''

The red-haired woman's face popped into Collin's mind. "A real upstanding guy, huh?'' Collin muttered in disgust.

"He's not selling drugs to kids, but he wouldn't win husband-of-the-year, either.'' Sam snorted. "He traveled internationally putting together these deals. You know, a guy with a woman in every city.''

Collin agreed then hung up and scrubbed his hand over his face. Sydney walked into the den carrying a tray of lemonade and a stack of sandwiches. Once again he cursed Doug Green. He knew the type.

Did Sydney have any idea what her husband had been up to?

FEELING CALMER NOW, Sydney willed herself to remain detached as she placed the tray on the coffee table and sat in the wing chair facing Collin. The couch seemed too small and intimate. In fact, the whole den seemed too warm and closed-in with Collin's big body in it.

"Thanks.'' Collin grabbed a sandwich and a drink.

"Did you find another room or did you decide to head back to Charleston?"

Collin chewed the sandwich, giving her a steady look. "I told you I'm staying until I know you're safe."

"You don't have to do that." Sydney held her sandwich in limp fingers. "I can take care of myself."

He drained the glass of lemonade, then stared at her, his expression unreadable. "I haven't called anywhere about a room yet."

She swallowed and put down her sandwich. "Then you've decided to go home?"

He arched an eyebrow, that devilish gleam back in his eyes. "I've decided I can protect you better if I sleep on your couch."

The knot that had finally unwound in her stomach while she'd been in the kitchen tightened again. "Do you really think I need protection?"

His smile faded. "Yeah, it looks like it," he said gruffly.

Alarm filled her eyes and Collin set his sandwich on the table.

"We need to talk." He reached for her hands and squeezed them gently.

She pulled her hands away and stared at him, shaken by his tone.

"This isn't easy for me to tell you." He studied her face. "But I just talked to a friend of mine, the detective I used to find out about Doug being the donor for my transplant."

Dread climbed her neck. "A detective?"

"Yeah. He was checking into Doug's murder."

"What did he learn?"

"Some background information on Doug." He propped

his elbows on his knees. "Did you know Doug had been married before?"

His voice was so calm Sydney thought she must have misunderstood him. "No, he wasn't," she said. But she immediately knew she was wrong when Collin dropped his head forward, feigning a sudden interest in his shoes.

Sympathy softened his voice. "Her name was Gina Waters. She lives in Charleston."

Sydney released a pain filled breath, shocked by his words. The extra checking account in Charleston—had it been for his ex-wife?

"There's more," he said, his gray eyes searching her face. "He had a record, had been arrested for fraud, accused of violating FDA standards—"

"No, that can't be true." Her heartbeat seemed to slow to a dull, aching throb as the extent of Doug's deception sank in.

"It's true, Sydney," he said in that same calm voice. "I'm sorry I have to be the one to tell you. I know how much you loved him."

Sydney buried her face in her hands, unable to look at him any longer. Pain rolled through her. Part of her couldn't believe Doug had been married, that he hadn't told her about his first wife. But with everything that had happened, all she'd learned since Doug's death, she knew it was true. He had lied about his feelings for her, he had another name, the vasectomy, another wife. God, what else?

"I thought he might be having an affair," she finally admitted in a voice so low she wasn't sure Collin heard her. "I wondered…all those times he went on business trips, if he had someone else."

Collin's breathing faltered slightly. His expression grew grimmer as he waited for her to continue.

"I found things in his pockets, a handkerchief that smelled like perfume, motel receipts, a receipt for a gift he'd bought and hadn't given me...." She fought to keep the pain from her voice but heard the unmistakable anguish there, anyway. "I thought there might be another woman, but the arrests—I had no idea."

"He's been accused of violating FDA standards more than once," Collin said. "Probably one reason for the aliases."

The heat was suddenly suffocating. She reached for her lemonade, then pressed the cool glass to the side of her face. "I found a passport and driver's license with the name Doug Black on it underneath some things of his in the closet."

Collin's head snapped up.

"And a ticket to Brazil. The flight was scheduled for the day he died."

"Did you give this evidence to Raeburn?"

She set down her glass. "I didn't know what to do. I found it after the police insinuated they suspected me. I was afraid Raeburn would think I had a motive. He doesn't seem to be looking anywhere beyond me for the killer." Sydney balled her hands into fists, trying to control her emotions. She refused to fall apart in front of Collin. Maybe when he left—

"Would you show me the fake credentials?"

She froze, wondering why he wanted to see them. But Raeburn didn't believe her. Maybe Collin would. Maybe his friend would even help.

"I'll get them." She rushed into her bedroom, her hands shaking as she took the box from the closet. Then she paused on the way back and stared at Collin's face through the doorway. Sunlight streamed in the window, radiating off his skin. A curl of his dark brown hair tumbled across his forehead, adding to his rugged, sexy look.

If she showed Collin the things she'd found, she'd be giving him all her trust, exposing herself to the humiliation of his finding out more about Doug's lies. Then again, if she didn't, she might never learn who had murdered Doug and be able to move on with her life.

And she couldn't forget—someone had tried to kill her.

COLLIN WAITED for Sydney, his jaw aching from clenching his teeth. He'd forced himself to search Sydney's face for any clues she might be pretending shock when he told her about Doug's first wife and his record. But her reaction had seemed heartfelt, which made continuing this investigation even more difficult. He'd hated like hell to tell her about Doug's wife. What if they discovered something worse about the guy? Maybe he had a whole string of wives or lovers. Maybe he'd hurt so many innocent people he deserved to die.

He dropped his head, guilt slamming into him. How could he think that about the man who'd given him back his eyesight? The one person who'd allowed him to live in the light again, instead of eternally in that prison of darkness?

Sydney walked into the room and he lifted his head. She thrust a box filled with papers toward him. "The fake passport, the driver's license, some of the receipts and things I found in Doug's pockets are in there."

He accepted the box, then Sydney sat back down, watching him.

He opened the passport and studied Doug Green's face, the round cheeks, red hair and beard, the wiry mustache. It seemed strange this man had been married to Sydney. He'd pictured a more charismatic-looking man, a banker-

type in a suit with a red power tie. And Green's eyes—
they were a dull brown, nothing like his own. Doug had
the kind of face that remained emotionless, like the ones
Collin had seen on countless criminals he'd interrogated
over the years. The color, the inflection, the distance—
nothing like his own.

"That picture doesn't look like him," Sydney said in
a low voice. "At least, not the way I knew him."

"What do you mean?"

"His hair was sandy blond and he never wore a mustache or beard." She fidgeted with her hands. "I almost
didn't recognize him when I saw the picture."

Green had obviously meant to flee the country in disguise. But why? Could McKenzie have been telling the
truth? If Doug had finalized the deal with Norvek, received his money and cashed in his stock options before
the bogus licensing agreement had been discovered, he
could have retired somewhere out of the country with millions. Not a bad plan. But something had gone wrong.
What?

He studied the driver's license, but his vision suddenly
blurred, dulling into the gray and white patches he now
recognized as Doug's memory. Sweat popped out on his
forehead, and he clutched the table edge, letting the memory unfold.

*A woman with wavy, short brown hair stood with a
child on her hip, her face drawn, her expression heated
as she spoke to him. Tears streaked the toddler's face,
streaming from big brown eyes.*

But he couldn't understand what the woman was saying
and the memory disappeared as quickly as it had come.
He fumbled with the motel receipts from the shoe box
and more visions bombarded him.

*A woman with hair as golden as the sun, a tan miniskirt
that showed off her thighs, heavy makeup and glossy red*

nail polish. She tossed a pair of black high heels toward him as she sprawled on an unmade bed, her posture almost vulgar.

A young woman, maybe twenty, dancing around a motel room wearing nothing but a pair of bikini panties, shaking her breasts, her head thrown back, her eyes dilated as if she was high on something.

A woman in the shadows, red hair, tall and willowy, a whisper of seduction hanging in the air, the smell of anger...

"Collin...Collin." He jerked, shaking away the disturbing images. Sydney was jostling his arm. "What's wrong? Did you figure out what Doug was doing with this fake ID?"

His hand folded around the passport. "No, not yet." He studied another receipt, one from a jewelry shop in France. A two-inch diamond pin, a sea horse with an emerald eye. His fist closed around the piece of paper, the description of the pin nagging at his mind. He had seen one like it, but where?

Then he remembered. Marla Perkins. The blond woman at the festival, the one who'd said she and her husband were separated. She'd been wearing a sea-horse pin just like the one the sales ticket described. So Doug had had an affair with Marla.

If Doug had a string of lovers, it was possible one of them had murdered him. That his death had nothing to do with his illegal business dealings. No fury like a woman scorned, he thought, vaguely recalling the old quote—or like the wife of a cheating husband. Raeburn, he knew, would pounce on the latter.

Disgust ate at him with every detail unveiled about Doug Green's life. He had no idea how to cushion the blow for Sydney. "You know, Sydney, if you were right," he said in a cautious voice, "and Doug was having an affair, the other woman would be a suspect in his murder. It's possible she killed him out of jealousy."

Sydney shrank farther into the chair, small and vulnerable-looking. He felt like a jerk. "I suppose you're right." She shrugged. "But I don't have any idea who this other woman might have been."

One of your friends, he thought, the ugly taste of acid burning in his throat. *Marla with that cute little girl, Beth.* And there might be others. Maybe he could find out about Marla, see if she had an alibi before he revealed her relationship with Doug to Sydney.

He scrubbed a hand over his face again, his body aching with fatigue, his vision blurring.

"Collin, are you all right?" Sydney asked.

He nodded. "I'm fine. It's been a long day."

"I know. You probably should have stayed in the hospital to rest."

"I've had enough of hospitals to last me a lifetime." Her blue eyes filled with sympathy. "Don't," he said, not wanting her to worry about him. He noticed the shadows beneath her eyes. She'd admitted she hadn't slept very well the past two nights. "You look pretty tired yourself."

"Yeah, it has been a long day," she said softly.

For a minute they sat in strained silence. He wanted to touch her, to wipe the anxiety from her eyes, but he reached for the phone book, instead. "I guess I'd better see about finding that hotel."

She stood, her fingers feathering her long dark hair from her cheeks, her face drawn with confusion. "You can sleep on the couch if you want." Her gaze captured his, and for a second he recognized the desire, the need burning in her eyes. Then she quickly masked it, and he thought he might have imagined it.

She walked down the hall and returned with a pillow and blanket, then set them on the sofa and said good-night. But long after she'd gone to her room, her jasmine cologne lingered, seeping into his body and driving him mad with desire.

He couldn't sleep for wondering why she'd changed her mind and let him spend the night.

WATCHING COLLIN STUDY Doug's things had driven Sydney crazy. She washed her face and donned a simple cotton nightshirt as she contemplated the hypnotic pull of the man's steely gray eyes. She'd wanted him to say something, *do* something, other than sit there with that odd, faraway look on his face as if he'd been privy to a world of Doug's she knew nothing about.

Slipping between the sheets, she flipped off the light and stared at the moonlight spilling through the narrow gap in the curtains. The day's events, the fire, Collin's escape, the things she'd learned about Doug all jumbled in her mind. If Raeburn found out about Doug's infidelity, he'd arrest her. Or maybe he already knew. Perhaps that was the very reason he hadn't been looking for the real killer.

But if Collin believed her, maybe he and his friend would find Doug's murderer and this nightmare would be over.

She rolled onto her side and stared at the wall, trying to shut off her feelings and the connection she felt to the enigmatic man only a few feet away in her den. A man who claimed to want to help her. A man who had turned her inside out with his touch, who had kissed her so hotly that her body had melted into a puddle of longing.

It couldn't happen again. Because even though the man had given her the most extraordinary kiss of her life, he had Doug's lying, deceiving eyes.

Chapter Ten

When the first slivers of morning light streaked through the sheers of Sydney's den windows, Collin groaned and climbed off the couch, stretching his sore limbs. He hadn't thought he'd be able to sleep, but he finally had. Now he'd awakened with more questions running through his mind. The realization that Sydney was in the other room in a big warm bed had him heading for the shower.

After retrieving a new set of clothes from the car, he went into the hall bathroom, smiling at the sight of a pair of black nylons draped over the shower rod. He couldn't resist touching them. As his fingertips glided over the sheer material, he imagined slowly sliding them off Sydney's slender legs, then sweeping her into his arms and making slow, passionate love to her. His frustration mounting, he forced himself to remove the delicate stockings and file away the provocative thoughts.

He thought about her home and how it compared to the drabness of his apartment. He'd had to keep things uncluttered when he'd been blind, and colors and accessories hadn't mattered. Now he appreciated the simple decorative touches, even in the bathroom. Warmth radiated throughout the house.

But she'd shared this house with another man, who was

the only reason he'd come to Beaufort. Stripping off the borrowed jeans and his boxers, he climbed into the shower, adjusted the temperature and savored the feel of the warm water washing away the last remnants of smoke from his skin. Still fighting lustful thoughts about Sydney, he stepped out of the shower and toweled off, then dressed, making mental notes about the case.

Did Raeburn know about Green's affairs? If so, it explained why Raeburn wasn't hunting too hard for another suspect. He was probably building a solid case against Sydney. The only thing missing was the murder weapon. Sam had said the gun still hadn't been found. Was it the pistol he'd seen in Sydney's car the day she'd crashed into the ocean?

A few minutes later he'd rummaged through the kitchen and made a pot of coffee, hoping he'd have time to talk to the police sergeant before Sydney awoke. After that, he planned to talk to Gina Waters, Green's first wife.

He poured himself a cup of coffee and dialed Raeburn. Seconds later the man's husky voice came on the line. "So, Mr. Cash, you came here on vacation, right?"

Collin sighed. "That's what I told you."

"You always bring your gun when you take a vacation?"

He'd found it in the fire, Collin realized. "Yeah. You're a cop—don't you?"

"I wear it to bed," Raeburn admitted. "But that's not the point. I've been doing some checking on you, mister. You haven't worked since you were shot in the line of duty. So why did you show up here poking your nose around in this murder investigation?"

"I haven't been poking my nose around," Collin lied. "It was a fluke that I saw Sydney run off the road. After that, I got curious." He paused. "When you see someone almost die, it tends to raise questions in your mind. If you were in my shoes, would you have left it alone?''

Raeburn muttered a curse. ''I don't know what's going on with you, Cash, but I don't need a stranger messing up my investigation. If you know something about Green or his wife, you'd better tell me.''

''All I know is someone tried to burn down the place where I was staying, and I want to know what you've found out.''

''Nothing yet,'' Raeburn answered. ''The lab's still working on the tests.''

''No suspects? Anybody see anything suspicious?''

''All the nearby residents were asleep,'' Raeburn replied, sounding annoyed.

''What about McKenzie?''

''His wife bailed him out two nights ago. But she swears he stayed with her all night.''

''She could be covering for him.'' Collin clenched his jaw. ''And you'd better make sure he doesn't go near Sydney.''

''I'm covering it. What are you keeping from me, Cash?''

''Nothing.'' Collin sipped his coffee, deciding Raeburn was smarter than he'd originally thought. But he still didn't like him.

''I don't believe you,'' Raeburn said. ''I know Green worked in Charleston. It doesn't take a rocket scientist to put two and two together. Did you have him under investigation there?''

''We have a file on him.'' Collin's patience was growing short. ''Did you know he had an alias? That he'd been arrested for tax evasion and violating FDA standards?''

''I don't have to discuss what I know with you,'' Raeburn snarled. "So stay out of my case or I'll have you charged for interfering with an investigation."

"Listen, Raeburn, I don't intend to let Sydney wind up like her husband."

As he hung up the phone, he heard a gasp. He turned to see Sydney standing in the hallway. She was barefoot, wearing a sleeveless black shell and white shorts, the wet strands of her hair falling softly around her face. God, how he wanted to hold her and chase the fear from her troubled blue eyes.

"I'D LIKE TO MEET Doug's first wife," Sydney announced.

"I don't think that's such a good idea," Collin said in a cautious voice.

"Maybe not. But it's something I have to do." She studied the plain gold band on her left hand, twisting it around her finger. "I can't explain it, but I need to meet her."

Collin's eyebrows furrowed in thought for a long moment as he sipped his coffee. "Okay, but I'll go with you."

Sydney hesitated, unable to meet his gaze. "Do you think this woman might know something about Doug's death?"

Collin shrugged. "Who knows? It depends on how long it's been since she's seen him. She might not have had any contact with him in some time. But it can't hurt to question her."

Oh, yes, it can, Sydney thought, the dull ache inside her intensifying. But she would find the strength to do it, anyway. Doug Green had hurt her enough while he was alive. She wasn't going to let him destroy her now that he was gone.

After a strained breakfast, Sydney relented and let Collin drive her car to Charleston to meet Doug's first wife.

"Her name is Gina," Collin said quietly as they approached the city limits.

Sydney straightened the hem of her black shell, her throat thick as they turned into a tree-lined street with small, neat brick houses. Toys and tricycles littered the driveways and lawns, and an elderly couple weeded their flower garden. It looked as if the day would be void of sunshine, filled with grueling heat, stormy clouds and humidity made worse by the impending rain.

Collin slowed the car as they neared a two-story gray house with red shutters that desperately needed a coat of paint. He checked the address and her stomach pitched. If Doug's first marriage had truly been over, why had he kept it a secret?

"Are you ready?" He parked in the narrow drive, killed the engine and they both climbed out.

A small boy of about eight whizzed by on roller blades, circled the drive, then flew down the sidewalk. He circled back and stopped in front of them, his skinny body dressed in a faded T-shirt and worn jeans. "Hey, what ya'll doing here?"

A frail, brown-haired woman poked her head out the door. "Jaycee, I told you not to talk to strangers."

The boy shrugged and skated off. But not before Sydney noticed his brown eyes. They reminded her of Doug. Was he Doug's son?

The woman, wiping her hands on an apron, walked toward them. Her simple cotton dress was obviously chosen for comfort, not style. "Can I do something for you folks?"

Sydney felt as if her pride had been torn open and scattered on the hot pavement.

Collin offered her a reassuring smile, then turned to the woman. "We'd like to talk to you, Ms. Waters." Collin extended his hand and introduced them. "This is Sydney Green."

Sydney forced a smile past dry lips, studying the woman's features. She was pretty in an old-fashioned way, wavy, chin-length brown hair, green eyes, nice figure, nothing sensational, but not unattractive. Odd, she couldn't picture Doug married to this woman.

"We'd like to talk to you about your ex-husband, Ms. Waters," Collin said.

"You're not from the IRS, are you?" She took a step back. "'Cause I told those people I haven't seen or heard from Doug in four years. And I don't aim to pay off his debts."

Sydney relaxed slightly, grateful it had been a while since she'd seen Doug. "I don't understand," Sydney said. "What debts are you referring to?"

The woman narrowed her eyes. "Are you from the IRS or not?"

"No, Ms. Waters," Collin said. "We're not with the IRS. We just want to talk to you."

Sydney cleared her throat. "You see, Ms. Waters, Doug is dead."

Gina Waters brought her hand to her cheek, her mouth dropping open in surprise. "You're serious?"

"I'm afraid so, ma'am," said Collin. "He died a few weeks ago."

"How...what happened?"

"Maybe we'd better sit down." Collin gestured toward the old metal chairs on the porch.

"It's too dang hot to sit out here," the woman said, palming perspiration from her forehead. "I guess you might as well come on in."

Collin placed his hand at Sydney's elbow and they followed the woman inside. The smell of cabbage and roast beef filled the air and a clock ticked somewhere in the distance. Sydney twisted the ring on her finger, scrutinizing the modest vinyl furniture, the shabby appliances, a scarred oak table. Although the house was nice, it obviously needed some maintenance. Apparently Doug hadn't been providing his ex-wife with any financial support.

"Would you like some iced tea or something?" Gina Waters offered.

"No, thanks," Collin said. "Sydney?"

"Water, please."

The woman seemed glad to have the simple task to do. She took her time filling two glasses with ice and water from the sink. She clutched one herself, handed Sydney the other and led the way to the living room. Sydney positioned herself beside Collin on the couch.

"Now, who are you folks?"

"I'm Sydney Green, Ms. Waters," Sydney began. "Doug and I were married last year." Her fingers tightened painfully around her glass.

"I pity you, then," Gina Waters said. "That man didn't have a faithful bone in his body."

Sydney felt the color drain from her face. Unable to look at Collin, she forced her gaze to remain steady on Doug's first wife.

"And you haven't talked to Doug in the last year or so?" Collin asked.

The woman waved her hand dismissively. "When I left him, it was good riddance. How did he die, anyway?"

"I'm surprised you didn't know about his death. He was murdered," Collin answered. "The story was in all the papers a few weeks ago."

"I've got a kid to raise, mister. I don't have time to

read the paper." Mrs. Waters sipped her drink, then pursed her small mouth. "So he broke down and married again? I never thought he'd do that."

Sydney felt Collin's probing scrutiny, and humiliation burned her face. She traced a bead of water rolling down the side of the jelly-jar glass. "How long were you and Doug married?"

"About two years," the woman said, picking up a basket of green beans. "At first I thought we might last. Then he started coming home smelling like cigarette smoke and cheap perfume, said he was out on business dinners, told me all these cockamamy stories about getting rich." She started stringing the beans, tossing them into a bucket. "But I knew what kind of business he was doing," she said. "He was making it with everything in a skirt."

Sydney absentmindedly twisted her wedding ring again, the metal oddly cold and offensive.

"Then a man came by one day and claimed Doug had been working with his research company. Said Doug was fudging paperwork, violating FDA standards—that was how he was going to make money."

"Did you ask Doug about it?" Collin asked.

"Didn't have to. The police came looking for him. Then he ran off." The beans pinged off the side of the bucket. "I figured he'd gone to that woman over in Summersville. She was the only regular one he kept. The others were just one-nighters."

The breakfast Sydney had eaten curdled in her stomach as the last of her feelings for Doug died. How could she have been such a complete idiot and not seen his lies? *Because you saw what you wanted to see. A handsome man who whispered all the right things, who promised you a rose garden and a house full of kids—and left you with nothing but thorns.*

"Ms. Waters, thank you for your time. We're sorry we disturbed you." Collin turned to Sydney. "Are you ready to go?"

Sydney stood and placed her glass on the rickety table, trying to forget her trip down misery lane. "Yes. Thanks, Ms. Waters."

"Police don't know who killed Doug?" Gina asked, glancing at Sydney.

"Not yet."

"Ought to try Doug's mistress. Maybe she lost it when he married you, instead of her," Gina suggested. "After all, she'd been warming his bed for so long, she figured she'd be the next in line for marriage."

"You have a good point." Collin withdrew a notepad from his pocket. "Do you know her name?"

"I can do better than that," Gina offered. "I can give you her address. Doug didn't even try to act discreet where this woman was concerned. She even called here a few times asking for him."

Sydney scanned the pictures on the side table while the woman located the address. A snapshot of the little boy caught her eye. He was about two years old, his big brown eyes bright with excitement as he reeled in a fish. Sydney couldn't leave without asking about him.

"Ms. Waters, is that boy, Jaycee…is he Doug's?"

The woman's face softened. "No, thank the Lord. He was my first husband's son. Roy was a good man." *Unlike Doug.*

The words lingered in Sydney's mind as she and Collin drove away. And she wondered if she'd ever be able to trust a man again.

COLLIN'S HANDS were wrapped so tightly around the steering wheel his fingers ached, but he couldn't show his anger in front of Sydney. Damn Doug Green for all the low, underhanded things he'd done, for the women he'd hurt. Especially Sydney. Even if Green had given him back his eyesight, it appeared to be the *only* good thing the man had ever done. Seeing the anguish in Sydney's eyes fueled his anger. And the case wasn't over. Not by a long shot.

Perspiration dampened his neck, soaking his collar. Now they would meet the woman Doug had been having an affair with. And if his suspicions were correct, Sydney's friend Marla had probably slept with him, and no telling how many others. If one of the women hadn't killed him, one of their husbands or boyfriends could have, which complicated the case even more.

He flipped the radio to a soft-rock music station, hoping to soothe some of the tension from the car, then stole a glance at Sydney. She hadn't spoken or looked at him since they'd settled in the car, and they'd been driving for half an hour. They'd be in Summersville in another five minutes.

Choosing his next words carefully, Collin cleared his throat, then spoke in a low voice. "I know this is rough on you, Sydney."

His comment snagged her attention. She threw a look of disbelief his way, then resumed staring out the window.

"You don't have to meet this woman, you know," Collin said. "I can visit her or we can turn her name over to Sergeant Raeburn and let him question her."

Sydney sighed, long and hard. "I have to face it," she said with surprising conviction. "Doug was murdered and someone is threatening me. I won't be able to rest until his killer is found."

"But you don't have to actually meet this woman," he said quietly. "You can leave it up to Raeburn."

"I have to do this." She heaved another sigh. "That stupid cop thinks I killed Doug. He's not going to listen to anything I have to say. If it were up to him, he'd lock me up and stop hunting for the real killer."

Collin reached over and covered her hand reassuringly. But after meeting Raeburn, he had a feeling she was right.

SYDNEY SAT MOTIONLESS in the car while Collin turned onto the quiet two-lane street, searching for the address Gina Waters had given him. They passed a low-rent housing development, some vacation rental property for sale, then moved on to a nicer part of town. He found a side street that lead to a row of high-rise condominiums. Very upscale. Roxy DeLong, Doug's other woman, lived in one of these.

Her fingers tingled, a reminder of Collin's touch. His sympathetic touch, she reminded herself. He was probably feeling sorry for her, wondering how she could have allowed a man to make such a fool of her. A question she'd like the answer to herself.

They pulled into the complex, and she half hoped the woman wouldn't be home. Her insides were already torn in shreds. Doug's mistress would only add salt to her wounds. But putting off the inevitable would only drag out this ordeal. And she was ready to get it over with. To hell with her pride—she didn't have any left, anyway.

"You're sure you don't want to wait in the car?" Collin turned to her. "I know this can't be easy for you. I hate to make you go through this."

"I may have been a fool, Collin, but I'm not going to let Doug destroy me." She climbed out of the car, blinking back the tears stinging her eyes. She refused to give in to the hurt—not in front of Collin.

The elevator seemed to crawl up the floors of the high-rise building. Her stomach spasmed as it lurched to a stop. The doors opened with a grating screech, and the hallway loomed ahead, a corridor of endless white walls. When Collin took her hand in his, she was too numb to pull away. She took solace in the physical comfort and told herself she'd think about the ramifications later.

Finally they stood outside the door of the woman's apartment, and Sydney fought the emotions bombarding her. She imagined Doug sliding a key into the door, walking in to share a tryst with this woman while she waited at home, the loving and trusting wife. As soon as the door opened, Sydney realized Roxy DeLong was exactly the kind of woman Doug would have liked. Tall and willowy with big breasts, hair a fiery red, showy clothes and perfect makeup.

"Hello, what can I do for you?" the woman drawled, ignoring Sydney and focusing on Collin.

Collin introduced them and the woman arched penciled eyebrows at Sydney. "I'm surprised you showed up here, honey. I didn't think you'd have the backbone."

Anger surged through Sydney. "Sorry to disappoint you."

Surprise flashed in Roxy's green eyes. "Doug always said you were so sweet—that was why he couldn't resist you. He didn't mention you had a feisty side, too." The compliment sounded vile coming from the woman's painted mouth. Sydney felt Collin put his hand to the back of her waist protectively.

"May we come in?" Collin asked in a polite tone.

Roxy shrugged. "I don't have long, but sure. We may as well get this over with."

Roxy DeLong did not offer tea or any other sort of refreshment, although judging from the plush decor of her apartment, if she had, the refreshments would have been served in Waterford crystal. The woman obviously had expensive tastes, and Sydney realized with a sickening clarity that Doug had probably paid her handsomely for her...assets.

When they were seated on a white leather sofa, Roxy sat facing them in a leopard-skin chair. She crossed her slender legs and angled herself so Collin would have a perfect view of her exposed thighs, including the black garter belt she didn't try to hide.

"So what is it you want? Doug's dead. I don't see how I can help you."

"We...talked with Doug's first wife, Gina Waters," Sydney said, not really sure where to start.

"Oh, her." Roxy flipped open a gold cigarette case and extracted a cigarette.

"Yes. She told us you and Doug had been together for quite a while," Collin explained.

"What's it to you? You a cop?" Roxy poised the cigarette seductively.

Sydney clenched her hands in her lap. "He's a friend of mine," she said, interrupting whatever Collin had intended to say. "You see, someone has been threatening me. Since you obviously knew Doug so well, you might be able to give us information that would help find his killer."

"Honey, the only thing I can tell you about Doug is how good he was in bed." Roxy paused, flicked a gold trimmed lighter with her initials embossed on the side and took a drag of the cigarette. "But then, I guess you know that."

Sydney squirmed, gritting her teeth. Collin didn't bat an eye at Roxy's blatant sexual behavior. The man couldn't be immune to Roxy's charms, could he? Doug certainly hadn't been.

"How long had you and Doug been seeing each other?" Collin asked in a detached voice.

"About five years." Roxy flicked ashes into a crystal ashtray. "Long before he married *you*," she muttered as if the thought of Doug with Sydney left a rancid taste in her mouth.

"So you were having an affair while he was married to his first wife, then continued to see him after their divorce," Collin said.

Roxy simply shrugged.

"Then he met Sydney and married her?" Collin asked.

"Yep." Roxy blew a ring of smoke in the air. "Rotten SOB. He should have married me. I gave him what he needed." She punctuated the words by pressing her hand over her breasts. "That's why he kept coming back even after he married you, Sydney. He was obsessed with you, liked all those sweet pictures you took, said he loved you." She pressed her breasts again. "But he kept coming back to me, 'cause you couldn't satisfy him the way I could."

Sydney stood up. "This is a waste of time, Collin. Let's go."

Collin rose and placed his hand at the curve of her back, offering support. "Did you know anything about Doug's business dealings, Ms. DeLong?"

"Heavens, no." Roxy rolled her eyes. "We didn't discuss business. We were busy doing other things. Fun things."

In spite of the air-conditioning, perspiration soaked Sydney's neck. And Roxy's strong perfume turned her stomach. "I said let's go."

Collin thanked the woman for her time. Sydney didn't wait for him. She rushed into the hallway, flinching at the harsh sound of Roxy's laughter echoing off the apartment walls behind her. Collin followed silently on her heels.

When they reached the elevator, she wrapped her arms around herself as they rode the elevator and found their way to the parking lot. A blast of afternoon heat hit her in the face, making her whole body flush. Once inside the car, she began to tremble. Collin reached for her. She knew he meant to offer comfort, but she held up her hands, warning him off. A sympathetic touch would only trigger her emotions past the breaking point. "Just take me home, please."

Collin's silence came as a welcome relief; his probing eyes showed her more understanding than she could accept. Finally he turned on the engine and pulled out of the lot.

Dark thunderclouds rolled across the sky. Lightning streaked jaggedly above the distant palms. Sydney welcomed the storm, taking refuge in the sounds of thunder, as if the sky's angry roar cried out her own pain. Then the rain began to fall and she felt the release of her own tears. Embarrassment heated her cheeks and she turned away, facing the window, hoping the road conditions would hold all of Collin's attention. Pressing her hands to her cheeks, she swiped away the moisture, hating herself for crying over Doug, for grieving over his death when she'd been grieving for their marriage months before he'd been killed. No, she wouldn't feel guilty for moving on with her life, she decided. Knowledge of Doug's numerous lies had obliterated any feelings she'd harbored for him.

And when they crossed the mile-long bridge over Johns Island, she pulled the wedding ring off her finger, opened her window and threw the meaningless band into the raging sea, tossing with it the last vestiges of her love for Doug.

COLLIN KNEW THE MOMENT Sydney's tears began to fall, and his chest tightened painfully. He started to reach for her, but she shrank away as if she didn't want his comfort. He ground his teeth, frustration filling him. If he hadn't been a gentleman, trained as a cop, he would have belted Roxy DeLong right on her two-thousand-dollar nose job for her cruel barbs. But Sydney had surprised him with her courage and the way she'd left the apartment, with her head held high.

When he heard the window slide down and the whistle of the wind, he glanced sideways. Sydney tossed something out of the window. She fidgeted with her left hand and he noticed the missing wedding band. So, she'd finally taken it off.

A strange feeling of relief washed over him, but guilt quickly followed. Sydney was vulnerable. She needed understanding and compassion, not passion or jealousy. And he'd better remember it.

The rest of the drive passed in awkward silence, the howling wind and slashing rain forcing him to keep his attention on the road. His fingers ached from clenching the steering wheel, and he wanted to draw her in his arms so badly he thought he'd die. When they reached her house, he had no idea what to do.

Sydney bolted from the car as soon as he parked in front. He jumped out and followed her up the drive. She was fumbling with the keys when he reached the entrance. He eased the key ring from her fingers and opened the door, then flipped on the light, bathing the foyer in soft light. He placed his hand at the back of her waist, ushering her in from the downpour, shuddering with restrained emotions.

"Sydney, I'm sorry you had to go through this," he said softly. "But now we have another suspect besides McKenzie. Roxy might have killed Doug."

She turned to him then and the look she gave him reeked of anguish. And need. He could sense the pain Roxy's words had caused, knew the kind of insecurity you could feel when your sexuality was disparaged. He couldn't let her think she was undesirable when she was the most desirable woman he'd ever met.

"I can't believe I didn't know," she said, her voice breaking. "I was such a fool."

"Shh, no, don't," he whispered. He touched her shoulders lightly, then pulled her into his arms and she whimpered, her big blue eyes lost and troubled. He cupped her chin, lifting her face so he could brush her mouth with his own, so he could taste the sweetness of her lush lips and breathe in her essence. She parted her lips, desire and vulnerability shadowed in the soft flutter of her eyelashes, and he lowered his mouth, hungrily drinking in her dewy taste. One kiss meant to comfort, only one, then another. His need grew, pressing into her, her soft compliance like a dam bursting between them, her eagerness trapping him with want. She dug her nails into his back and moaned, trembling and leaning into him as if she could no longer stand being without his touch.

He drove his tongue into her mouth, taking, accepting her passion, their hands clinging and seeking. A shudder rippled through her. He drew back, saw the shadows still haunting her lovely face and knew he couldn't take her, not like this, not when she was so vulnerable.

She would regret it. She would wonder tomorrow why she'd let herself be seduced, and he would feel like a heel.

And the memories of their lovemaking would be tainted. It had been so long for him and he wanted her desperately, but he wanted her to want him. Not as a replacement for the husband she'd lost, nor a figure to erase a traumatic day, but as a friend, a lover....

Her hands caressed his back and he eased his own around her face, gently stroking her jaw, kissing her cheeks, slowing the pace, allowing them both time for their raging emotions to dissipate. Then he pulled her into his arms and simply held her, resting his hands at her waist. "Sydney, I want you—you know that."

She closed her eyes and nodded against his chest.

"But not like this, not tonight when you're upset."

"But I—"

He silenced her protest with a gentle kiss. "I do want you. You can feel how much." He pressed his arousal against her. "But if we make love tonight, you'll be sorry in the morning." He paused, hating it when she lowered her head as if embarrassed.

"Don't," he whispered, kissing her eyelids. "We're both adults, we both want it, but the timing isn't right. When we make love, Sydney, and we *will* make love," he said, lifting her face and forcing her to look into his eyes, "I don't want you to have regrets the next day. I want you to wake up in my arms and yearn to do it all over again." He kissed her nose, her cheeks, her mouth. "Again, again and again."

Her lips curved into a smile beneath his and he pulled away. "You look tired." The remnants of his passion lingered in his husky voice. "Maybe you should rest for a while."

Her voice sounded rough when she spoke. "What are you going to do?"

He shrugged, then tucked a strand of hair behind her ear. "I'll take a drive, give you some time by yourself."

"I guess I could use that," she said softly.

He squeezed her arms, then forced himself to release her and walked to the door. "Do you mind if I come back later? I'd feel better if you weren't alone."

"I'm fine," she said in a weak voice.

"But you may still be in danger," he said, knowing he would never forgive himself if he let his personal attraction to her interfere with his determination to protect her.

She chewed her bottom lip, the gesture provocative and vulnerable at the same time. "I guess you're right."

He smiled. "Good. Now lock the door when I leave."

She clutched the doorknob and he kissed his finger, then pressed it to her cheek. "I'll be back in a little while. You get some rest."

He felt her watching him as he strode toward his car. The rain had slackened considerably, but the air hung thick with shadows and heat and darkness as more clouds rolled in. The skin at the back of his neck prickled, and he paused, his instincts warning him something was amiss. Was he wrong to leave her alone?

He stopped a few feet from his car, pivoting to scan the surroundings, then glanced at Sydney, his uneasiness growing. She lifted her hand in a small wave and his gut tightened. Maybe he would sit in the car and watch her place for a while, make sure no one had been waiting for him to leave. He turned to cover the small distance left to his car and pressed the remote unlock button on his key chain.

Suddenly a deafening explosion rent the air. Metal and glass pelted the walkway. Sparks and fire splintered in front of Collin. He was thrown backward, hurled through the air. Seconds later he hit the pavement with a painful jar and realized, just before his head connected with concrete, that a bomb had blown up his car.

Chapter Eleven

Sydney staggered in the doorway, her heart thundering at the sight of Collin's body being thrown backward. Bits and pieces of burning metal and rubber rained through the air. Flames and smoke billowed like a thick, black cloud. She ran forward, stumbling over the fiery parts of the car. "Collin!" She screamed his name over and over, coughing at the stench of the smoke.

Collin groaned and she dropped down beside him, ignoring the sting of the pavement on her knees as chaos descended around her. Neighbors ran out of their houses screaming, "Everyone okay over there?"

"Call 911!" she shouted as she ran her hands over Collin's face, then down his arms. "Oh, my God, Collin. Are you hurt?"

He groaned again. "I'm all right." Raising slightly, he pulled her into his arms.

Sydney strained against him, trembling and wanting to hold him, but anxious to make sure he hadn't been hurt. "Are you sure? You're not burned or cut?" She pressed her hands down his chest, probing and feeling for injuries, then gasped at the bloody gash on his forehead. Other small nicks and scrapes marred his arms. "Your forehead, it's bleeding."

He caught her hands in his and sat up, hugging her against him. "It's not bad, Sydney, just a flesh wound."

"That was a bomb, wasn't it? You could have been killed." Her voice broke.

"Shh, don't cry." He thumbed the tears from her cheeks. "Come on, help me up. Let's move away from the heat."

She nodded, sliding her hands under his arms, the heat from the blaze scalding her back. Relief filled her when Collin stood and leaned against her, unharmed except for the cuts and minor scratches.

"I don't understand what's happening. Why would someone want to hurt you, Collin?" She dropped her head against his chest on a sob. "You're a stranger here in town. No one here even knows you."

"I don't know why, either." Collin gently wrapped his arms around her but anger hardened his voice. "But I'm going to find out."

"Gracious alive!" Seventy-five-year-old Millie Blake yelled from across the street, "The fire truck's on its way. Are you okay, Sydney?"

"Yes," she shouted back, waving at Millie as she tried to come down her porch steps, hampered by arthritis.

"Stay back, ma'am," Collin yelled. "Everyone, please stay back."

Sydney noticed Mr. Zimmerman watching from his porch. Two other neighbors huddled together in their yards, looking anxious and worried. She gave a silent thanks Kelly hadn't been out taking Megan for a stroll when the explosion had hit.

Together she and Collin walked back to the house, the crackling of the car fire behind them, the acrid smell burning Sydney's nostrils. When they reached the porch, Sydney turned and saw pieces of charred black metal scattered across the lawn. Slivers of metal and rubber had hit the porch. Her heart constricted. Collin could have died.

"I wonder who did this," Collin said matter-of-factly, scanning the area.

"And why." Sydney's breath caught as a frightening thought dawned. "It's because of me, isn't it? Because you've been helping me ask questions about Doug's murder." The realization horrified her. Who would want her dead badly enough to come after her and Collin?

"We don't know that, Sydney." Collin stroked her hair from her face. "Just try and stay calm."

She traced his jaw with her finger, memorizing the strong lines of his face. "I can't believe how close you came to being kill—"

He pulled her into the doorway, away from the neighbors' eyes, and captured her lips with his, cutting off her words, his mouth devouring hers hungrily as if he needed to feel her warmth as much as she needed to know he was alive. She clutched his back, angling her head sideways, parting her lips and moaning when he slipped his tongue into her mouth and explored the tender recesses. The rest of the world faded into oblivion as her need flowed into his.

The brush with death, the flames hissing behind, the memory of Collin being hurled through the air, the danger—all culminated in a desperate desire to hold him. She wanted him, all of him, wanted to feel his bare skin against hers....

But if Collin was in danger because of her, she should make him leave here, leave Beaufort, go back to Charleston.

She ended the kiss, her body throbbing as she pulled away. A siren wailed and flashing blue lights bounced across the planes of his face. The conversation would have to wait.

"I guess the cavalry has arrived," Collin said. He was trying to calm her with his light tone. He had no idea how endearing the gesture was.

The police car screeched to a stop in front of her house, the fire truck on its heels. Firefighters rushed from the truck, the bomb squad and Sergeant Raeburn quickly following. The men snapped to business, yelling orders. "First put out the fire," the fire chief called.

"Seal off the area. Evacuate the people."

"Check the surrounding area for other bombs!"

Sydney watched as a team of men searched the area for other explosives while the firefighters douched the flaming car. A paramedic insisted on examining Collin and cleaning the cut on his forehead.

"Ma'am, we need to search the house and your property," one of the men said.

She waved them forward, the enormity of the situation settling in as she watched the team explore the neighboring yards. Whoever had planted the bomb had meant to hurt Collin, and maybe her, but they could also have hurt her neighbors, innocent people.

Once the fire was extinguished, Collin moved to stand beside her. "They didn't find another bomb," he said, sounding relieved. "They're going to start investigating the blast site, take samples, bag evidence and examine the remains of the car. It may take a while."

Sydney sank onto the porch swing, her mind a jumbled mess.

"Are you okay, Sydney?"

She nodded, too numb to speak as she tried to make sense of all the horrible things that had been happening lately.

He patted her shoulder. "I'm going to talk to Raeburn, see if they have any idea what kind of bomb was used."

Collin went to talk to the investigators and she fought tears. He had wanted to help her find Doug's killer, but now he'd put himself in jeopardy. Because of her.

She studied his back, his muscular physique, the powerful way he walked. Desire curled in her belly, strumming her nerve endings with a want so basic and primitive it shocked her.

But she couldn't follow through on the attraction. If she wanted Collin to be safe, she needed to send him packing. As soon as the chaos ended and Raeburn finished talking to him, she would tell him to go.

COLLIN TRIED TO REMAIN focused on the men examining his car, aware that Sydney was sitting on her porch looking pale and terrified as police roped off her house with yellow tape and turned it into a crime scene. For once, he was glad to see Raeburn and the bomb squad, grateful not to be the prime investigator. Being emotionally involved definitely clouded his thinking. He'd almost picked up a piece of suspicious-looking wiring with his bare hand, a mistake he hadn't made since his early days on the force.

"What triggered the explosion?" Raeburn asked Collin.

"My remote key," he said, studying the pieces of metal piping scattered in the wet driveway. "You think it was black powder?"

Raeburn nodded. "Probably. Rain may hinder things, but I'll let you know after the team reconstructs the bomb." He rubbed his hand over his belly, his girth stretching the buttons on his uniform to the limits. "Any ideas who did this, Cash?"

Collin shook his head. "It has to be related to Green's

murder," he said. "But if the bomber used black powder, I know it'll be hard to trace. Any Tom, Dick or Harry can buy it at the local hardware store."

"Probably used that piping." Raeburn pointed to several scraps on the ground. "And bits of electrical tape are everywhere. Simple stuff, easy to buy."

"How about McKenzie?" Collin asked. "He's a scientist. Wouldn't be too hard for him to figure out how to construct a bomb."

Raeburn stuffed a piece of gum in his mouth. "Could be. We'll bring McKenzie in for questioning."

Collin couldn't believe Raeburn was actually agreeing with him.

The sergeant glanced back at Sydney, his ruddy complexion turning bright red with the afternoon heat. "What have you and Mizz Green been up to today? You been nosing around?"

Collin recalled the conversations with Doug's ex-wife and mistress. If Raeburn were any kind of cop, he already knew about them. The affair with Roxy would definitely give Sydney a motive for killing her husband, except he really believed Sydney hadn't known about the other woman. And Roxy, of course, was another suspect. Deciding he'd better not withhold information, he forged ahead, determined to end the case as soon as possible. "We rode over to Charleston. Sydney's husband was married before."

"I know about his ex." Raeburn's bushy eyebrows shot up. "But Mizz Green, did she know?"

"Not until I told her." Collin narrowed his eyes at a fragment of piping one of the investigators was examining. "There's more. A mistress by the name of Roxy DeLong."

Raeburn chomped on his gum, unimpressed. "Anything else you've been holding back?"

Collin shook his head as he thought about Marla, but decided to wait until he had a chance to question Sydney about her and the husband from whom she said she was separated.

"You should talk to Roxy DeLong. She thought she was next in line to marry Green. She might have killed him for spite."

"I think I've got me a pretty good suspect already," Raeburn said "Money, infidelity." Raeburn shaded his eyes with his hand and lumbered toward the front porch. "All I need is the murder weapon."

Collin blew out his breath angrily, following Raeburn as he ambled up the steps. Sydney rose, her face anxious as she watched them approach.

"Mind if I ask you a couple of questions?" Raeburn propped one hip against the porch railing.

Dust streaked Sydney's face and stained her clothes where she'd wiped her hands. Her big eyes widened with fear.

"What have you been up to today, Mizz Green?"

Sydney lifted her chin, then, in a dull voice, repeated the story he'd already told Raeburn.

Sweat rolled down Raeburn's beefy arms as he listened. "I guess you were pretty mad when you found out Doug had been sleeping around, huh?"

"I wasn't happy about it," Sydney said in an uneven voice.

"What did your husband say when you confronted him?"

"I didn't confront him." Sydney knotted her hands in her lap. "I just found out about the affair and his ex-wife today."

"You're sure about that now?" Raeburn asked sarcastically. "'Cause I think maybe you already knew. Maybe you and Doug had a big fight, and maybe he was a little ugly to you, Mizz Green, and you couldn't stand it no more."

"That's not what happened," Sydney said, her voice rising in pitch. "I told you I just found out—"

"I think you knew about the other women, you killed Doug, and then made it look as if there'd been an intruder. When Cash here showed up asking questions and talked about this other woman, you acted all surprised."

"No." Sydney's pale cheeks looked hollow. "No, that's not true."

"Raeburn, she answered you—"

"Then you decided he was asking too many questions and you got nervous, so you set fire to the inn—"

"No!" Sydney said.

"And he escaped. Then you tried to blow up his car."

"That's a lie." Sydney searched Collin's face, doubts and worries darkening her eyes.

Collin's temper flared. Raeburn was doing his job, jumping to the same kind of conclusions and questions he would if he were in Raeburn's shoes. But damn it, Raeburn was wrong. He'd stake his reputation on it.

"Sydney was with me all day," Collin interjected. "There's no way she could have planted the bomb."

"How about this morning?" Raeburn suggested.

"I stayed the night," Collin said, realizing how the admission sounded when Sydney winced and Raeburn's brow furrowed.

"I see," Raeburn said.

"No, you don't," Collin said, fighting the urge to deck the officer. "I was worried about Sydney's safety. I slept on her sofa. End of story." He punctuated his words by jamming his finger at Raeburn's chest. "And she and I have been together all day, so there's no way she could be responsible for the bomb."

The fear in Sydney's eyes disappeared slightly. He wished he could do something to alleviate all the shadows.

Raeburn merely grunted, his jowls shaking as he pulled Collin aside. "I don't know what your game is, Cash, but I think you'd better start thinking with your head, instead of what's behind your zipper." With that, the sergeant walked off to join the other investigators, and Collin muttered a curse.

When he turned to Sydney, his body throbbed at the caring way she gazed at him. He had to hold her, had to make sure she was within reach. Hell, there were no guarantees in life. He might die tomorrow or even tonight. And he wouldn't want to leave this world without making love to her at least one time.

As THE INVESTIGATORS finished their work and impounded the remains of the car, Sydney tried to gather her shattered nerves. Collin had defended her in front of Raeburn. His vote of confidence touched chords of longing and affection in her that hadn't been touched in a long time. He'd admitted that his relationship with her was strange, all tangled up with Doug, and she'd thought she could keep her feelings at bay, but a surge of wanting rose up that refused to be dismissed. Her love for Doug had died, was no longer a source of guilt eating away at her, but could she have feelings for another man so soon?

And if someone had connected the two of them with Doug's murder, they might be watching them now.

His gaze found hers and he smiled slowly, then walked up the porch steps, his shoulders hunched as if he was tired, his gaze steady.

"I'm sorry about your car," Sydney said, staring at the ashes.

He shrugged. "It was an old Bronco. About time I replaced it."

She smiled at his attempt to make light of the matter, then opened the door and went inside. He followed, his masculine scent mingling with the smoke from the bomb, reminding her of his close call and how she'd felt when she'd seen the blast throw him to the ground. She turned to face him when they entered her den. "Thank you for defending me in front of Raeburn."

"I told the truth," Collin said in a low voice. He stroked her chin with the soft pad of his thumb. "You and I were together all day." His eyes grew dark and pensive. "And I saw how shocked you were when that bomb exploded."

The memory of flying metal and sparks caused a tremor to run through her. He must have sensed it because he moved closer to her, putting his hands on her waist. "Collin, I really think you should go," Sydney said, starting to back away.

"What? You think I'd leave you alone now, after a bomb exploded in your driveway?"

"You can't stay here—it's not safe," Sydney said, hating the fear in her voice.

He stared at her for a long moment, his expression unreadable, then ran his finger gently down her jaw. "Do you really want me to go, Sydney?"

She swallowed, trying to make her voice work. "I don't want you to be hurt because of me," she finally said. "I couldn't live with myself if…if something happened to you."

"I'm a big boy," Collin said. "I make my own decisions, Sydney, and there's no way I'm leaving you now."

He lowered his mouth, his lips seeking hers hungrily, and Sydney succumbed as he drew her nearer. She felt the slight stubble on his jaw as he brushed his face against her cheek, then inhaled the smoke lingering on his skin. Her hands tangled in his hair, holding him tightly with all the passion and worry that had been building in her chest for days. His arms slid around her, his hands stroked her back, the long column of her spine, then they cupped her bottom and he pulled her firmly against him, tucking her into the heat of his arousal.

"No, we can't," Sydney said, jerking away. She pressed her hand over her chest, heaving for air, her breathing unsteady.

"Why not?" Collin asked, his hands fisting beside him. "Is it because you're still in love with Doug?"

She stared at him in shock, the blood roaring in her ears.

"Even after all the things he did to you, you're still grieving for him," he said in a voice filled with defeat.

"It's not like that," she whispered fiercely. "But I told you, I couldn't stand it if anything happened to you. And ever since you met me, weird things have been happening."

"Weird things started happening *before* I met you." Collin ran a hand through his hair.

"What do you mean?" Sydney asked, surprised by the seriousness of his voice.

He paced across the room. "Maybe you'd better sit down."

"Why? Is there something you're not telling me?"

For a long second he merely stood there, looking as if he was trying to decide whether or not to break some awful news to her.

"Come on, Collin, you might as well spill it." She

swung her hands around, suddenly furious. "Whatever you have to tell me can't get much worse, can it? Doug was murdered, the police think I did it, he had a mistress, an ex-wife, he cheated his own company..." Her voice was starting to sound hysterical so she paused, striving for calm when she felt like screaming.

"It's not about Doug. It's about me," he said calmly.

She wrapped her arms around herself. "What are you talking about?" Her eyes widened with suspicion. "You're not married, too, are you?"

He gripped her arms in his hands, his face tormented. "No, Sydney, I'm not married." He coaxed her toward the sofa and sat down beside her, his hands resting on his knees.

"I didn't tell you this when I first came because I didn't want to frighten you. But since the transplant I...I've been having these visions. I think I'm seeing Doug's murder in them."

Her heart pounded. "I don't understand. Are you telling me you're psychic?"

"No, it's even stranger than that." He paused, as if searching for the words. "After the transplant, when the doctor first unwrapped the bandages from my eyes, I saw a man being shot."

His eerie tone chilled her to the bone.

"I thought it was impossible at first, that maybe I was hallucinating from the drugs they'd given me during surgery, but it's happened again since."

"But how could you...?"

He explained about the doctor's theory and the experimental drugs. "So it's not only you that's keeping me here, Sydney. I have to know if what I'm seeing is really Doug's murder, if I'm a witness."

Sydney stared at him, too stunned to speak. He really believed he was an eyewitness to Doug's murder?

"I know it sounds bizarre." He covered her hand with his, and her skin tingled. "But I saw the gun, Doug falling on the green rug."

Sydney gasped and stood, putting some distance between them. This was crazy talk. There had to be an explanation. But how could he have known about the green rug?

"When did you see the rug?"

"In this vision I've been telling you about. There was blood all over it."

"But I changed that rug before you came here. How would you know, unless…" Unless he'd been in her bedroom before, *unless he had killed Doug.*

The back of her thighs hit the edge of the end table as she stumbled away from him, fear ballooning inside her. "You…you saw his murder or you killed him?"

His eyes darkened. "Wait a minute, Sydney—"

"Oh, my gosh. You killed him, then you came here after me? If it's because you think I saw you, I didn't. I didn't see anyone." Her pulse raced as she glanced at the door, planning her escape. Bits and pieces of the past few days swept through her mind: the graveyard, his questions about Doug, his showing up when McKenzie was at her apartment…

Collin held his hands up pleadingly. "Look, Sydney, your imagination is running wild. You know I didn't kill Doug."

"I don't know anything," Sydney said, backing away. "Except that the way you showed up at the graveyard that day was eerie, and then you were following me when my car crashed into the ocean—"

"And I rescued you," Collin reminded her in a calm

voice. "Think about it—why would I have done that if I wanted to kill you?"

Her mind struggled to make sense of it all. But how could he have seen Doug's murder if he hadn't been there? Could his story be possible?

"If I had killed Doug, Sydney, and wanted you out of the way, too, I would have let you drown that day. There would've been no reason for me to drag you from the water." He gestured toward the door. "And what about the fire and the bomb? Why would I do those things to myself?"

"To throw suspicion off yourself," Sydney said.

Collin's eyes darkened with hurt. "You don't really believe that, do you?" He shook his head, his voice heavy with emotions. "Tell me you don't. You know I would never hurt you." He inched forward, and Sydney froze, her back pressed against the doorjamb.

"I think you know deep down inside I care about you. Listen to your heart, Sydney," Collin urged softly.

A lump rose in her throat. "I did that before, with Doug." Her voice broke. "But he lied, over and over and over…"

Collin stroked her hair, his touch tender and reassuring, and Sydney sensed he wouldn't hurt her, knew he was telling the truth.

"I'll give you my doctor's name and you can call him yourself," Collin suggested. "Ask him if I'm telling the truth." His breath fanned her face and Sydney trembled, clenching her hands by her side so she wouldn't touch him.

"Trust yourself, Sydney," he coaxed in a husky tone. "I know Doug hurt you, but I'm not Doug." He lifted her chin, forcing her to look into his eyes. The eyes were the windows of the soul, her grandmother used to say.

"Look at me. I may have Doug's eyes, but I'm *not* Doug. I won't hurt you, ever."

No, his eyes were kind, full of feelings. And the desire lacing his voice sent a ripple of sensual delight through her. Her fear receded slowly, gradually, leaving an onslaught of need in its wake. Aching, hungry need.

"Come on, Sydney. Trust me." He paused, his fingers trailing gently down her arm. Caressing. Soft. Coaxing. His lips brushed hers with such sweet tenderness that she lost her breath. "Trust yourself, sweetheart."

The warmth of his smile echoed in his voice and Sydney found herself leaning into him, touched by his patience, seduced by the magic of his fingertips on her bare arm. But still he waited, his dark gaze filled with longing, the heat in his smile unraveling the protective web she'd spun around her heart.

"The car crash almost killed you, and I almost got blown away today. Someone knows we've been snooping around together, hunting for clues about Doug's murder." His jaw tightened with restraint and his finger stroked her chin, his other hand slowly dancing along her spine. "After all those months of darkness, Sydney, I want to hold you, to feel that you're real, that we're both alive."

He caressed her temple with the pad of his thumb and Sydney sighed, knowing if it was dangerous to be with Collin, she was ready to face the worst. She'd been cold and lonely when Doug had been alive, empty and unsatisfied. But Collin could take away the aching loneliness. Could fill the emptiness with pleasure and warmth.

She slowly raised her hand and placed it against his jaw, stroking the stubble-roughened skin. Her simple touch was all the encouragement he needed. He swept her into his arms, slanting his mouth over hers greedily. His hands kneaded her back, stroked her shoulders, cupped her bottom. Passion quickly blazed through her, warmth pooling in her abdomen, her hesitation gone as her own hands clutched his arms. Her fingers dug into his hair and she opened her mouth, meeting his tongue with her own, excitement flaring as they melded together. Sydney sighed in contentment, for the first time in months feeling as if the dark void in her life could be filled with light.

Collin nibbled on her earlobe, kissed the soft, sensitive skin on her neck while his hands roamed up from her waist to cup her breasts, kneading and massaging them with his palms. "I've wanted you for so long," he whispered hotly.

"I want you, too," Sydney mumbled. He pulled back and studied her, his eyes intense with raw desire.

"You're sure?"

The concern in his voice drove her wild with desire. "I'm sure." She took his hand and led him to her bedroom, then left him standing by the doorway while she drew the curtains and turned down the comforter on the bed. When she glanced back at Collin, he was watching her, all male need and want. The realization that he was waiting for her to take the lead astounded her, aroused her even more, and she knew that, as powerful and strong as he was, he would never hurt her. He was an honorable man with a sexual magnetism that bordered on dishonorable, a man who ignited her passions by simply walking into the room. He lit the group of candles beside her bed, and a thrill of frightened anticipation touched her spine. She'd always wanted to make love by candlelight. And she was so totally enthralled by the blatant look of lust in his eyes her nipples puckered, pushing against the constraints of her bra.

"I want to see you," he admitted softly. "I lived in the darkness for so long. I want to enjoy every inch of you."

His heartfelt admission twisted her insides, freeing her shyness, and she slid the material of her cotton shell off her shoulders, watching with delight as a devilish gleam lit his handsome face. "You take my breath away," he whispered hoarsely.

Then he moved toward her, his hands gently raking over the curves of her body, her own hands racing down his back as he bent and kissed her breasts. Soft flesh met muscular, primal urges danced with fantasies of hot sex and bold loving, and Sydney moaned when he slipped her shorts over her hips, then found her breast with his mouth and laved her nipple. His hands molded her flesh as his lips closed around the pouty point through the thin lacy bra.

She clung to him, her knees buckling, and he caught her in his arms, holding her upright as he moved to the other breast and suckled her, strong and hard as if he couldn't get enough of her taste. Then his fingers skimmed over her heat, sliding between her thighs, stroking the soft skin between her legs, and she cried out his name, hungry to feel his bare skin beneath her fingers.

Sensing her need, he tossed his shirt to the floor. The strength of his broad, muscular chest mesmerized her, and she whimpered when she finally touched his hot skin. She ran her hands over his shoulders, down his arms, and fire ignited at her fingertips when she encountered his rough, hair-dusted skin. She circled his taut nipples with her fingers, and he threw back his head with a guttural groan that made her want to push him down on the floor and ravage him as she'd never ravaged a man before. She didn't care that he had Doug's eyes, that he might be helping her out of some misguided need to repay a debt.

She only knew that his touch was explosive, his hands a mystical form of ecstasy as they drew her down on her bed and stripped away the remaining thin barriers of her clothing. Then he lowered his head and placed his mouth at the heart of her passion, and she arched and cried out his name, telling him how she desperately needed to feel him inside her.

He brushed kisses along her swollen heat, then parted her thighs and drove her mad with hunger when his mouth closed over her again. When she thought she could stand it no more, he stood, stripped off his jeans and boxers and rose above her. She closed her hand around him and he moaned, pure male satisfaction etched on his face, and she thought her body would explode from want. His glorious sex brushed her thigh as he moved, and when his hot gaze searched hers for affirmation, she whispered his name and cupped his buttocks with her hands, smiling when his taut muscles flexed in her palms. He took her mouth, hungry and hard, and coaxed her with his hands and body, tasting, teasing, eliciting moans of pleasure that had her bucking and begging him to enter her.

But still he teased and plundered her body, suckling and devouring her with his hands and mouth. He stroked her sensitive heat with his fingers, separating her femininity, then delving and exploring and filling her to the core with desire. Then he entered her, first slowly, then hard and fast, his breath tickling her bare skin, his passion meeting hers.

"Look at me, Sydney," he said as he lifted her hips and filled her once again. "I want you to see it's me inside you."

"I know who it is," Sydney whispered, pulling him against her. She dug her nails into his back as he stroked her most sensitive places, making her come alive with yearning and with love. "It was never like this, Collin, never..."

A smile curved his lips. "I'm going to make you forget any other man," he whispered, flicking his tongue across her nipple. "I'm going to make sure you want only me." His tongue encircled her nipple again and again. She felt the building tension rising within her, curling and spiraling through her, exquisite torture. She wanted to prolong the pleasure, to keep the inevitable at bay, but he seemed to sense she was on the brink and moved harder, thrusting in and out of her body and loving her with a fiery rhythm that had her exploding within seconds.

Then he groaned her name and covered her mouth with his, drew her legs around his waist and drove into her one more time. Her body convulsed into a maelstrom of colors, her insides quivering with joy, and when he met her at the peak, she called out his name and nearly wept with the ripples of pleasure his own release gave her.

Then he folded her in his arms and held her, loving her again and again all through the night, and she knew he had ruined things for her, because he would leave when the murder case was solved. And after tasting true passion, she would never again want to be with another man.

SYDNEY HAD RUINED HIM for any other woman.

In the early-morning hours, Collin stared at the beautiful woman lying against him, her bottom tucked firmly into his arousal. He was mesmerized by her sweetness and the memory of her placing her trust in him. She had reasons to doubt him, a past experience that would make anyone hesitant to trust, yet she'd given him her body with more passion than he'd ever imagined. He wound a lock of her sable hair around his fingers and brushed his lips across her shoulder, inhaling the jasmine smell that would always remind him of her. He'd vowed never to need anyone again, and when the case was solved and Sydney was safe, he'd have to walk away.

But for now, he wanted to hold her and savor every moment. Sadness swept through him at the thought of leaving her, but he couldn't give in to his feelings for her, feelings he suspected bordered on love. He'd depended on others, but he never would again.

Guilt nagged at him for not telling her the complete truth about himself. Now that she'd shared her bed with him, he had to tell her he was a cop. In spite of all his vows not to get involved with her, he *knew* she was innocent.

And Raeburn knew he was cop. With the bomb explosion, he needed to assist the investigation. Someone wanted him dead, and if the murderer thought he and Sydney were on to something, he'd come after her again. He might even panic and speed up his plans.

She moaned softly and curled into his arms, rolling over and cuddling against him, one leg draped over his thighs. He cupped her face in his hands and kissed her, watching as her dark lashes fluttered and she opened her eyes. Maybe she'd trust him enough now to tell him about the night of the murder.

"Good morning, beautiful," he said in a husky voice.

"Good morning," she whispered, a smile lighting her eyes as she snuggled face-to-face with him. Naked body to naked body.

She should smile more often, he thought, realizing it was the first time he'd seen her look so relaxed. He traced his finger down her arm and grinned when she nestled closer to him. He lowered his mouth, ready to find ecstasy in her arms again, but then remembered they needed to talk, so he kissed her gently and pulled away.

The doorbell rang and he silently cursed at the interruption. Sydney seemed stunned and they both glanced at the clock—6:00 a.m.

"Pretty early for a visitor, isn't it?"

"Unless it's Kelly and she has a problem with Meg." Sydney pushed back the covers, then blushed, as if she'd forgotten she'd slept nude beside him all night. He grinned, his eyes feasting on her naked body. But the doorbell sounded again, and she reached for the long satin robe draped on a nearby chair. Quickly slipping it on, she fumbled with the belt. "Kelly used to be a nurse, but I swear, when Megan is sick, she totally freaks."

He laughed softly. "They say parents do that with their own kids."

"I'll see what she wants. Maybe she needs some Tylenol or something."

She hurried from the room, but an uneasy feeling hit him, and he grabbed his shirt and jeans and yanked them on. Surely if it was someone who wanted to harm Sydney, he wouldn't ring the doorbell. But cop instincts exploded in his head and he strode into the den, surprised when she opened the door and Raeburn stood on the other side with a woman officer beside him.

"Morning, Mizz Green." Raeburn tipped his bald head.

Sydney clutched her robe to her throat. "Sergeant Raeburn, what are you doing here?"

Raeburn glanced from Sydney to him, a leer on his face, and Collin wished he'd stayed out of sight.

"I'm here on official police business." Raeburn hooked a thumb in his belt loop. "Is that the way you city cops interrogate suspects, Cash? You get 'em in the sack hoping they'll talk?"

"Shut up," Collin said, his voice lethal.

Sydney gasped and looked at him, her eyes wide. "What? You're a cop?"

Raeburn chuckled. "Me, I like to do it the old-fashioned way, take 'em down to headquarters and book 'em. But I guess you guys from Charleston get down and dirty."

"What do you want, Raeburn?" Collin asked, quickly buttoning his shirt.

"You're...a policeman?" Sydney asked again in a weak voice.

He hated the look of betrayal in Sydney's eyes. "I can explain, Sydney."

"You'll have to do it at the station." Raeburn reached for his handcuffs, and panic slammed into Collin full force.

"And why is that?" Collin asked.

"'Cause Mizz Green here is under arrest." He dangled the cuffs in front of him and grinned. "For the murder of her husband."

Chapter Twelve

"You're arresting me?" Sydney's legs threatened to give way beneath her. She put a hand on the wall to steady herself. "But I'm innocent. I told you that before."

"I suppose you have a warrant?" Collin asked.

Raeburn held up a piece of paper. "This is for her arrest. We'll be back with a search warrant." Collin snatched the paper and studied it, his expression grim. Sydney's stomach nose-dived.

"Says here you have probable cause?"

"I sure do," Raeburn said, jangling the handcuffs. "Mizz Green, I suggest you put on some clothes so we can go."

Sydney tried to speak, but the words clogged in her throat, hurt and betrayal swamping her. This wasn't happening. She wasn't being arrested, Collin wasn't a cop, he hadn't used her....

Collin reached for her. "Come on, Sydney, I'll go with you."

Fear plowed through her. "But I didn't kill Doug."

Raeburn made a smacking sound with his mouth. "That'll be for the courts to decide."

"And I suppose you think I set off that bomb, too." She ran shaky fingers through her tousled hair and glared at Raeburn. "As if I'd know anything about making a bomb."

"Sydney, you'd better not say anything else," Collin warned.

Her control almost snapped at his dark look. Her lips still felt swollen from his kisses. Whisker burns marked her pale face. She wanted him to hug her and love her and tell her it would all be all right.

But he had lied to her. Used her and lied to her. "You...you're really a policeman?"

He winced. "I'm sorry, Sydney, but...yeah, I am."

The air whooshed from her lungs like a balloon deflating.

"I can explain," he said hurriedly. "I'll go with you and we can talk while you change."

"No." She backed away from him, holding one hand up. "No, I don't want you with me." She clutched her robe more tightly, hurt almost overpowering her. She'd trusted him. She had given herself to him, heart and soul. *Fool me once, fool me twice...*

"Mizz Green, Officer Chandler here will escort you to your room to get dressed," Raeburn said in a smug tone.

"That's not necessary," Collin snapped. "Just give her a few minutes, Raeburn. She'll answer your questions." Collin touched her elbow to guide her, but Sydney jerked away.

A wave of dizziness washed over her and sweat popped out on her face. She turned, blindly stumbling through the den to her bedroom, heaving for air, her heart breaking. Raeburn was arresting her, taking her to jail for killing Doug, and Collin—the man she'd finally trusted—was helping him.

Bits and pieces of conversations with Collin skated through her mind—he'd wanted to repay Doug, he'd insisted on going with her to meet Doug's ex-wife, he'd made up that crazy story about having the transplant and those visions, and she'd believed him. He'd had every opportunity to tell her he was a policeman. At least Raeburn had been open with his inquisition, not deceitful. He hadn't charmed his way into her bed for answers.

Reality crashed around her and her palms grew clammy, her stomach queasy. She rushed into the bathroom and dropped to her knees in front of the toilet, retching violently. She trembled uncontrollably, her stomach roiling, her head pounding, her heart shattering into a million pieces.

A gentle hand touched her shoulder. She knew it was Collin and the bile rose again, but she swallowed it and pushed away his hand, drawing on her anger to give her strength. "Get out of here," she said coldly. She stumbled to the sink, splashing cold water on her face and ignoring the man who refused to leave, who stood silently behind her, waiting…watching. The man who had betrayed her.

"I'm sorry you had to find out like this," Collin said in a voice laden with regret. "But I was going to tell you, Sydney. Please, just listen."

She whirled around, hands on her hips. "When were you going to tell me? When they locked me up? When they sentenced me for a crime I didn't commit?"

"Sydney, don't. It's not like that, I swear," he said. "I swear. I didn't use you, I'm going to help you—"

"You're saying you didn't get close to me to find out who killed Doug?"

He ran a hand through his hair and released a shaky breath. She saw the answer in the turmoil darkening his eyes. "I am going to help you," he said again, more forcefully this time. "You have to believe that."

"I don't have to believe anything anymore. You're a

liar, just like Doug." She started to push past him, but he grabbed her arm.

"Listen to me, Sydney. I'm not like Doug. Everything I've told you is the truth. I was blind, I had the transplant. I witnessed the murder."

She refused to look at him. "Let me go, Collin."

"I believe you're innocent and you need to believe me. I want to help you," he said, forcing her to listen. "When I found out Doug was murdered, yes, being a cop, I wanted to solve the case. At first for Doug—"

"You would side with him, wouldn't you," she said bitterly. "I guess all you slimeballs think alike. You use women, gain their trust, sleep with them—"

"Stop it, Sydney. I know you're upset, but I'm not like Doug," Collin argued. "I swear—"

A loud knock cut him off and Sydney stared at the bedroom door, knowing Raeburn waited on the other side.

"Mizz Green, we need to go now," the woman officer said through the door.

"We'll be right out." Collin gave Sydney a pleading look.

Sydney pointed to the door. "Please go. I have to get dressed now."

He shoved his hands in his pockets and studied her for a long, silent minute, and Sydney remembered all the wicked and wonderful ways he'd loved her during the night. All lies...just like Doug. The knock sounded again.

"It's not over, Sydney," he said quietly.

"Yes, it is," she said in a rough whisper. She went to the closet and grabbed some clothes, then stepped back into the bathroom and closed that door, shutting him out forever.

COLLIN LEANED AGAINST the wall and squeezed his eyes closed. His head ached, but the pain was nothing compared to the desolation he felt when Sydney closed the door. She was shutting him out. He knew it, and he knew it was all his fault. He should have told her the truth sooner, but things had gotten complicated when…when he'd fallen in love with her.

It wasn't just lust, not merely sexual attraction. He knew it deep in his soul, and as much as he'd vowed not to need anyone ever again, he needed Sydney. Needed her love, her sweet trust…which he'd blown. Now he had to prove to her that his feelings were real, that his intentions had been honorable.

She opened the door and he grimaced at her sickly green pallor and the look of despair in her eyes. Winning back her trust would be a difficult task, complicated now by this stupid arrest. He had to clear her of the charges, but first she had to face Raeburn and the booking. He wanted to help her through the ordeal, but she gave him a scathing look and he knew she wouldn't allow it.

She ignored him and walked from the room, her head held high. He winced when her bottom lip quivered. He noticed that her hands were curled into fists, the same hands that had roamed his body and brought him such pleasure only a few hours before.

"I'm ready," she said to Raeburn in a bland voice.

The sergeant held out the cuffs and Collin's temper flared. "You don't need those and you know it!" he snapped.

Raeburn glanced at the woman officer and she nodded her acquiescence, then she guided Sydney to the door. "I'm going with her," he told Raeburn as they walked to the police car. He noticed Sydney's neighbor, Kelly, pushing a baby stroller down the sidewalk. When she saw the police car, she stopped and gaped. Sydney made a proud show of lifting her chin and smiling at Kelly, but Kelly's face turned chalky white, her body frozen in place beside her child as she watched Sydney climb into the police car.

"When we reach the station, Cash, I expect you to tell me everything you found out," Raeburn said in a sardonic voice.

Collin ground his teeth, realizing Raeburn really thought he'd slept with Sydney for information. And even worse, Sydney believed it, too.

THE NEXT TWO HOURS passed in a blur for Sydney. The police ride, the escort into the precinct, the dozens of questions, the booking—fingerprints, the photograph, the small room with the wooden table, metal chairs and cold blank walls...it was everything she'd imagined and seen on TV, except it was real. Finally numbness had settled in and she pushed the pain aside, concentrating on surviving the rest of the day, one dark, humiliating moment at a time.

"I've explained what happened that night a dozen times," Sydney told Raeburn and the female officer. At least the woman wasn't quite as daunting, but the creases in her coppery skin suggested she had no sympathy.

"Yes, we have your statement, but under the circumstances we thought you might be willing to cooperate now," Raeburn said in his deadpan voice.

"I can't tell you anything different because nothing has changed," Sydney argued in frustration.

"Give it up, Mizz Green. I know you drew up divorce papers before your husband died. And we found the murder weapon. With your fingerprints on it."

They'd found the gun. Sydney dropped her hands to her lap in defeat.

"It was on the shore near where your car went into the

ocean,'' Raeburn continued, pounding his fist on the table. "It *was* in your car, wasn't it? You'd meant to ditch it that night, but then you had the accident.''

Sydney shook her head. "I didn't kill Doug. And I drew up the divorce papers, then changed my mind. I wanted to save my marriage.''

Disbelief hardened Raeburn's face.

It was hopeless. "I think I'd better get a lawyer,'' she said.

Raeburn's nostrils flared, but he nodded curtly and stood, then he and the other officer left her in the room alone. She stared at the scratches and foul words someone had carved into the table and knew her soul was just as scarred as the ugly wood. Her body still reeked of Collin's scent, and her heart had been shattered from his deception. And if Raeburn had his way, she'd spend the rest of her life rotting in jail.

"OKAY, RAEBURN, tell me what you have.'' Collin glanced at Sydney through the small window of the interrogation room. She seemed pale and bereft. And utterly alone.

"You first, Cash. You are going to cooperate now, aren't you?''

"Yes,'' Collin said. "But I expect the same from you. The Charleston police are working with me on this.''

Raeburn nodded. "I figured as much. Did you have a case on him in Charleston?''

"We were investigating him for fraud.''

"I see. Anything else you can give me?''

Collin told him what he'd learned about Doug's first wife and mistress. "They both have motives. Have you checked to see if they have alibis for the night Green died?''

"I have someone on it," Raeburn replied. "But Mizz Green's fingerprints were the only one's on the murder weapon."

"For God's sake, at least consider the possibilities. There was another woman, Marla..."

"Perkins," Raeburn supplied. "She didn't have anything to do with Green's murder."

"How can you be so sure?"

Raeburn shrugged. "'Cause she's my niece, Cash. And you'd better leave her alone."

"But I think she was having an affair with Green." Collin folded his arms, watching Raeburn for his reaction.

"So? Her husband was gone all the time, and Randy ain't worth a dime."

"You knew about her relationship with Green?"

Raeburn nodded, obviously deciding not to reveal everything he knew.

"You have to suspect her or her husband. Maybe he found out—"

"They both have alibis," Raeburn stated. "They were at my house the night Green was killed. My wife and I hosted an anniversary dinner, and all the family was there."

Collin rubbed his chin thoughtfully. What if Raeburn was protecting his niece or her husband? It would explain his hurry to arrest Sydney. Raeburn could easily have planted the evidence, found out about Collin and been worried he'd break the case. *Or maybe I'm just grasping.*

"How about McKenzie?" he asked, remembering the beady-eyed man. He'd certainly seemed unstable.

"He has an alibi," Raeburn said. "His wife says he was home with her all night."

"She could be protecting him."

"Look, Cash, face it. Green's wife is a murderer. She

had divorce papers drawn up a month before her husband died.''

Collin pretended interest in one of the Wanted posters on the wall as he tried to gauge his reaction.

''She had motive, opportunity, and now that we've recovered the murder weapon, it's an open-and-shut case.''

''You're sure the gun's the same one that killed Green?''

''Yeah. It was found on shore right close to where Mizz Green's car went into the ocean. It matches the bullets that killed Green.'' Raeburn hitched his pants higher. ''And if you'd stop letting your hormones affect your brain, you'd see she tried to kill you, too. Twice.''

''That's ridiculous.''

''The fire? The bomb at her house? I don't think so.''

''Well, I do.'' Collin had to trust his instincts. Even if his partner had screwed up and died because of a woman. Sydney was no murderer.

But he had seen the revolver in her car. Someone had obviously planted the pistol there, then tampered with her brakes and caused the accident, hoping the gun would be found and Sydney would be indicted.

He peered through the glass door and saw her making a phone call. To her lawyer, he hoped. Unfortunately she needed one since Raeburn had already tried and convicted her.

''I want to talk to her,'' Collin said.

''I guess that'd be okay,'' Raeburn complied, ''as long as you share any information you get.''

''I will,'' Collin said. ''But before you close the investigation, think about this. My guess is someone's framing her. I suggest you check out that mistress and Green's first wife or look at McKenzie again, also Green's business dealings and Steve Wallace, the CEO of Norvek.''

I'm calling Sam. We're going to find the real killer, then I'm going to shove it in your face, Raeburn. And pray that Sydney will forgive me.

SYDNEY BLANCHED when Collin entered the small room. Another interrogation tactic, she thought morosely. Maybe they thought she would crack with Collin, be so smitten with his sex appeal she'd spill her guts—as she had been, she thought, her chest aching again at her own stupidity.

The heavy door closed as Collin walked in. She folded her hands in front of her on the wobbly table, bracing herself for another inquisition. He moved slowly, his posture rigid with tension, and she focused on a scarred indentation it the wood, despising herself for even noticing his discomfort.

"I know you hate me right now, Sydney," he said in a solemn voice. "I guess I can't blame you. But you're wrong about me." The chair creaked as he sat down opposite her. When she didn't respond or look at him, he continued, "I didn't sleep with you for information—"

"Don't talk about last night," she said, glaring at him with all the fear and anger she'd been bottling up inside. "I want to forget it ever happened."

"I can't forget it," Collin said roughly. "And whether you want to admit it or not, our making love changed things."

Sydney winced. "It was sex."

Collin scrubbed his hand over his chin. "It wasn't just sex, Sydney, and we both know it." He folded his hands on his knees. "And nothing about last night was simple, especially our lovemaking."

"Sleeping with you only proved what a fool I was," Sydney said in a shaky voice.

"You're not a fool. And our being together wasn't a mistake. It was—"

"Don't say it," Sydney said in a strained voice, as if the memories sickened her.

"Look, Sydney, admit it or not, when I made love to you, when you clung to me with passion, when I came inside you, it was the best night of my life—"

"Stop it!" she shouted, her voice breaking.

He reached for her hand, but she shrank away, and he sighed. Then he said in a gravelly voice, "I love you. I should have told you sooner—"

"Don't tell me any more lies." Her breath whistled out as she strove for control. "Just tell me why you're here."

He ran a hand through his hair again, and she forced herself not to watch his hands, not to think about them touching her and the way she'd reacted last night. "I believe you're being framed, Sydney, and I want to help you."

"I think you've already done enough."

"Do you have a lawyer?"

"I called Grady Jackson—he's the only attorney in Beaufort—but he won't be back in town until tomorrow."

Collin drummed his fingers on the table. "Will you let me call someone in Charleston for you? There are a couple of good criminal attorneys."

"You think I'm going to need one?" she asked, the seriousness of the situation really hitting her.

"Yes." He shifted, the chair groaning under his weight. "I intend to find the real murderer, but it may take some time. Meanwhile, you need to secure someone."

"I'll wait for Grady," Sydney said, deciding she didn't trust Collin enough to accept his help now.

He seemed to read her mind. Disappointment clouded his features. "If I'm going to find out who's setting you up, you have to tell me everything you know about the murder.''

"I gave a statement, Mr. Cash. I'm sure Sergeant Raeburn will let you read it,'' she said bitterly. "And I'm not saying another word until my lawyer arrives.''

He fisted his hands on the table in front of her. "I will read the statement, Sydney, but I want you to talk to me about Doug. Why didn't you tell me you'd filed divorce papers?''

She clasped her hands together. "It didn't seem important. I told you I thought he might be having an affair.'' She looked away, recalling the long, lonely nights she'd spent wondering where Doug was. And what she had done to drive him away. She didn't feel that guilt anymore. Although Roxy's comment that Doug had really loved her confused her.

But her relationship with Doug seemed light-years away. Collin had helped her forget him, only to break her heart again.

"Sydney?''

"I didn't tell Doug about the papers,'' she answered tightly. "I decided to give our marriage another try.''

He cleared his throat. "Okay. About Doug. We've already uncovered an ex-wife and a mistress. Either one of them could have committed the crime. McKenzie also had a motive. We know Doug had an alias and a one-way ticket to Brazil for the day he died. Obviously Doug knew he was in trouble, knew someone was on to him, so he was planning an escape. It could have been Roxy DeLong or someone from work.''

"I guess he had a lot of enemies,'' Sydney admitted.

"Tell me about this deal he was putting together. I know the product debut was postponed, and McKenzie mentioned Doug might have forged the licensing agreement. Were there any other co-workers who might have wanted to kill him? Someone who stood to gain a lot of money over the deal?"

"Steve Wallace," Sydney said, remembering how upset Steve had sounded on the phone. "He's the CEO of the company. He called and wanted to know if I had any of Doug's files. He said there was some question about the patent and the licensing agreement, that he suspected Doug might have told another company about the product, then sold the formula to the highest bidder."

"So Doug conned Norvek Pharmaceuticals," Collin said, contemplating the theory.

"Steve had invested his life savings," Sydney replied. "I'm pretty sure he would earn millions in stock when the public offering was held."

"Money is a motive," Collin agreed. "I'll pay Mr. Wallace a visit."

Sydney studied him, watching his mind at work, wondering if he really would solve the case. If so, she had to tell him everything she knew. She couldn't forgive him, but she didn't want to spend the rest of her life in jail for a crime she hadn't committed.

"I found some files, too," she admitted, not surprised when Collin's gaze swung up to meet hers. "Doug had a bank account in Charleston and several Swiss accounts. They were loaded."

Collin's chair squeaked as he leaned forward. "He must have been planning to leave town after he received his cut of the money." He reached out to touch her, but Sydney drew back, folding her hands in her lap. Collin's disappointed look twisted her stomach into knots, but she couldn't allow herself to feel sorry for him. He had hurt her.

"Would you mind if I looked at those files?"

"Not if you think it would help."

"Anything could be a help," he said. "Where are they?"

"They're on disk in a shoe box in the bedroom closet. That is, unless the police confiscated them when they searched the house." Sydney shuddered at the idea of Collin in her house, going back into her bedroom where she'd foolishly given him her body, where she'd finally thought she'd found love again.

"I promise I'm going to solve this case, Sydney," he said in a husky voice, as if he, too, remembered their passionate night and felt the same as she did. "I'll do everything I can to get you out of here this afternoon. Please try to trust me."

She stood, her heart aching, blinking back the unwanted tears stinging her eyes. Last night he'd begged her to trust him, to trust herself, and she had. Only to discover this morning he'd deceived her.

"Just find out who killed Doug," she managed to say in an even voice. "Then your debt will be paid and you can go home." With that, she walked to the door and met the guard, refusing to look back at Collin as the uniformed officer led her down a long hallway to the cell where she would probably spend the night. And maybe the rest of her life.

COLLIN TOOK A TAXI to Sydney's, recalling the frustrating afternoon while the sights and sounds of the town buzzed by his window. He'd tried to set up a meeting with Steve Wallace, only to be told the man couldn't see him until the next day. Then he called Sam, gave him all the information he had to date, and Sam promised to call him back as soon as he could. After that, he spent two hours trying to make bail for Sydney, but the judge presiding in

Beaufort was unavailable, like Sydney's lawyer and Wallace. The three of them must have been on a fishing trip somewhere together, Collin thought in frustration.

Leaving Sydney at the jail was the hardest thing he'd ever done in his life. But staying wouldn't find Doug's killer, which was the only way to help Sydney. He let himself into her house and scanned the rooms, angry at the sight of Sydney's belongings scattered from the police search. Sydney's scent lingered in every corner. Then he walked into the bedroom and saw the unmade bed, the tangled sheets, and remembrances of their lovemaking overwhelmed him. Forcing himself to continue his mission, he straightened the covers, then opened the closet door and pulled out the box. Obviously the police had been looking for weapons, not Doug's business files.

He quickly searched the contents. Two computer disks lay inside, along with the fake ID Sydney had shown him. Slipping on a pair of gloves to avoid fingerprints, he put the disk in the computer and opened the files. Just as she'd said, Doug had several international accounts. He jotted down the account numbers, then scanned the other files. Notes on business dealings with two earlier companies filled two folders. Doug had been dishonest and cunning in the measures he'd taken to make his bogus agreements appear legit. Somewhere along the way he'd probably paid off someone in the FDA. Money talked.

After two hours of poring over the data, he finally shut off the computer, then stuffed the disks in his pocket to keep for evidence. Apparently Doug had forged signatures on licensing agreements and required FDA approval forms, then marketed them to pharmaceutical companies as done deals. He'd sold the products while still in the research stage. When the research companies cut deals with the larger pharmaceutical companies, they received advances, as well as stock options. Doug received both, then skipped town and changed names before the forgeries were discovered. One of the companies had managed to obtain the proper FDA approval and keep their product going, so he'd made a bundle off the stock, but the second company had gone belly-up. As would Norvek Pharmaceuticals if he'd pulled the same scam.

Exhausted, a headache wearing him down, he dropped his head and rubbed his neck, the muscles tight and knotted. He'd figured out a little bit about Doug's business dealings, but who had killed him? The problem wasn't that he had no other suspects besides Sydney—the problem was he had too many. Why had Raeburn been in such a rush to arrest Sydney when there were other suspects? Did the sergeant have his own agenda? Maybe he was an investor himself. Curious, Collin accessed Norvek's files and found a list of investors. Sure enough, Raeburn was on the list.

Hmm, no wonder Raeburn couldn't wait to close the case. When the pharmaceutical deal went through, he'd instantly double his investment at the offering. So would several businessmen in Beaufort who'd invested, including the two men he'd met at the festival that day.

Knowing he couldn't do anything else until the next day, Collin stretched out on Sydney's sofa, unable to lie down in the bed where they'd made love, the bed that still held the scent of their passion. But his mind filled with images of Sydney, and the thought of her locked up in a jail cell burned his gut.

Even if Sydney never forgave him, he would see that she was free. Free to resume her life without him. He rubbed his hand over his face in despair and turned off the den light, welcoming the darkness.

He'd hated the black emptiness once, but tonight he

didn't mind it. The darkness served as a cool retreat from the pain and blinding light of reality he'd awakened to this morning. He'd vowed not to need anyone ever again, but he'd come here and fallen in love. And he had no idea how he'd go on without Sydney.

SYDNEY STARED at the concrete wall, her body curled into a ball on the narrow cot in the cell where she'd lain awake all night. When morning had come, she'd prayed she'd be released, but now morning had stretched into afternoon, and with it, her hopes had died. Her muscles and body ached from the chill of betrayal and fatigue, but the rest of her felt numb and lifeless. Would this be her home for the next few months? Or years?

She tried to push aside her negative thoughts and avoided the dark gaze of her cellmate, a scary mooselike woman with a tattoo of a snake on her arm and a nose ring that shimmered in the dim light of the jail cell.

Collin's promise to get her out faded with every passing hour. *Trust me, Sydney,* he'd said—but he wouldn't come through for her. His promise was just another lie. She wished she'd had time to shower before she'd been locked inside. The scent of Collin's lovemaking had lingered on her skin for hours, then they'd made her shower with the other women, and the harsh scent of the jail soap had replaced it, permeating her skin. The smell and humiliating memory of the leering women made her feel ill.

Heavy footsteps on the concrete floor shuffled toward her, but she lay still, praying it wasn't Raeburn with more accusations. Noises from the other cells and a grunt from her own cellmate forced her to glance at the door.

"Mrs. Green, you need to come with me."

Keys jangled and clinked and the metal bars screeched opened. She stood, seeing the sour face of a woman guard with a short, round body and hands the size of a man's. "Come on," the woman barked.

"Where are you taking me?" Sydney asked, hating the fear in her small voice.

"Take me with you, girlie," her cellmate yelled.

The guard glared at the woman, then took Sydney's arm. "Someone posted your bail."

Sydney followed the woman on wooden legs, her skin crawling at the stares and catcalls of prisoners in the other cells. The guard escorted her through two sets of double doors and into a holding area, then ordered her to sit.

Collin appeared in front of her, looking freshly showered, dressed in a pair of khaki pants and a navy polo shirt. Her heart broke all over again. Self-consciously she tugged at her rumpled clothes and hair, her predicament making her flush with humiliation.

"Your bail's been posted," he said, his eyes raking over her. "Are you okay?"

"You mean you posted it?" she asked in dismay.

A muscle ticked in his jaw. But he spoke softly as he guided her down the hall, "Yeah, I've been worried to death about you. Are you all right?"

She blinked as unwanted tears pooled in her eyes. "I'm fine."

He smiled and gently reached out to tuck a strand of hair behind her ear. "Come on, Sydney. I'm taking you home."

She pulled away. "I don't want to owe you anything."

He paused as if she'd struck him, then proceeded out the door. "Don't worry. The money was some I'd put aside for a house."

She trailed behind him, determined to set him straight. They climbed in her rental car and he drove toward her house, the silence between them strained and awkward.

"I'll pay you back," she said tightly. "Doug had plenty of money and I'm getting an insurance check for my car."

"Your accounts will probably be frozen until after the case is solved," he said in an almost apologetic voice.

Her chest heaved with surprise. They could do that? Freeze her accounts?

"I'll pay you back," she said again, her voice even steelier.

A muscle tightened in his jaw again, but he didn't look at her until they'd pulled into her drive and he'd cut the engine. Then he reached out and touched her hair.

She shrank back. "Don't."

He drew his hand away, his eyes filled with an emotion she thought might be hurt, worry. Even concern. But how would she know? Their relationship had been built on lies.

"I tried to get you out of there last night, Sydney, I swear I did, but the judge was out of town." He paused as if he was hoping she'd say something, but she gripped the door handle, fighting to keep her emotions at bay.

He continued, his expression troubled, "I've set up a meeting to see Steve Wallace today. And I've also called my friend in Charleston. He's going to help us."

Sydney cleared her throat. "There is no 'us,' Collin."

"Damn it, Sydney, I care about you." He reached for her again. "You have to believe that. I could never have made love to you like that if I didn't care—"

"Stop it!" She threw open the car door, her throat clogging with grief. "I don't have to believe anything you say. You not only have Doug's eyes, you have his character flaws. You're a liar, just like he was."

"Sydney, that's not true, I love—"

"I appreciate all you've done, but please leave, Collin. I won't be a fool again. It's cost me too much already." She ran up the sidewalk, the sobs she'd tried to hold in all night racking her body. Kelly's lights were on, and she started to go to her place, to cry on her friend's shoulder. But the humiliation of being carted off in a police car overwhelmed her. She couldn't face her friend yet. She just wanted to be alone.

Chapter Thirteen

"I'm going to prove you wrong," Collin muttered to the closed door, Sydney's rejection tearing him apart. He surveyed Sydney's yard, the debris and yellow police tape a reminder of the explosion. She wanted him to leave her alone, but how could he when he knew she was in danger?

He couldn't. But he also couldn't sleep on the sidewalk, and Sydney obviously wouldn't invite him back into her house for the night. Remembering the rental-car company around the corner, he started walking, letting the evening breeze and fresh air revive his battered body and mind. A few minutes later he'd rented a small station wagon. He called Sam, but had to leave a message, then went back to the precinct to see if Raeburn had discovered anything more. The only thing he managed to learn was that Roxy DeLong had an alibi for the night of Doug's murder. A dead end. But he still didn't know about Gina Waters.

He grabbed a hamburger from a fast-food place, picked up some extra clothes and toiletries at a small department store, then parked the car near Sydney's, situating it behind a big willow tree so she couldn't see him. While he chewed the tasteless burger, he listed all the suspects involved in the case, wondering which one of them had killed Green. Or if the killer was even on the list.

Damn. Green certainly had enough enemies. Collin wished Green was still alive so he could beat the hell out of him for hurting Sydney.

SYDNEY STRUGGLED with the feeling of violation she experienced when she saw that the police had done a thorough search of her home. Adrenaline pumping through her, she cleaned each room, putting everything back in order. After practically scrubbing her skin raw in the shower to rid herself of the stench of jail—and the lingering scent of Collin—she dressed for bed, then checked her messages from the studio.

Three people had canceled appointments for portraits. She'd scheduled very few bookings since Doug had died to give herself some time to grieve, but the news of her arrest had probably spread quickly. People obviously didn't want a murderer photographing their children. She couldn't blame them, but she'd thought the people in town were her friends. Anger knotted her stomach at the unfairness. With a surge of fury, she tackled her closet, determined to discard anything even remotely associated with Doug.

Three hours later with a stack of his clothes and other personal items moved to the extra bedroom, she crawled into bed. Tomorrow she would talk to Grady Jackson. The town lawyer, she hoped, could advise her what to do. But the police had to find the real murderer, and if Raeburn believed she'd killed Doug, he would have given up the search. Was Collin really going to help her?

The telephone shrilled and Sydney froze, then realized it might be the lawyer returning her call, so she picked up the receiver.

"I warned you to leave Doug's murder alone," the gruff voice said.

Sydney's heart stopped beating. "Who is this? Why are you doing this to me?"

"You'd better listen or you're going to regret it." Then the voice clicked into silence and Sydney exhaled, her hand trembling as she put down the receiver.

She considered phoning the police and reporting the call, but remembered the officer's reaction the last time she had. Instead, she turned on the lamp and stared at the ceiling, listening for any sounds of an intruder, wishing that Collin was there to protect her through the night.

A feeling of hopelessness invaded her and she closed her eyes, too exhausted even to cry. She'd thought she lived in a town where people took care of one another, had wanted to raise a family here, but the town no longer held the appeal. Someone here wanted to see her rotting in jail or dead. And she didn't know whom to trust or turn to.

Except Collin. He'd said he believed her. But he'd slept with her to find out more about Doug's death. Still, he said he suspected someone was framing her. Was he telling the truth or using their relationship as a ploy to persuade her to tell him more, hoping to trap her? Had he believed she'd murdered Doug at first and then changed his mind?

The worry and stress of the day drained her of energy and hope, and she finally drifted to sleep. But she tossed and turned all night, her dreams haunted by visions of Doug and blood, Collin and fire, and a small cell where she might spend the rest of her life.

COLLIN DOZED OCCASIONALLY, keeping tabs on Sydney's house during the night. When morning came, he decided he had to get busy. The sooner he cleared Sydney's name, the sooner he could straighten out their personal relationship. After checking into a hotel, he quickly showered and dressed in a pair of khaki pants and a dress shirt. He wanted to look presentable to talk to Steve Wallace.

Thirty minutes later he'd made the drive and sat in the plush waiting room, listening with interest as the receptionist transferred calls to the various employees and smoothly answered calls about the delay of the weight-loss product hitting the market.

Finally Wallace escorted him into his office. The man's expensive suit and lavish office fit the image of a high-profile company.

"What can I do for you, Mr. Cash?" Wallace leaned back in his leather chair and crossed one leg over the other.

"I'm investigating Doug Green's murder."

"I see." Wallace rolled a gold pen between his fingers. "I've already told that other detective everything I know."

"I'm sure you have, but I'd like to talk about the deal Green had with you. You never know when some small detail might materialize that could be important."

"I can speak about general matters, but some things are confidential," Wallace said in a cautious voice.

"Mr. Wallace, Ms. Green has already told me your concerns about her husband. She also shared with me files about Doug's business dealings, as well as information on his bank accounts."

"Then what more can I add?"

"You can tell me about a man named Spade McKenzie. He came to Ms. Green's house and threatened her, saying that her husband had forged the licensing agreement for this weight-loss drink."

"I'm aware of McKenzie's allegations," Wallace said. "He came here declaring the same thing."

"Is he telling the truth?"

"I'm not sure." Wallace continued to fiddle with his pen. "So far, I haven't found proof to substantiate that his claims are false. McKenzie has a patent agreement, but so did Doug, dated prior to McKenzie's. As for the licensing agreement, it was with the university. Doug's agreement named another scientist, a man named David Waters, as the inventor."

Knowing Doug had been married to Gina Waters, Collin registered the name in his head, figuring David Waters was another alias. "Did you talk to Waters?"

"Apparently he's off in South America on some cruise and hasn't been located," Wallace said with a wry laugh. "So I contacted Sydney to see if she could find some of Doug's files. However, I suggested to McKenzie that we go through the Patent and Trademark Association to settle the issue, and our attorney suggested we settle out of court."

"If you offered a settlement, then you had reason to believe McKenzie's claims?"

"We thought it would be in everyone's best interest to keep the dispute low-key."

Which meant he probably knew Doug had been underhanded, but he'd managed to keep the matter from the public eye. A shrewd businessman.

Wallace made a clicking sound with the pen. "But unfortunately Mr. McKenzie hasn't been very agreeable so far. His wife came with him to the second meeting. They brawled right here in the office. I thought I was going to have to call security."

"What were they fighting about?"

"She wanted him to accept the settlement. In fact, she insisted. It made me wonder if he was lying and she wanted him to take the money and run."

Collin contemplated that notion for a minute. He'd thought the killer might be a woman. If it wasn't Doug's mistress or first wife, perhaps Mrs. McKenzie had killed Doug to gain notoriety and more money for her husband.

"Is there anything else, Mr. Cash?" Wallace asked, standing as if ready to dismiss him.

"Just one thing. Are you going to bring out the product as you planned?"

Wallace smiled. "Absolutely. We've received clearance with the FDA. In fact, the delay has hyped interest. I predict our stock will be even more valuable."

Collin nodded and left, rolling the information he'd just learned around in his head. It only broadened the list of suspects. Now he'd added McKenzie's wife and Wallace. If Norvek's stock went up, he'd be willing to bet Wallace would be the first one to profit. And with Doug out of the picture, Wallace would rake in millions.

ANXIOUS ABOUT SYDNEY, Collin drove straight to her house. He rang the doorbell, not caring if she planned to throw him out, but knowing he had to see her and make sure she was safe.

When the door swung open, Kelly, Sydney's neighbor, greeted him warily. She held her baby on her hip.

"Who is it, Kel?" Sydney called.

"It's me, Sydney." Collin brushed past Kelly.

Sydney sat cross-legged on the floor of the den in the midst of notebooks, papers, clothes and various other items, obviously sorting them into boxes. "What are you doing here?" Sydney asked, shooting him an angry glance as she continued to pack the items.

"I was worried about you," he said in a low voice.

Her hands stilled momentarily, the only sign that his

words had affected her. "Well, as you see, I'm fine. And I'm really busy, so you can show yourself out."

He didn't budge. "Did you talk to that lawyer yet?"

She glared at him. "I have an appointment with him tomorrow."

Collin breathed a sigh of relief. He hoped she wouldn't need a lawyer, but it was better to be safe.

Kelly moved into the room and sat on the sofa, cradling the little girl in her lap. Collin noticed an appointment book and picked it up. "Was this Doug's?"

Sydney nodded, stuffing various shoes in a box.

He touched the outer binding, then flipped open the pages, skimming the dates and names. Various pharmaceutical companies, appointments at the university.... "I'm surprised the book wasn't confiscated when the police searched your house."

"It was hidden in the closet, near the box. I found it this morning."

Collin nodded, but the gray and black lines of the pages bled together and his eyesight blurred, darkness smothering the light as flashes of different people floated in front of him.

McKenzie and a woman, his wife, arguing heatedly with him...a man in a white lab coat, a doctor holding a chart and discussing one of his drugs...a woman in white flirting with him, but he couldn't see her face, couldn't see the doctor's face...

"Collin? What's wrong? Did you find something?"

The visions faded. Collin blinked to clear his sight and saw Sydney standing beside him, studying the book over his shoulder.

"Did you show this book to Wallace? Or Raeburn?"

Shadows darkened her eyes. "No, like I said, I just found it."

"Do you mind if I keep it and read through it? It might give us some clues."

"Go ahead." She was so close to him he could smell her jasmine scent. He wanted to soothe the haunted look from her face.

Then Kelly stood, interrupting the moment. "I think I'll leave you two alone."

"You don't have to go," Sydney said, looking panic-stricken.

The phone rang and Sydney froze.

"Have you gotten any more threatening calls?" he asked, guessing the answer by the fear in her eyes.

She bit her lower lip. "Yes, last night."

Anger burned his throat as he answered the phone.

"Cash, is that you?"

He grimaced. "Yeah, Raeburn, what is it?" Sydney rested her hands on top of the box, watching him.

"I need Mizz Green to come down here to answer some more questions."

"What *haven't* you asked her?" Collin's tone hardened.

"It's about McKenzie," Raeburn said in a snide voice.

"You brought him in about the bomb?"

"Not exactly," Raeburn said. "But we found him. He's dead."

Collin squeezed the receiver so tightly his fist ached.

"Tell Mizz Green she can come down of her own accord or I'll send a car."

"We'll be there in ten minutes!" Collin snapped. He slammed down the phone, dreading telling Sydney the news.

"What is it?" she whispered.

He looked into her eyes. "McKenzie's dead. Raeburn

wants to talk to you.'' He sighed, his voice full of regret. "We have to go, Sydney."

She pursed her lips and nodded, squeezing her eyes closed briefly as if to gain control.

"Who's McKenzie?" Kelly asked.

"He worked with Doug," Sydney explained.

"You want me to go with you, Syd?" Kelly's eyes filled with tears. She placed a hand on Sydney's arm.

"The police station is no place for a little one." Sydney brushed a kiss across Megan's forehead. The baby gurgled and swatted her chubby hand, and Collin's chest squeezed. He'd like to see Sydney with her own child, happy and carefree, loving and—

"Let's go." Sydney grabbed her purse and he followed her to the door, thinking about Sydney and a baby. Maybe his baby. He quickly dismissed the idea. Sydney was making it very plain she didn't want anything to do with him. She certainly wouldn't consider having his child. Then he stopped, stunned at his own thoughts. He'd never contemplated marriage or having a family. And the fact that he had just imagined a future with Sydney shook him to the core.

"I TOLD YOU I was at home that night," Sydney said.

Raeburn snorted. "Did he know too much? Is that why you did it?" Raeburn asked as if he hadn't heard her. "Or were you afraid he'd lay claim to the money and you wouldn't get it, after all?"

"She *was* at home all night," Collin interjected. "Because I was with her."

Raeburn's ruddy cheeks reddened. "Cash, I don't get it. Did sleeping with her blind you to her manipulations?"

"No, but since you brought it up," Collin bellowed,

"you know I was there. Hell, you dragged us out of bed the next morning."

Sydney shuddered at the memory and twisted her hands in her lap.

"Then who shot McKenzie?" Raeburn asked snidely.

"Maybe the same person who killed Green," Collin suggested. "If you'd quit trying to pin it on Sydney, you might find the real killer!"

Sydney stared at Collin, shocked at the degree of conviction in his voice. He really did believe her. And he was putting his reputation on the line for her.

A young officer popped his head into the office.

"I told you not to disturb me," Raeburn barked.

"I think you'll want to hear this. We received a call from Norvek Pharmaceuticals. Some crazy woman is there threatening the CEO with a gun."

Sydney gasped.

"Christ, what next?" Raeburn asked.

"It must be McKenzie's wife," Collin said.

Raeburn sighed. "I'm on my way."

COLLIN AND SYDNEY followed Raeburn, making double time behind Raeburn's police car with its siren wailing. When they reached the Norvek building, blue lights were flashing across the glass front, a crowd had gathered, and most of the people inside had been evacuated. A SWAT team stood by, preparing their strategy.

"She's on the fifth floor," a uniformed officer told Raeburn.

"Stay here, Sydney," Collin said, following Raeburn.

Sydney clutched his arm. "Collin?"

He turned quickly. "Yeah?"

Her eyes were luminous. And so beautiful. And worried. "Be careful."

He smiled and squeezed her hand. Her whispered warning gave him hope. Maybe she cared, after all.

SYDNEY STAYED STILL for all of five seconds. Then she rushed forward, knowing if Collin confronted Steve, she had to be there. This whole situation revolved around her. Or rather, her dead husband, who refused to remain buried.

Raeburn and Collin were pushing the elevator button when she raced up to them. "I thought I told you to stay outside," Collin snapped.

"How did you slip past those guards?" Raeburn asked.

She ignored the question. "I won't get in the way," Sydney promised. "But this is about me. I have to be there."

"You'd better stay in the background," Raeburn warned.

"He's right, Sydney." Collin shot her a black look. "The woman is armed—that means she's dangerous." He reached out and stroked her cheek with his thumb. "Promise me you won't interfere."

"I promise," Sydney said, her breath catching.

The elevator dinged and the doors opened. Raeburn led the way and policemen quickly filled the hallway. Raeburn pointed for her to stand behind them. "Let me have that bullhorn."

Raeburn snatched it from the officer and raised it to his mouth. "Mrs. McKenzie, this is Sergeant Raeburn of the Beaufort Police Department. We'd like to talk to you."

The door swung open to reveal a short, skinny woman with stringy brown hair and a baggy old-fashioned dress waving a gun. Steve Wallace sat glued to his chair, his face ashen.

"Talking won't do any good!" the woman cried. "It's too late for that."

Sydney held her breath as Raeburn tried to coax her into surrendering. "We found your husband, Mrs. McKenzie," Raeburn said. "It wasn't a pretty sight. Do you think Wallace killed him? Is that why you came here?"

"He cheated my husband, just like that no-account Doug Green did!" Mrs. McKenzie shrieked. "We deserved better. We worked hard all our lives."

Collin reached for the bullhorn. "Let me talk to her."

"Mrs. McKenzie, this is Collin Cash. I talked to Mr. Wallace earlier about the problem you had with the deal for the weight-loss drink."

"My husband created that formula—he should have been given credit!" the woman wailed. "And he never signed no licensing agreement with that Mr. Green."

"I understand that," Collin said calmly. "And I understand how upset you must have been. But please put down the gun, ma'am."

"I tried to persuade him to take the settlement," she whimpered. "I tried, but he wouldn't listen to me. He wouldn't settle, said Mr. Wallace here wanted him to go through that patent association. All that red tape—it'd take forever...." Her voice broke into sobs and Sydney's heart went out to her.

"Mrs. McKenzie, don't you see that hurting Mr. Wallace isn't going to help?" Collin asked.

"But now Spade is gone!" she cried. "He wouldn't listen to me and we argued..." Her voice transformed from a wretched sob into an angry, fevered pitch. "I told him what to do, but he wouldn't listen. I told him to get rid of Green, to stand up for himself, but he was such a wimp...always a wimp."

"It's all right, Mrs. McKenzie, we'll help you," Collin promised. "Just put down the gun, and we'll make sure everyone learns your husband invented the formula." Collin inched his way into the room and Sydney held her breath, but he continued talking softly, waving his hand in a calming gesture. "We'll investigate Green's files and see if he forged the agreement. We'll make sure everyone knows the truth. Wallace will cooperate, won't you, Wallace?"

Wallace's chin bobbed up and down.

"And any money due you will be placed into an account for your family. You have kids, don't you?" Collin asked.

"Yes." The woman's face crumbled as she lowered her head, sobbing. Collin moved like lightning, wrestling the gun from her. She didn't struggle. She wailed, then collapsed into his arms in a heap, her body racking violently with sobs.

Tears streamed down Sydney's cheeks in a surge of pity for the woman and the depths she'd gone to. Raeburn and the other officers moved in, quickly taking charge. Collin braced the woman around the waist so she wouldn't fall, then handed her over to two officers.

"Mrs. McKenzie, you killed your husband, didn't you?" Raeburn asked.

The woman nodded again, her pale face red and swollen. "I wanted him to stand up for himself, to get what was ours...."

"And what about Doug Green? You killed him, too?"

"He deserved to die for what he done to my husband!" she screeched. "That man deserved to die!"

Sydney pressed her hand to her stomach. Despite all the pain Mrs. McKenzie's actions had caused her, compassion for the couple overwhelmed her. The husband

dead, the wife arrested—their children would be trauma-
tized. Another disastrous legacy from Doug.

WHEN COLLIN DROVE Sydney back to her house, she
stared listlessly out the window. Physically and emotionally exhausted and more confused than ever, she couldn't
think of a word to say.

"Raeburn will drop all the charges against you," Collin
said as he pulled into her drive. "Once they record Mrs.
McKenzie's confession."

Sydney nodded, grateful but numb from the evening's
ordeal. Collin parked the car, then walked her to the door.
She fumbled with the key and he took it and let them in,
then he stood in the doorway as if he didn't know what
to do.

She turned to him, her heart lodged in her throat.
"Thank you for everything you did," she said weakly.

He shook his head. "I'm glad it's over for you, Sydney."

"Me, too."

"You look exhausted."

She fingered her hair away from her face, leaning
against the doorjamb, suddenly too tired to stand.

He brushed a gentle kiss on her forehead. "Get some
rest, okay?"

"I will." She looked into his eyes. This would be the
last time she would see him. "I appreciate your finishing
the case and…and for believing in my innocence."

She saw a host of emotions in the dark gray depths of
his eyes, but confusion clouded her mind. Doug and all
his lies…Collin and Doug's eyes, Collin holding her, loving her all through the night—

"I fight for the things I care about, Sydney. And

whether or not you believe it, I'm not like Doug. I'm not a liar."

Her lower lip trembled. "I suppose you'll be going back to Charleston now that your debt is paid."

He shrugged, then lifted a finger and stroked her chin, his voice thick. "I never meant to hurt you. I care—"

She swallowed against the lump in her throat and cut him off, "Goodbye, Collin."

Then she hurried inside and closed the door, her heart constricting as she watched him through the window. He walked down the steps, then turned and stared at her house for a long time, his expression troubled, the planes of his face shadowed in the moonlight. Then he climbed into his car and drove away, his taillights disappearing down the road, leaving nothing but the empty darkness behind.

She sagged against the door, feeling as if she were breaking in two, hating herself for ever entertaining the idea of a future with another man.

COLLIN SPENT A TORMENTED NIGHT at a small hotel on the outskirts of town, the plain walls and furnishings a reminder of his empty apartment and life back in Charleston. He'd wanted to stay with Sydney so badly he ached, had contemplated begging her for forgiveness, but the strain and exhaustion evident on her face had stopped him from pressuring her. He didn't want her to succumb to him out of fatigue or duress. He wanted her love.

And she'd been saying good-bye.

He rolled over in the bed and clutched the pillow, remembering the scent of jasmine but inhaling the odor of utilitarian laundry soap, instead. He couldn't blame Sydney for not trusting him. Look at all the trouble her first husband had caused. The only decent thing the man had ever done was give Collin his eyes. And now, Collin wondered if that had been a blessing or a curse in disguise.

THE NEXT MORNING Sydney went through the motions of living, even dragged herself to her photography studio. With the news of her arrest, she wasn't surprised no one had called to reschedule an appointment. She guessed the morning paper hadn't received the news of McKenzie's wife's arrest in time to print it, but still, she knew the townspeople would be wary. Her reputation had been tainted. It would take time to build business back up. Or maybe she would move, she thought. Someplace where no one knew her. A place where she could start over and leave the shame and humiliation of the past few weeks behind her.

COLLIN HAD TO MAKE SURE the case was tied up, but first he drove by Sydney's. When he didn't see her car, he swung by her studio. The rental car was there, parked out front. He itched to go in, but decided to give her time, so he spent the day at the police station. Something had been nagging at him all night, but he wasn't exactly sure what it was.

After much arguing, Raeburn allowed him to see the things confiscated from Doug's pockets the night of the murder. With gloved hands, he examined Green's keys, a motel receipt, two parking tickets, a few bills, then his wallet, frustrated when the contents revealed nothing. Damn, he wished he knew what he was looking for!

The hairs on the back of his neck stood on end. There was something he still didn't understand—if McKenzie's wife had killed Doug, why would she want to kill Sydney? Sydney hadn't known about the forged deals. Mrs.

McKenzie had been incoherent. She'd hated Green, she'd said he deserved to die, but had she ever truly confessed?

He refolded the billfold but the leather felt stiff in one spot, so he opened it again and found a small photograph lodged in one of the slits for credit cards. He carefully examined it, expecting to find a picture of Sydney. Instead, he discovered a worn photograph of a baby, a baby with big brown eyes. His fingers tightened around the snapshot. He'd seen those eyes before. Then he flipped the picture over and read the words scribbled: "To you, Daddy."

Green had a child with someone else. Someone who stood to inherit Green's estate. Especially if Sydney died.

He headed to the door, his heart pounding. He had to see Sydney immediately. She might still be in danger.

DECIDING TO CALL IT a day, Sydney grabbed her briefcase and walked to her car. The town seemed unusually quiet. The streets were practically empty, as if everyone had decided to take a rest. Or maybe they were all avoiding her, she thought, then chided herself for being paranoid.

The sweltering heat sucked the air from her lungs. She climbed in the rental sedan, knowing she should begin the search for a new car soon, but feeling too apathetic to get excited about the prospect.

Dusk settled around her, obliterating the hazy remnants of the sunset. As she turned onto the main road, she glanced into the rearview mirror. A utility vehicle was bearing down on her. She turned right at the stop and so did it. Her pulse jumped. She turned onto a side street and the car behind her also turned. Then she made a U-turn at the next block and the vehicle behind her did the same.

The relief she'd experienced the night before faded into fear as the car drew closer. The nightmare wasn't over, after all. Someone was following her.

Chapter Fourteen

Sydney's gaze darted to the rearview mirror, her mind screaming with panic. McKenzie was dead and his wife was in jail—who could be after her now? She wove around the winding road, maneuvering through the small town until she thought she'd lost her tail. When she cut across three intersections and didn't see the utility vehicle, she exhaled shakily and sped toward her house.

Her imagination was probably working overtime, she realized as she stopped in the driveway.

A car door slammed behind her and she glanced up and recognized Kelly's red Cherokee. Thank God, Kelly was walking toward her. Sagging against the steering wheel, she steadied her breathing, then climbed out of her car.

"Hey, Sydney," Kelly said. "I picked up some Chinese and a bottle of wine. Mrs. Bailey's keeping Megan tonight. Want some company?"

"I would *love* some company," Sydney said, thankful she wouldn't have to face her empty house alone. "Come on in."

Kelly retrieved the bags of takeout and the wine and followed Sydney inside. "I'm glad it was you." Sydney helped her friend unload the cartons of food. "I was getting paranoid. For a minute I thought someone was following me."

"God, it's no wonder. You've been through so much. I heard on the news they arrested a woman for Doug's death."

"Yeah, McKenzie's wife."

Kelly removed dishes from the cabinet as Sydney explained the incident at Norvek. Then she filled their plates while Kelly poured wine in two crystal glasses. They sat on the couch in the den. "Thank goodness, it's over," Sydney said. "I actually felt sorry for the woman when they took her away. She was crying so hard she was barely coherent."

"It must have been terrible for you," Kelly said sympathetically. "And being arrested, I didn't know what to do. I wanted to help, Syd."

Sydney reached over and squeezed Kelly's hand. "Thanks, Kel. Your friendship means a lot to me."

Tears pooled in Kelly's eyes. "And yours means a lot to me, Sydney."

Kelly wiped a tear from her eye, then settled down and took a bite of chicken. "Where's that hunk who's been hanging around here?"

"Who? Collin?" Sydney sipped her wine, then shrugged. "I don't know. Probably back in Charleston by now."

Kelly seemed thoughtful for a minute. "I thought you two had a thing going. Was I wrong?"

Sydney sighed, raking fried rice around on her plate with her chopsticks. "It's complicated."

"Meg's spending the night, Sydney," Kelly said softly. "I have all night."

She and Kelly had always shared everything, so Sydney found herself pouring out the whole story, all about the transplant, Collin's being a cop, her feelings for him and even the visions he'd described.

"That's unbelievable." Kelly waved her chopsticks in the air. "Is he still having them?"

"I don't know. Now that the police have Doug's murder solved, maybe they'll stop and he can go back to his normal life." She took another sip of wine and yawned.

"You look tired, Syd."

"I am," Sydney admitted. "The last few weeks have been so stressful." She stretched her legs and kicked off her shoes. "But I'm grateful Doug's killer is in jail and I'm not. Maybe my nightmares will finally go away."

Kelly raised her glass for a toast. "Let's drink to that."

Sydney frowned as their glasses clinked. "Although something's still bothering me about McKenzie's wife."

"What?" Kelly asked, her eyebrows knitted.

Sydney scratched her temple in thought. "She never actually said she shot Doug, just that he deserved to die."

Kelly finished her food. "I'm sure the police will drag the truth out of her. Don't worry about it tonight, Syd. You deserve to relax."

Sydney traced her finger around the rim of her glass, for the first time since Doug's murder, trying to envision her future. A future that didn't include a man. Especially Collin Cash, the man who'd taken away the sting of Doug's betrayal, given her a few fleeting moments of passion and hope, then left her with a broken heart.

COLLIN'S MIND REELED. The memory of Doug's love affairs surfaced and an uneasy feeling tightened his chest. Marla. The mistress. There was someone else. He'd never asked Sydney about her friend Kelly or her baby's father. What if Doug had fathered the baby? It would explain why he'd found the photograph of Kelly's baby in Green's wallet.

Snippets of his conversations with Sydney raced through his head. "Kelly used to be a nurse...."

He stared at the picture again. A woman's voice drifted into his mind. *"I need to talk to you, Doctor."* Darber had sounded annoyed. *"Wait in my office."*

Right before Darber had removed his bandages He'd asked Darber who the voice belonged to and Darber had said, "Just a nurse." But Darber had sounded edgy and the voice somehow seemed familiar. Could Kelly have worked with Darber? The eyedrops he used—they were manufactured by one of the companies Doug had worked with. He hadn't thought much about it at the time. He picked up his cell phone and called the hospital in Charleston.

"Dr. Darber is with a patient," the receptionist said.

"Tell him it's an emergency. This is Collin Cash, one of his former transplant patients—"

"Just a minute, sir. I'll page him."

Soft music piped over the phone and he gritted his teeth, but within seconds, Darber's smooth Northern voice came on the line. "Darber here. What's wrong, Mr. Cash? Are you having vision problems? Headaches—"

"No, it's not my eyes," Collin said.

Darber sighed into the phone. "Then what's wrong? My nurse said this was an emergency."

"It is," Collin said. "I need to know if a woman named Kelly worked for you as a nurse. I don't know her last name...."

"Kelly Cook, yes, she was one of my nurses," Darber said. "But if this isn't an emergency—"

"It is," Collin said sternly. "It may be a matter of life

and death. You see, Doctor, I found out the name of my donor.''

Darber's anger radiated in his voice. "I warned you not to do that.''

"I know, but it was important to me.'' He explained about Doug's murder and his trip to Beaufort, giving a brief version of everything that had happened since, including the connection he'd made with the eyedrops. "Did you know Doug Green personally?''

Darber's breathing sounded labored. "Yes. Two of the companies he worked with supplied me with drugs.''

"So it's possible Kelly might have met Doug when she was working for you.''

"They knew each other,'' Darber concurred. "Although I don't see where you're going with this.''

"I'm not sure, either,'' Collin said. "It's just a hunch. But thanks, Doc.''

He hung up, the uneasiness he felt growing. Snatching his keys, he headed toward the door. If he was right, Megan was Doug's child. She would inherit a small fortune if the Norvek deal went through. But Kelly was Sydney's friend. He hoped he was wrong.

He broke every speed limit in town as he raced to Sydney's studio. When he saw the deserted parking space, he slammed his fist against the steering wheel. He should call her at home, warn her to sit tight until they could talk. Then what would he do—tell her that her dead husband had yet another lover? And a child? With her best friend, too. Not exactly a way to endear himself to Sydney.

He felt ill thinking about it. If he was wrong, if Kelly truly was a friend, Sydney and Kelly would never forgive him. But if Sydney was in danger...

He spotted a pay phone, swerved into a parking spot and jumped out, then dialed her number as fast as he could. The phone rang once, twice, three times, four, then finally someone answered. A voice he feared he recognized.

"Can I speak to Sydney?" he asked, working to keep his voice calm.

"She can't come to the phone," the woman answered. "Why don't you come over here, Mr. Cash."

His heart thudded to a stop. *Kelly.* The woman's soft, Southern drawl hammered into his subconscious, and Collin's hand tightened around the phone. The images of the town faded. Once again the cloudy shadows, the grays and blacks blurred before him, replaced by the shimmering light of metal glinting in the darkness. Another vision. He was being swept back in time to the murder he'd witnessed.

Kelly's face was cast in shadows, haunted by anger and fury as she lifted the gun and pointed it at him. He trembled, holding out his hand, shock riveting his body as he tried to coax Kelly to put down the weapon. But she smiled, a peaceful look washing over her as she pulled the trigger. He clutched his chest, his body bouncing backward, blood seeping from the wound. She fired again. He tried to call for help, then saw himself falling, collapsing onto the hard, cold floor. More blood, draining from his body, trailing onto the green Oriental rug. His head lolled to the side, his breath ragged. He closed his eyes, knowing he was going to die.

Jerking himself back to reality, Collin dragged in deep breaths, then pressed the phone back to his ear. "Kelly, are you still there?" Silence. "Kelly, hello, are you still there?"

A beeping tone pierced the awful quiet, then the phone went dead. He jumped into his car, praying as he raced toward Sydney's. *God, please let her still be alive.*

SYDNEY LAY STRETCHED OUT on the sofa, more relaxed than she'd been in weeks. "This wine is wonderful. This is the first time in ages I feel like I could go to sleep and sleep forever."

Kelly smiled and cleared the dishes. "I bet you will sleep a long time tonight."

"Leave those and I'll do them later," Sydney said, starting to get up.

Kelly waved her off. "No, I don't mind. You lie there and rest."

Sydney drained the glass, then placed it on the table. "You're such a great friend, Kel. I don't know what I would have done without you the past few months."

Kelly paused, an empty plate in her hand. "We've helped each other," Kelly said softly. "Having Meg all alone has been so hard."

"I know," Sydney said. "Have you thought any more about contacting the father? You could at least get child support."

Kelly shook her head. "He didn't want anything to do with her. He's completely out of the picture now."

"I'm sorry, Kel. I really am."

"Me, too," Kelly said, wiping away a tear.

A knock sounded at the door and Sydney jumped.

"I'll get it," Kelly offered.

But the door swung open, and Collin burst into the room. "Sydney..." He paused, looking first at Kelly, then at her. "I needed to see you," he said in an odd tone. "Are you all right?"

"I'm fine." Sydney waved a hand, feeling dizzy. "Just tired, but Kelly and I have been having wine.... What are you doing here? I thought you'd left for Charleston."

"I couldn't leave with things unsettled between us,"

Collin explained. He turned to Kelly and Sydney squinted through blurred vision. Her head was starting to hurt.

Collin's jaw hardened. "You put something in her wine, didn't you?"

Kelly backed toward the sofa table, a strange look in her eyes. Sydney tried to sit up, but the room tilted. She grabbed the sofa edge for support. "What's wrong, Collin?"

"I know what happened, Kelly." Collin stepped in front of the sofa, positioning himself between her and Kelly.

"What exactly do you know?" Kelly's normally cheery voice turned cold.

Collin stared at her. "I saw you murder Doug Green."

Sydney gasped. Kelly pulled a small pistol from her waist and pointed it at Collin.

"How could you see it? You weren't there." Kelly's voice shook with rage.

"I have Doug's eyes," Collin said. "I've been having visions of the murder."

"Kel, what are you doing?" Sydney tried to stand, but Kelly waved the gun toward her.

"You'd better not move, Syd. Then I won't have to hurt you," Kelly warned.

"What?" Sydney swayed drunkenly. "Kelly, I don't understand. Why do you have a gun?"

"She killed Doug," Collin replied.

"Shut up!" Kelly shouted. "You weren't supposed to come to Beaufort."

"I'm not sure why she murdered him, but I think it has to do with Megan," Collin said quietly, leveling a look at Kelly. "Megan is Doug's baby, isn't she, Kelly?"

Kelly nodded and Sydney gasped, then pressed her hand to her stomach, shock riveting through her.

"Yes, he was her father," Kelly said, her voice furious. "But he wouldn't even acknowledge her. Can you imagine that? A father so despicable he wouldn't even admit he had a child. Megan's such a sweet baby—she deserved better than that." The pain in her voice tore at Sydney. And the realization that Doug had fathered a child with her best friend sent her mind reeling.

"That's why you killed him," Collin said. "Because he wouldn't take care of Megan?"

"Oh, it was more than that," Kelly said, waving the gun back and forth between Collin and Sydney. "It was way more than that."

"Tell me about it," Sydney said, her chest tight. "I thought we told each other everything, Kel."

Kelly twisted her mouth sideways, her chin trembling. "He loved me, you know. He did, that is, until he met you, Sydney."

Sydney's stomach churned. "Doug didn't know the meaning of the word love, Kelly."

"Well, he was mine first. And I had his baby. I met him when I was working for that eye doctor," Kelly explained.

"Darber, the one who performed my eye transplant," Collin said.

"Yes." Kelly swiped at her face angrily, giving up any pretense of control. "I'd been working for Darber for a couple of years. Then I fell in love with Doug. He was so smart, so industrious. I knew he was going to make millions."

"And the two of you had an affair," Collin supplied.

"I thought we were going to get married." Kelly had a faraway look in her eyes. "I knew some of Doug's deals weren't on the up-and-up. But I didn't care. I was raised dirt poor and I wanted better, and Doug could give it to me. Then I found out Dr. Darber was overcharging rich patients so he could afford to perform surgery on other people who couldn't afford it.''

Collin frowned. A piece of the puzzle he hadn't detected.

"So Doug and I decided he'd be perfect to help us out. We blackmailed him into giving experimental drugs to patients, ones Doug was trying to market. Darber would sign off that they'd passed clinical tests, and Doug could get the FDA approval in record time.''

"Then he'd sell the product, make a lot of hype about it, the stock would escalate, and he'd cash his stock in before anyone found out about the fraud," Collin added.

"It was a great plan," Kelly said.

"Why did you come to the clinic the day Darber removed my bandages?''

Kelly laughed wryly. "I wanted to see if your eyes looked anything like Doug's, if they would haunt me forever.''

"I don't understand all this," Sydney said, feeling weaker by the minute. "Why didn't you sue Doug? You could have won child support.''

"She couldn't go to court for fear they'd find out about the other activities," Collin explained.

"You think you're so smart, Mr. Cash. I never dreamed you'd come here looking for Doug's murderer.''

"Well, you were wrong, weren't you?" Collin took a step toward her. "You tried to kill me with that fire and the bomb, didn't you?''

"I wanted you to go away," Kelly said, her voice petulant like a child's.

"And what about me, Kelly?" Sydney asked. "Did you want to kill me, too?''

Kelly made a pitiful moaning sound. "I didn't...I don't

want to kill you, Sydney. But I can't go to jail and give up Megan. She's my life.''

Sydney remembered Doug's vasectomy and the pain overwhelmed her. He'd had a child with Kelly. "I thought you were my friend, Kelly.''

The pupils of Kelly's eyes darkened with fury. "I hated you at first," she admitted. "You were the reason Doug wouldn't marry me. When I came here, I was going to warm up to you to make Doug nervous. Then I got to know you, and I actually liked you.''

"If you like me, how could you do this to me?" Sydney asked in a ragged whisper.

Kelly's face twisted with rage. "Because Doug offered me money, *money*, to go away, to have his baby and stay out of his life so he could marry you!''

Sydney pressed her hand to her mouth, rocking back and forth, feeling woozier with each passing minute. Not only had Doug betrayed her, but so had her best friend. No, Kelly wasn't a friend at all; it had all been a pretense, more lies. Just like Doug. And Collin. The room blurred, spun around her. She closed her eyes, fighting the nausea.

"But he offered me a pathetic amount, pennies compared to the money he'd earned." Kelly's hand shook with the gun. "And then he married you. Married *you*, when we could have been a family, when I had his little girl.''

"You framed Sydney for Doug's murder, didn't you?" Collin asked, his voice menacing.

Kelly made a mewling sound and brushed at her eyes. "It was the only way, Sydney. I couldn't go to jail and leave Megan motherless. And with you in jail, I thought I could get Doug's money for Megan." Kelly began rambling incoherently, her hand shaking as she kept the weapon trained on Collin.

"So you're going to kill me now?" Collin asked, inching toward Kelly.

"And me, Kelly—are you going to kill me, too?" Sydney asked. "When will you stop?"

"I don't want to kill you, Syd," Kelly said. "But Collin, he has to die. And...and I'll frame you for it. I'll say Collin realized McKenzie's wife didn't kill Doug, that you knew Collin was on to you, so you killed him. It won't take much to convince Raeburn." She gave Sydney a pitying look. "And when that sleeping pill takes effect, you'll sleep for hours. You may not even know when the police get here and find him dead. Then it's off to jail for you, Sydney, and Meg and I can leave town."

"But I'll tell the truth," Sydney argued.

A harsh laugh escaped Kelly. "It'll be my word against yours, and you know the police won't believe you, not after they find this gun in your hand. And not after I give you a shot of this wonder drug I have in my purse."

"What drug?" Collin asked.

"It's not on the market yet, because it has a few nasty side effects to be worked out." Kelly smirked. "It messes your memory up so you don't know your own name. Sydney'll probably admit to killing you and Doug."

Sydney gasped. "Kelly, don't do this. Please don't do this. You need help."

But Kelly raised the gun, the planes of her face hard and determined, her eyes wild. Collin gave Sydney a beseeching look. In that split second, Sydney saw the love shining in his eyes and knew he would take the bullet for her if he had to. But she loved Collin, and in spite of his deceit, he was a decent man, a man she could depend on. A man who had loved her more in one night than her husband had in two years.

She couldn't let Kelly kill him.

She dived forward, praying she could distract Kelly long enough for Collin to grab the gun.

"No!" Collin bolted sideways to stop her, but too late. The gun discharged, and Sydney cried out and slumped to the floor when the bullet found its mark.

Chapter Fifteen

"Sydney!" Collin dived at Kelly, praying he could block Sydney from the line of fire as the gun discharged again. Dear God, he had to save her!

The shot went wild. Collin knocked Kelly's arm upward and sent the gun flying. When it hit the floor, it skidded several feet away.

"Let me go!" Kelly tried to jerk away, but he grabbed her wrist and pinned her against him. His heart pounded with fear. Sydney was lying in a heap on the floor with her blood spilling onto the carpet. *No, Sydney, no, please don't die....*

Kelly sagged against him as he tightened his grip. "You're going to jail for this," he ground out. "And you'll stay there for a long time."

"It wasn't fair!" Kelly cried. "I only wanted things for my baby."

"Be quiet," he growled. "And tell me what you put in Sydney's drink."

Kelly didn't answer. He jerked off his belt, wound it around her arms, dragged her to a chair and tied her to it. "I asked you what you put in her drink. A sleeping pill, narcotic? What?"

"It was just a sleeping pill from the hospital," Kelly answered in a hollow voice.

He grabbed the phone and punched 911, kneeling beside Sydney. "I need help," he said. "Send an ambulance and the police. A woman's been shot. Hurry!" He rattled off the address, taking Sydney's pulse and praying at the same time. *Please, dear God, please let her be alive....*

He found a weak pulse, and his chest heaved in relief, then he gently rolled her over. Blood poured out of the wound, soaking her blouse. He ripped the material apart to examine the damage. The bullet had hit her upper body, above the heart, near her shoulder. He ran to the kitchen and grabbed towels, then pressed them to the wound.

"Collin..." Sydney murmured groggily.

"Yes, love, I'm here." He tucked her hair behind her ear, his throat thick with emotion.

"You're okay?" She reached up and brushed his cheek.

He nodded, so touched by her concern for him that he couldn't speak.

"I..." She coughed and he pressed his finger to her lips.

"Shh, it's okay, I'm going to take care of you," he whispered, his eyes filling with moisture. "The ambulance is on its way."

Her eyelids fluttered, and he kissed her forehead gently. "I'm sorry, sweetheart, so sorry."

She called his name again weakly, and he lowered his head so he could hear her.

"What is it, honey?"

"I...I love you."

He gently laid her head in his lap, wanting to say the words back, but emotions clogged his throat. Then she lost consciousness and his breath locked in his chest. He placed his head over her heart, weeping when he felt the soft rhythmic beating, even though it was weak.

"How many pills did you give her?" Collin croaked.

Kelly wrestled against the chair. "Just two."

"She'd better make it." He kept pressure on the wound, ignoring Kelly's sobs as he held Sydney and prayed the ambulance would make it in time.

HOURS LATER Collin sat beside Sydney's hospital bed, frantic with worry, staring at the clock as the minutes dragged by. He watched the slow rise and fall of her chest. The doctor had said she'd come through the surgery fine, but she needed rest. He was waiting for her to open her eyes so he could see for himself.

She'd seemed so pale and lifeless on the long ride to the hospital. The three words she'd whispered to him had played over and over in his head, balm to his wounded soul. Damn it, why hadn't he told her he loved her? Well, it would be the first thing he'd tell her when she woke up. Would she be able to forgive him for lying to her? Would he still remind her of Doug's deceit?

When they'd arrived at the hospital, she'd been whisked off to surgery. He'd paced the waiting room and almost lost his mind. When he'd gotten the news she'd made it through surgery, he'd bought a dozen yellow roses, then held them the whole time she'd been in the recovery room, nearly crushing the fragile blooms as he'd paced some more.

Now the roses sat on the table beside her, wilting. His fingers curled around a cup of cold coffee. He sipped at it just for something to do with his hands.

He'd called Raeburn. Kelly had confessed to everything. She'd admitted to knowing enough about cars to tamper with Sydney's breaks and the fire had been easy to set, but McKenzie had helped with the bomb. She'd promised to help him get credit for the weight-loss product if he made the bomb. Darber had turned himself in. He'd cried like a baby when he heard Kelly had tried to kill Sydney, had blamed himself for not blowing the whistle on Kelly and Doug for blackmailing him. He would undergo a medical review for unethical practices.

The rustle of sheets caught his attention and he froze. But she'd barely stirred. He reached out to cover Sydney's free hand with his own.

"I need you, Sydney," he said softly. "I didn't want to need you. I didn't want to need anyone ever again." Moisture stung his eyes and he remembered his own stay in the hospital, those long, dark hours of waking up all alone. Of wanting someone to be with him, someone who cared. Now he'd found that special someone, and he'd never let her go.

And if she came up with some garbage about saying those three little words because they'd been in danger, he'd tell her she was the one lying this time. She loved him, he knew it; he'd seen the emotion brimming in her eyes right before she'd dived in front of the bullet to save his life. It should have been the other way around, he thought, with helpless fury. He was supposed to have protected her, taken the bullet, not her.

He gently stroked the soft skin beside her eyes, letting his fingers trace a path down her cheek, memorizing each and every feature of her lovely face. "Please wake up and look at me, sweetheart."

An hour later, exhausted, he laid his head down on her bed, careful not to disturb her, but wanting to feel the reality of her next to him. He closed his eyes, letting go of all his old demons as he drifted off to sleep.

"COLLIN." SYDNEY FOUGHT to speak through her dry mouth. She struggled to move, then felt a hand squeeze hers. "Collin," she whispered again.

He slowly raised his head. Fatigue lines were etched around his eyes, and a frown pulled at his mouth. How long had she been asleep? What had happened?

"You're awake. I can't believe it," he said. "I must have fallen asleep."

She smiled slowly, wanting to reach out and touch his face, but when she tried to raise her hand, a jolt of pain rocked through her. She groaned and his eyes darkened with worry.

"Don't try to move, Sydney," he said. "You're going to be sore for a while. You've had surgery."

He moved closer to her and cupped her face in his big strong hands. "I was so scared you wouldn't wake up."

She bit her lip, recalling the scene at her house. "What happened? Is Kelly all right?"

"She's fine." He fought the anger in his voice. "She confessed to everything. The police have her in custody."

Sydney nodded, feeling the loss deep in her soul. "I really thought we were best friends," she said sadly. "I can't believe I didn't see through Doug. Or her."

"It wasn't your fault, Sydney. Doug was a master at deception. He even fooled his business associates." Collin brushed a tendril of hair from her face and pressed a kiss to her temple. "And as for Kelly, I never suspected her, either. Not even once."

Sydney glanced away, tears pooling in her eyes. Sunshine peeked through the clouds, brightening the white-washed walls, but depression pulled at her.

"I know you're hurt right now," Collin said. "You've been through a lot, Sydney. But you'll survive this, too, sweetheart."

It sounded as if Collin was saying goodbye. She'd told him she loved him—she remembered that much—but he hadn't said the words back. He'd promised to keep her safe and to find Doug's killer. Now he'd accomplished his goal, paid his debt—

"What's going on in that mind of yours?" Collin asked softly, tugging a strand of her hair until she looked at him.

"I was thinking about the investigation. Now that it's over I suppose you'll be going back to Charleston."

Collin shrugged. "I can do police work anywhere."

Tears burned her eyes again. She wished he'd leave so she could let them fall.

Instead, he traced small circles on her cheek with the pad of his thumb. "But I don't want to be just anywhere," he said softly. "I want to be with you, Sydney."

She felt a seed of hope. "You do?"

"I do." He hesitated, then cleared his throat. "I spent all last year alone in a world of darkness. It was the worst year of my life." He grimaced at the memories, then forced them away, knowing they both had to focus on the future.

"My world's been pretty dark, too," Sydney said softly.

His gaze locked with hers and her eyes sparkled with understanding. "I love you, Sydney." Then he lowered his mouth and claimed hers with a kiss so gentle and sweet the tears she tried to keep at bay seeped through her eyelashes.

"I know you said I was like Doug...."

"You're nothing like Doug."

One corner of his mouth lifted in a lopsided smile. "I have mixed feelings about having his eyes, Sydney. I don't want you to look at me and see him."

"I don't," she whispered. "I see you, only you and

your gorgeous bedroom eyes." She squeezed his hand. "Besides, if it wasn't for the transplant, I never would have met you. In a way, Doug sent you to me. Maybe to make up for all the bad stuff."

He brought her fingers to his mouth and kissed the tips of each one gently. A soft hum of awareness stirred in her abdomen.

"I don't want to pressure you or rush you," he whispered.

"I don't mind being rushed."

His smile grew wide. "But I want to marry you, sweetheart."

She brought his hand to her mouth and kissed his fingers, each one in turn, just as he had kissed hers. "I hope you believe in short engagements."

He chuckled and dropped another kiss on her forehead, then stroked her cheek and covered her mouth with his, devouring her with a long, hungry kiss. When he finally pulled back, Sydney inhaled the heady scent of his passion, brimming, ready to explode. She'd never been happier.

"Collin?"

"Yeah?"

"I want to use the money in Doug's accounts to start a fund for people in need," Sydney said. "For transplant patients."

Some deep emotion registered on his face. "I want a family, too," he said, growing serious.

This time *she* smiled. "We could work on it right away."

"I'd like that." His eyes twinkled momentarily, then his face became serious. "Child and Family Services took Megan and put her in foster care. Kelly doesn't have any family. I think she's going to be in jail for a long time."

"So little Meg will have to live with strangers." Sydney's voice broke.

"I know how much you love her, Sydney. But she was Doug's, and it would be hard for you to forget what Kelly did."

Sydney studied his face, so full of compassion and understanding. "*You* wouldn't mind that she was Doug's?"

He shook his head. "She's an innocent little girl. A beautiful, innocent little girl who adores you." He kissed her on the cheek. "Almost as much as I do."

Her love for Collin overwhelmed her. How could she ever have thought this compassionate man was anything like her deceased husband? "I love you so much, Collin."

"And I love you." He leaned over to kiss her again, then raised his head so their faces were only inches apart, their breaths mingling.

"Do you think Kelly will give up custody?" Sydney asked.

Collin shrugged. "She became hysterical when they took Megan away. She told me that if she went to jail, she'd rather you raise her baby than strangers."

Sydney closed her eyes on a sob and Collin cupped her face in his hands again. "Of course, we can still work on a baby of our own. Just as soon as you get well."

"I'm feeling better already." She laughed softly and slid her fingers through his hair, drawing his face to her for another kiss. Her lips parted and when his warm mouth closed over hers, pleasure pooled and ebbed in her body, making her forget the pain of her injury. He tasted her hungrily, greedily, his tongue seeking and dancing with her own, and when he finally pulled away, she was breathless.

The aching loneliness of the past year disappeared with his gentle touch, and suddenly she couldn't wait for the future. She fingered a lock of hair from his forehead and smiled. ''Go ask the doctor when I can go home.''

If you enjoyed what you just read,
then we've got an offer you can't resist!

Take 2 bestselling
love stories FREE!

Plus get a FREE surprise gift!

Silhouette

INTIMATE MOMENTS™

A mugging leaves attorney
Alexandra Spencer with a head
injury—and no recollection of her
recent divorce. Dylan Parker's
investigation into the not-so-random
attack is nothing compared to
the passion he feels for the woman
who once broke his heart. Can he
find answers before losing himself
to Alex—again?

MEMORIES AFTER MIDNIGHT

BY LINDA RANDALL WISDOM

Silhouette Intimate Moments #1409

DON'T MISS THIS THRILLING STORY,
AVAILABLE MARCH 2006 WHEREVER
SILHOUETTE BOOKS ARE SOLD.